100 WAYS TO MAKE YOUR WIFE HAPPY

JEMIMAH JONES

Why You Should Read This Book

In the day to day of our relationships, a lot of stuff can get swept under the rug. Combine that with the fact that a lot of partners don't really get to know each other on a deep level at the beginning of their relationships (or at any point) and you could be highly prone to emotionally stepping on your partner's toes without knowing it.

For best results, clear all distractions from your environment. Turn off your phones, close the laptops, and switch off the TV. Make sure the kids are asleep and the dog is taken care of. Clear out any and all extraneous things that could potentially ping their way in to the space that you are creating and handle them ahead of time.

Here, in this book we discussed in detail about the 100 Successful ways to make your wife or girlfriend happy all the time.

LET'S
BEGIN

- This trick is quite old, but it's still very effective. Yes, Compliment her in front of your friends. When you ask your friend and his wife to join you for dinner or lunch, be open and Compliment her, with something as simple as "You look beautiful" or "You're a terrific cook" and you put a smile on her face that doesn't easily fade.

- If your wife has a hobby or passion that you've always effectively ignored, boost her esteem by showing some interest in it. You don't necessarily have to take part yourself, but showing up to watch some of her soccer games or providing positive feedback about her blog will make her feel valued. Mutual respect is the glue of successful relationships, so if you've been acting as though her interests are trivial or incidental, it's time to start showing them some enthusiasm.

- Write some romantic love letters to your wife. You can be serious, or fun and playful, doesn't matter, as long as you're spontaneous and sincere. Go ahead and put your thoughts in writing, and let her read about how much you love her.

- Remember the dates of very special occasions like her birthday, your anniversary, the first time you met, the first time you kissed, the day you proposed, remember these dates, the memories and circumstances, and do something special or prepare something nice and sweet for your wife while you and your wife reminisce.

- Put your arms around her when she needs comfort, holding her silently.

- Occasionally bring home her favorite flowers specially on those days when there is No occasion and on those days when she is feeling low. Even her favorite cake/ice-cream are as effective as favorite flowers.

- Make use of your simple cooking skills and make her bed-in-breakfast. Even a good cup of coffee/tea can be a turn-on and easy to grab her love.

- If she packs you a lunch box everyday. You can occasionally put a small note after you are done, saying Thank you in a sweet/romantic way. Just be sure that she is the one who opens it after you go back home and not your mother/mother-in-law/maid.

- You will definitely earn brownie points if you are good in giving a massage be it head or back.

- Kiss your partner before one of you leaves home. Add a hug while you're at it! Two minutes that start your day off right. And, don't forget to kiss when one of you come home!

- Communication is key. Be a good listener and understand her needs. Be helpful in any way you can without being too submissive.

- Keep her trust at all costs. Leave no gray area when it comes to other female relationships, money and your word.

- Ask for a list of 5 things that she is desired to be done in the home and plan to do them as soon as possible.

- Call, email or text her when you're apart so she knows you are thinking of her.

- Speaking of arguments, you may want to consider letting her win in most arguments, by giving in and keeping quiet, women tend to resist agreeing to their "man" in an argument, if they feel they can win it by endless talking. So spare yourself and your wife the agony, and let her win. There are wives who are quick to realize mistakes, but you show them first that you love them and that you are willing to listen to them let them win the argument.

- Keep yourself fit and be in good body shape so she's especially proud to be with you and also she feels happy when she is going out with you.

- Physically touch her every day and even if it's only for a minute or two. This small things create some magic.

- Be sensitive enough to ask her if you offend or hurt her sexually in any way or any you have offend her through words.

- You don't just commit to marrying her, you commit to her baggage, her priorities, her needs and her dreams. When women say I do, we do it wholeheartedly, and we expect the same commitment from our husbands.

- She wakes you up during the wee hours, excited and/or anxious, does not make the mistake of ignoring her and going back to sleep. During these moments, no matter how tired or sleepy you are, you need to show her that you're OK with talking and that you're actually open to listening to her. We. wives remember these moments, and our husbands' reactions linger. You can't run out of topics to talk about, and if your wife is the shy and quiet type, initiate the conversation, and reward yourself and your wife this beautiful element in a marriage.

- Women tend to be hard on themselves regarding their looks. We are afraid we don't measure up in your sight. But if you look into your wife's eyes and tell her she is beautiful, you will make her day!

- Your wife is not a robot! She gets tired too, you know. So what if she's a stay at home wife or mom, and you bring home the bacon, she does her share of work and contributes to the relationship. She helps you by not splurging on senseless expenses, she budgets for your home, and if she's the type, she cleans up after you. By all means, help her with her work and/or chores. If you really can't, find a way to make her work easier, and if you can, more enjoyable.

- Be especially helpful to her when she is not feeling well and care her like a child.

+ You work on your jokes and making people at the office and your boss cracks up, you should also make it a habit to make your wife laugh. Find out, the soonest you can, about what she thinks is funny, and make her laugh whenever you can. When my husband and I fight, and he's just tired of my nagging, all he does is say something funny, that I can't resist laughing, and I forget about the fight and the issues.

+ Whatever she does, be a friend to her and support her. If she can't it, find a way to stress how much you support her and that she can rely on you for help, and you're the person to back her up no matter what.

- Try to make her comfort and kiss her lips daily but before that brush your teeth's regularly and clean your tongue regularly, especially before you intend to kiss her lips.

- All couples fight. In fact, it is perfectly healthy--if the fighting is productive. Don't say hurtful things that you will regret. I know, easier said than done. But remember, this is someone you married and love. Never, ever mentioned the D-word in the heat of the fight. Take 20 minutes, or however long it takes to cool off, and make things right.

- Allow your wife to teach you things without being defensive. Even though you know those things pretty well, just pretend and act as you have not come across such things in your life.

- Love passionately your partner. And have sex as it relieves you from the tension and headaches of daily life, and it also keep you contended. Scientific studies conducted by world class universities like Yale and MIT have proven that healthy sex rejuvenates your body and increases the efficiency of body to double to work even vigorously, and keeps you concentrated at your work.

- Call her from work and say, "I've been thinking of how good I have it with you in my life. Thanks for all that you are as a woman and all that you do for me and our family."

- Make the time to set specific family and personal goals with her to achieve together for each year and it really makes sense between a husband and wife relationship.

- Exhibit humility, admit your mistakes, and ask for forgiveness. She'll appreciate that!

- When you are together in bed, just brush her hairs and compliment her hair and eyes.

- When she asks how your day went, don't just say "fine" rather than just spend few minutes with her and actually elaborate her fully what exactly happened today.

- This is very important thumb rule, try not to argue over money. Peacefully discuss future expenditures instead.

- Make your wife feel like she's the center of your world all the time, and especially so when she's with you. Don't ignore her because you're having a fun conversation with another attractive girl or with your colleagues or something else. When your girlfriend is around you, it doesn't matter who or what is around, make sure your attention is focused on your girl.

- While your wife studies her face in the mirror, come up behind her and gently kiss the back of her neck. Say, "God broke the mold after He made you. You are so beautiful."

- Always try to be honest to your wife at least to the extent of 99%, As a old proverb says "Honesty is the best policy" which suits best for an relationship. Being honest to your wife itself saves you from the critical position in a relationship.

- Make a strong eye contact when she is talking to you and when you are talking with her.

- Be helpful, both before and during the time you have visitors in your home. If you're not sure of what to do, ask your wife "What can I do that would help the most?"

- Refuse to compare her unfavorably with others. This is bit critical and much important one, every human hates when we compare them with others. So don't compare your partner with others.

- Be supportive by helping her to finish her education and personal goals that are important to her.

- Don't forget to hold her hand in public like you used to when you dated her.

- Show your love and affection to her mostly without sexual intentions and respect her feelings.

- Be careful of choosing your words while you converse with your partner, especially when you are angry.

- Kindly Make sure that she has money to spend in any way that she would choose.

- Just Hold her close and verbally express your love when she is hurt or discouraged.

- Show interest in her friends, and if they are trustworthy, give her time to be with them. Respect their friendship.

- Do something active together to lift her spirit —even taking a walk hand-in-hand.

- Find and frame an old photo of your early dating or married days. Give it to her for her nightstand or desk.

- You dated your wife before marriage? and fell in love?. Date her now to STAY in love.

- Show your love and affection for her especially in front of friends and relatives.

- Be polite and kind. Often we're kinder to strangers than we are to our spouse.

- Surprise her by suggesting a marriage seminar or weekend retreat you can attend together.

- Call, email or text her when you're apart so she knows you are thinking of her.

- Don't ignore the small things that bother her and let them build into bigger issues.

- Honor her by not disagreeing with her in front of the children.

- Whenever she is sick or not well, just take care like a mother and I'm sure she will give back that love in triple.

- If you want to make your wife feel happy in the relationship, you need to focus on one thing girls want most in a guy, his protective element. When your wife feels secure when you're around, and when she feels like she can depend on you for anything, she'd instinctively feel happier to be in love with you.

- Don't focus on the physical features of another woman and It really dishonors your wife.

+ Allow her to express herself freely, without fear of being called illogical or dumb.

+ Don't tease and belittle her, saying "I was just joking" when she doesn't find it funny.

+ Pro-actively do things that makes her feel cherished as a woman and as a wife.

+ Your wife wants to hear about your life. She wants to know what is making you happy and what is stressing you out. This is how she connects with you. She actually cares about what you had for lunch and the strange thing you saw on the way home. Don't reply to your wife's questions with one word answers. Elaborate.

- Sit close to her, even when you are just watching television.

- Maintain good grooming habits so you look and smell good. It shows you care.

- Be an involved partner in helping with the children and spending time together.

- Give your spouse time to unwind after she gets home from work. Your evenings will be much more enjoyable.

- Remember to tell her or call her as soon as you know you are going to be late from office.

- Book her a session at a luxurious spa and better still, join her. She will not only enjoy the spa session, but will be happy that you came along with her.

- Scratch her back, rub her feet, or her rub her neck—whatever she'd prefer.

- Sometimes in cold mornings where the alarm goes off and neither of you wants to move, just hit the snooze button, roll over and put your arm around her and cuddle her.

- Always remember to hug and kiss your wife before you leave for work in the morning, even she is still snoozing in bed.

- A case study states that Girls prefers a Bike ride / Car drive with her loved ones all times. So have a romantic bike/car ride with your partner at least twice a week.

- Remember Favorite Foods of your lovable wife, so that whenever she is low or sick, you can either cook or order her Favorite Foods and make her happy.

- If you are well enough to compose a song or sing a song for your wife either on valentines day or any special day's it pretty good.

- Take care of your wife's mother and father like your parents and am sure it will make your wife double happy.

- Pick up some tradition, Every year for your anniversary just pick up some doughnuts from the same bakery.

- Create a jar filled with "Love Coupons." Make the coupons redeemable for hugs, kisses, back rubs or any number of special favors. Give the jar to your lover and let him/her redeem the coupons over time.

🔸 Willingly accompany your wife to family events. Granted, that you are bored among all her cousins, aunts and uncles. But make a sincere attempt to look happy at a family wedding and your wife will be sure to appreciate the gesture.

🔸 Take care of your wife like a baby during her Menstrual cycle.
🔸 Whenever you plan for a movie or restaurant, let the choice of choosing what movie and which restaurant always be with your wife.

- Write some note on the bathroom mirror with dry erase marker or in the shower with shower crayons. It's always a great way to start the day. Even you can make use of sticky notes also.

- Start saying random I Love You's to your wife at unexpected moments and this means them a lot in their fruitful heart.

- Find out your wife's favorite perfume and gift it to her for no particular reason.

- Pray for her every day and make it a point to pray with her when she is troubled.

- Share your favorite family memory photos together in all social media like Facebook, Instagram, WhatsApp, Pinterest, etc.

- Try to take some random funny selfie's daily with your lovable wife.

- Create an habit of appreciating small silly things and minor achievements of your wife always.

- On Weekends, take charge of your home like taking cooking or cleaning department and give rest to your partner.

⬇ Maintain eye-contact with your wife whenever you talk with her and it creates a strong relationship bond.

⬇ Whenever she is low and seek for an advise, just be a good listener and try to resolve her problem and be always an solution giver.

⬇ There is nothing wrong with going out with your friends. But, if you have plans with your wife, don't back out on her for your friends. If you're a workaholic, make sure it is obvious that you are still her number one. Keep in mind that your wife should be always your first priority.

- Show her that she matters more to you than any one you could be with, that threatens her security in your marriage.

- Plan a mini-honeymoon every quarter, where the two of you can spend quality time together. This also works out effectively in relationships.

- This might be looks silly but an effective one, just play video games with your wife once a week and you will experience the love and happiness.

- Use Romantic, funny pet names that she likes to call and use those nicknames daily with her.

- Sometimes just go for a walk around the block by holding hands and talk about your day and make love while walking.

- Extend the birthday celebration of your wife, instead of celebrating birthday; start celebrating Birth Week.

- Go an entire day without criticizing anything about her. Instead, try to notice her doing something that you really appreciate, and tell her how much you value her.

- If you don't know what will make her happy, ask her. Ask her what she wants which will make her feel important and appreciated. We always assume that the other person knows how we feel and what we do to make them feel loved, but it is not always automatically true.

CONCLUSION

To summarize the 100 ways in short for easy understanding, we categorized the 100 ways into 5 basic thumb rule.

- Physical affection - Touch, hugs, kiss, sex.
- Affirmation - Using words of appreciation and gratitude for what you do.
- Gifts - Buying flowers, nice dinner, jewelry, etc.
- Acts of service - Doing things around the house, cooking, cleaning, fixing things.
- Time together - Spending quality undivided time together doing things you both enjoy.

ONE LAST THING...

If you enjoyed this book or found it useful I'd be very grateful if you'd post a short review on Amazon. Your support really does make a difference and I read all the reviews personally so I can get your feedback and make this book even better.

Thanks again for your support!

10393161R00023

Printed in Great Britain
by Amazon

KANT'S *CRITIQUE OF*
AESTHETIC JUDGEMENT

Continuum *Reader's Guides*

Continuum's *Reader's Guides* are clear, concise and accessible introductions to classic works of philosophy. Each book explores the major themes, historical and philosophical context and key passages of a major philosophical text, guiding the reader toward a thorough understanding of often-demanding material. Ideal for undergraduate students, the guides provide an essential resource for anyone who needs to get to grips with a philosophical text.

Reader's Guides available from Continuum

Aristotle's Nicomachean Ethics – Christopher Warne
Aristotle's Politics – Judith A. Swanson and C. David Corbin
Berkeley's Principles of Human Knowledge – Alasdair Richmond
Berkeley's Three Dialogues – Aaron Garrett
Deleuze and Guattari's Capitalism and Schizophrenia – Ian Buchanan
Deleuze's Difference and Repetition – Joe Hughes
Derrida's Writing and Difference – Sarah Wood
Descartes' Meditations – Richard Francks
Hegel's Philosophy of Right – David Rose
Heidegger's Being and Time – William Blattner
Heidegger's Later Writings – Lee Braver
Hobbes's Leviathan – Laurie M. Johnson Bagby
Hume's Dialogues Concerning Natural Religion – Andrew Pyle
Hume's Enquiry Concerning Human Understanding – Alan Bailey and Dan O'Brien
Kant's Critique of Pure Reason – James Luchte
Kant's Groundwork for the Metaphysics of Morals – Paul Guyer
Kuhn's The Structure of Scientific Revolutions – John Preston
Locke's Essay Concerning Human Understanding – William Uzgalis
Locke's Second Treatise of Government – Paul Kelly
Mill's On Liberty – Geoffrey Scarre
Mill's Utilitarianism – Henry West
Nietzsche's On the Genealogy of Morals – Daniel Conway
Plato's Republic – Luke Purshouse
Rousseau's The Social Contract – Christopher Wraight
Sartre's Being and Nothingness – Sebastian Gardner
Spinoza's Ethics – Thomas J Cook
Wittgenstein's Tractatus Logico Philosophicus – Roger M White

KANT'S *CRITIQUE OF AESTHETIC JUDGEMENT*

A Reader's Guide

FIONA HUGHES

continuum

Continuum International Publishing Group
The Tower Building   80 Maiden Lane
11 York Road   Suite 704
London SE1 7NX   New York NY 10038

www.continuumbooks.com

British Library Cataloguing-in-Publication Data
A catalogue record for this book is available from the British Library.

ISBN: HB: 978-0-8264-9767-3
PB: 978-0-8264-9768-0

Library of Congress Cataloging-in-Publication Data
A catalog record for this book is available from the
Library of Congress.

Typeset by Newgen Imaging Systems (Pvt) Ltd, Chennai, India
Printed and bound in Great Britain by CPI Antony Rowe

In fond memory of Michael Podro [1931–2008], art theorist and passionate philosopher, in conversations with whom reflective judgement became 'a feeling of life'.

CONTENTS

ACKNOWLEDGEMENTS

This book is a product of many years' work on the *Critique of Aesthetic Judgement*. In particular, I learned so much over many of those years from jointly teaching the text at the University of Essex along with Michael Podro, whose very *modus operandi* was an exhibition of reflective judgement. Our audience was a mixed group of Philosophy and Art History M.A. students, whose questions and suggestions helped us gradually clarify how reflective judgement operates. In more recent years I have taught the text to upper-level undergraduate students at Essex and discussed a range of related issues with M.A. and Research students. I am grateful to all of these students, whose perseverance and willingness to express puzzlement have helped me make some progress in determining the indeterminate. I am particularly grateful to Michael Podro for his support as an interlocutor, colleague and friend.

The preparation of the final copy of this book led to a fruitful and enjoyable cooperation with a number of readers. Principal among these were James Corby, Maria Prodromou and Elin Simonson, each of whom read the text in its entirety and gave me extensive comments, valuable suggestions and corrections. The acuity of their suggestions, enthusiasm for the project and generosity in time and attention was remarkable. I am also very grateful to Dana MacFarlane and to John Walshe for helpful suggestions on aspects of the book. Finally, I would like to thank the team at Continuum, especially Sarah Campbell, Tom Crick and P. Muralidharan (in order of my acquaintance with them) for their efficient and helpful handling of this project. Despite all of this, any mistakes are, without doubt, my own.

CHAPTER 1

CONTEXT

1 KANT'S ROLE AS A LATE EIGHTEENTH CENTURY REPRESENTATIVE OF THE ENLIGHTENMENT

Kant came at the end of the period now referred to as 'The Enlightenment'. Like his forerunners, he sought to establish a rational basis for human experience. His particular contribution was to found a style of philosophizing known as 'critical' philosophy or critique. Kant, like other enlightenment thinkers, saw that while reason was a counterweight to the forces of dogmatism and mysticism, reason could itself become dogmatic if it was taken as an absolute foundation. Critical philosophy seeks to establish the importance of reason, while limiting its excesses through anchoring it in experience. Kant's distinctive way of achieving this goal shared by other Enlightenment philosophers was to trace experience back to grounds that make it possible, a *priori* conditions or the principles that govern knowledge and morality. Such principles are necessary if there is to be any experience whatsoever, but they are in no way sufficient conditions of experience. Principles must be applied within experience, just as the latter is always open to rational critique. Thus Kant expressed his commitment to experience at the same time as insisting that it can be analysed from a rational perspective. I will be emphasizing that, for Kant, if the principles governing our project of knowing things in the world and our moral actions, respectively, are to be established, each must be traced back to a distinctive cognitive faculty. Understanding is the most important mental capacity we possess when we aim to achieve knowledge, while reason is paramount in moral matters. The identification of principles for our cognitive and moral projects will require establishing the subjective grounds of their possibility, alongside an analysis of the principles that arise from those grounds and make experience possible. This is the dual focus of Kant's

1

critical response to the Enlightenment problem of establishing a rational basis for experience.

2 KANT'S OTHER CRITICAL WORKS AND THE STRUCTURE OF THE *CRITIQUE OF AESTHETIC JUDGEMENT*

The *Critique of Pure Reason* was initially published in 1781. This first critical work aimed to establish the rational grounds of our everyday claims to have knowledge about objects in the world. Kant argued that the validity of claims to knowledge must be traced back to the faculty of understanding, the basis for a system of principles which establish the form of experience in general. Anything that we might know and that counts, in his technical use of the term, as 'experience' must fulfil the following criteria: it must have some quantity, that is, must have some extension in space and time; it must make some qualitative effect or impression on our senses; it must stand in some relation to other things; and it must be capable of being experienced as possible, necessary or actual. These are the formal criteria of the experience of any object whatsoever and provide the necessary, though not the sufficient grounds of our experience of an object, for there must also be something given to us through the senses. In the second part of the first *Critique* Kant considers what arises if we try to ground our claims to know objects through a different faculty, namely, reason. In the theoretical context, reason is speculative and aims to think of the infinite as a totality. Yet the sensory world of objects comprises one thing after another and completion is not, in principle, attainable. Using reason to explain sensory objects leads to illusion and ultimately defeats our attempt to know them. However, reason makes a positive contribution to experience when it is used heuristically or 'regulatively', introducing a goal of completion as an ideal only. Using reason as a supplement to understanding, we aim to make knowledge as systematic as possible and this encourages us to expand our comprehension of the world.

The second critical text is *The Critique of Practical Reason*, which was published in 1788, one year after the second edition of the first *Critique*. Here Kant turns his attention to our capacity for moral action, which is grounded in the faculty of reason now in its practical, not its speculative guise. Practical reason is the foundation for agency and, ultimately, for moral agency insofar as it provides a principle for the assessment of whether or not what we aim to do is moral. The Categorical Imperative is the principle of morality and is presented in a number of different forms. Perhaps the most well-known version is expressed thus: if a maxim for action is moral, it must be possible to universalize it for all other judging subjects in all similar cases. Another formulation of the same idea is that we must respect humanity in all human beings, both in others and in ourselves.

A problem arises in that the first and second *Critiques* seem to present conflicting images of human existence, the first insisting on our mechanical determination in accordance with the laws of nature, while the second points to a realm of freedom in principle incompatible with nature. How is one and the same human agent capable of combining both these structures of experience?

Kant came to the conclusion that he needed to add another dimension which would make his philosophical critiques of cognition and morality consistent with one another through positioning them within a philosophical system. The third *Critique* is not only an additional component of critical philosophy, but the element that makes a system out of two books which would otherwise have, at best, shown two contingently related sides of our human existence and, at worst, would reveal the latter as fragmented and incoherent. The task of the *Critique of Judgement* (1790) is to bridge the gap between the principles of cognition and the principle of morality, showing that moral agents can intervene in the empirical world of objects. The specific field in which the resolution of the apparent conflict between cognition and morality will be addressed is, perhaps surprisingly, our appreciation for beauty. This is the subject of the first book of the third *Critique*, the *Critique of Aesthetic Judgement* where Kant identifies a third principal faculty, judgement, as making possible a link between the purposeless world of mechanical causality and the purposeful world of moral agency.

Judgement allows us to view the mechanical world in its empirical detail *as if* it were conducive to our moral agency, even though this must remain a heuristic interpretation, not a determination of the natural world. When judgement operates in this way, it is independent from the other principal faculties and counts as reflective judgement. When it is exercised under the direction of understanding or reason, judgement qualifies as 'determining'. The principle that guides reflective judgement is that nature is purposive for our judgement, that is, that we are capable of making sense of nature through the exercise of our judgement. Reason, as we have seen, leads to illusion when it seeks to explain experience as a totality. Understanding, meanwhile, achieves only a formal framework within which knowledge is possible, but which is ultimately not coherent with moral agency. 'The purposiveness of nature for judgement' opens up a new possibility, namely, that nature, while not the result of our own or any other rational purpose is, nevertheless, compatible with our intervention in the mechanical order of nature as moral agents exercising rational purposes. We can aim to realize our purposes within the natural world because that world is at least construable as conducive to, or purposive for, our capacity for judging.

But even if the purposiveness of nature for our judgement is a plausible or coherent idea, what could it possibly have to do with aesthetic judgement? Many readers of the third *Critique* have come to the conclusion that there can be no connection other than, at best, an associative one between such different issues as the order of nature in its empirical detail and our feeling of pleasure in the face of beauty. In 'Reading the Text' I will show how we can make sense of Kant's claim at the end of his first draft of the Introduction where he says that the 'Analytic' – in this case meaning the 'Analytic of Aesthetic Judgement' or the main body of the *Critique* prior to the 'Dialectic', not just the 'Analytic of the Beautiful' – is the working through of the idea of the purposiveness of nature. In short, I will argue that a beautiful object and in Kant's view, especially natural beauty, provides an instance where an object is congenial to our mental response, first, on the part of our cognitive power but also of reason, the basis of moral agency. If this is so, then although the beautiful object cannot prove that moral agency is possible in the natural world, it can intimate that such a bridging of the gap between cognition and morality may be possible.

Some have thought that the second part of the third *Critique*, *The Critique of Teleological Reason* is the place where a transition between cognition and morality is finally achieved. This is understandable as an interpretative strategy, because in judging teleologically we treat objects as if they were the result of, or at least conducive to, human purposes, especially of the moral kind, while at the same time seeking to expand our knowledge of them. This is surely a point when cognition and moral purpose converge. However, I will suggest that while teleological judgement certainly contributes to the systematic task of the third *Critique*, the deepest root of judgement's mediating role between understanding and reason is to be found only in the account of aesthetic judgement, for it is there that judgement is exercised as the power of judgement in independence from the other faculties. This *Reader's Guide* will focus exclusively on the aesthetic part of the third *Critique*, because both books are sufficiently complex to deserve separate treatments. But there is an even more important reason why the aesthetic part has to be investigated first: only an analysis of aesthetic judgement can uncover the power of judgement on which teleological purposiveness is founded.

3 THE EMERGENCE OF PHILOSOPHICAL AESTHETICS IN A SYSTEMATIC FORM IN THE LATE EIGHTEENTH CENTURY

There is plenty of evidence, some of it archaeological, for the view that appreciation for both natural and created beauty goes back almost as far as the beginning of human history. When western philosophy became established in the fourth century BC beauty was a topic from the outset. Admittedly, the evaluation of artworks in Plato's *Republic* is, at best, sceptical, but Aristotle had a much more positive view of their significance and wrote the first major western treatise on aesthetics, *The Poetics*. From then on, however, aesthetics hovered at the margins of the main philosophical topics of the western tradition, which was, from the outset, principally concerned with knowledge and morality. This is not to deny that there are instances – both important and interesting ones – of philosophical interest in aesthetics, but there is no continuous history of philosophical aesthetics until the late eighteenth century.

In writing the *Critique of Aesthetic Judgment* Kant brought aesthetics onto the centre of the philosophical stage. He not only wrote an extensive philosophical treatise on aesthetics – this had been done before by Shaftesbury, Baumgarten and Winckelmann, for instance – but, most importantly, he argued for the inclusion of aesthetics within the range of topics that count as fundamental for human experience, alongside knowledge and morality. Aesthetics was worthy of a critique because of being based on a principle that marks out a possibility not reducible to one of the other 'higher faculties', understanding and reason.

As we have seen, Kant not only included aesthetics within the system of the higher cognitive powers, he made the third *Critique* the condition of the possibility of his critical system. If judgement is not capable of mediating between understanding and reason, the possibility of the exercise of those powers becomes highly questionable. Aesthetics is the point at which the system concludes, but it is also the condition of possibility of that system, retrospectively establishing that the two previous critiques can harmonize with one another. Thus the Enlightenment project of limiting reason in the interests of experience culminates in the insight that knowledge and morality can only be safeguarded if it is also established that we have a power of judgement that mediates between them and aesthetics, I will argue, is the principal domain in which this new higher faculty is exercised.

4   THE POLITICAL CONTEXT OF *THE CRITIQUE OF JUDGEMENT* – CENSORSHIP AND REVOLUTION

When Kant was writing, it would be another century until the modern state of Germany was born. He lived in Königsberg, a city on the Baltic, which belonged to the kingdom of Prussia, the capital of which was Berlin. During the period when the first two Critiques were written, or, at least, in development, the King of Prussia was Frederick II, commonly known as Frederick the Great (1740–86). Frederick was considered an 'enlightened' monarch in that he governed by rule of law and not as an absolute despot. While there had been threats to the power of the monarchy since at least the time of the English Revolution in the seventeenth century, it was not until the late eighteenth century that the reality of that threat arrived in continental Europe. The French Revolution of 1789, inspired by the principles of Enlightenment philosophy, overthrew the local monarchy and put in question the legitimacy of the power of monarchs throughout Europe and beyond. Kant broadly sympathized with the republican principles on which the French revolution was founded. Political power would now be based on rationally determined laws, rather than on the autocratic power of an individual or cabal. His own political philosophy, especially 'Perpetual Peace', argued for the necessity of just such a rule of law not only within a nation, but also between nations.

However, Kant hesitated about the way in which the revolution developed into the 'Terror', when even supporters of the republic were condemned as its enemies. Moreover, he was in a potentially difficult position because however 'enlightened' a monarch might be, any non-elected sovereign would be bound to have some misgivings about the revolution's threat to royal power, never mind the threat of regicide. The situation was worsened as by this stage the prevailing regime under Friedrich Wilhelm II (1786–97) was overtly antagonistic to the project of the Enlightenment. It was not uncommon for writers to be thrown into prison for expressing revolutionary ideas and, at the very least, their works could be suppressed by the state censors. Thus Kant walked a fine line both in his own reflections on the revolution and in his dealings with the prevailing political powers.

There was not a great risk of the *Critique of Aesthetic Judgement* being censored, in contrast to his more political works. But this work has a political relevance, even though it may not always be evident. Kant's insistence on the irreducibility of individual aesthetic judgement and on the absence of rules – either divine or otherwise authoritative – for beauty indirectly speaks for the right of individuals to exercise their judgement as autonomous and mature judging subjects. The message is not, however, one of out and out individualism, for he also believes that there is an aesthetic community of judging subjects. This, too, can be seen as an implicitly political position, because it suggests that there is a community prior to the enforcement of order by a state power. For these reasons, Kant's aesthetics is compatible with and even reinforces and deepens his political commitment to the republican ideal.

5 THE WIDER CULTURAL ENVIRONMENT

Famously – or, rather, infamously – Kant did not venture more than a short distance from his native city of Königsberg and as this was hardly a centre of European cultural excellence, he was at somewhat of a disadvantage. Nevertheless, he was kept well informed of philosophical and cultural developments through reports in journals and through translations of some important texts into German. Thus he was aware of Hume's radical development of Enlightenment philosophy, questioning widely held presuppositions and assumptions still dormant within thinking that attacked dogmatism.

Kant was at more of a disadvantage when it came to the arts, for although his surroundings were not without aesthetic interest, he did not have direct access to any of the great artworks, all of which were to be found far from Königsberg. Unlike Goethe, he did not travel south to Italy to discover the treasures of the classical period, a journey that was fashionable for the educated elite. Kant may have had access to prints and engravings, as well as direct access to lesser known local works and, thus, some exposure to a range of visual artworks. Even so, his education in the visual arts must have been restricted by the medium in which he encountered images, the originals of which were often highly coloured and physically commanding works. It is thus not surprising that some of his most enthusiastic comments are directed not to the visual arts, but, rather, to poetry. When we consider that his sedentary lifestyle can have given rise to few opportunities for the experience of magnificent natural beauty or sublimity, we must be even more struck by the important role he gave to aesthetics.

CHAPTER 2

OVERVIEW OF THEMES

In the first part of this 'Overview' I begin by discussing the specific nature of aesthetic, as opposed to moral and cognitive, judgements. I go on to emphasize the way in which, for Kant, aesthetic judgements reveal 'the power of judgement' and how this characteristic gains a place for aesthetics within the system of critical philosophy. This discussion sets the scene for grasping the task Kant sets for the *Critique of Judgement* and provides readers with a context for the main issues addressed in the text.

In the second part I chart a way through the text by raising some particularly important interpretative issues. First, I discuss the sense in which we should understand Kant's claim in the 'Analytic of the Beautiful' that judgements of beauty are subjective. The answer I propose allows me to introduce the central motif of my reading, namely, such judgements are characterized by what I call a 'dual harmony': one side of which is the harmony between our mental faculties, while the other is that between our mental activity and a beautiful object. I go on to mention that, contrastively, in the 'Analytic of the Sublime' we learn how judgements of the sublime reveal a disharmony – again, both within the mind and between mind and world – which is highly significant for our moral agency. Secondly, interpreters often ask why Kant's investigation of aesthetic judgement does not conclude with the analysis of judgements of the beautiful and sublime. I suggest that one element of the advance in Kant's argument achieved by the 'Deduction of Judgements of Taste' is his description of the power of judgement as 'our very ability to judge'. The other element is the investigation of a pre-determinative relation between subject and object. Finally, I turn to the relative importance of natural and artistic beauty for Kant, suggesting his position may not be, and need not be, as polarized as many have thought. I hope that raising these issues, which will be discussed in detail in 'Reading the Text', will help prepare for the reader's engagement with the text.

1 AESTHETIC JUDGEMENT LIES BETWEEN KNOWLEDGE AND MORALITY

Up until shortly before writing the *Critique of Judgement* Kant believed that he had exhausted the scope of the project of transcendental philosophy, the aim of which was to establish the fundamental structures of human cognition and agency. On the one hand, we are beings in a natural world of objects governed by laws of cause and effect. In this respect, we, just like objects, are determined by the mechanical laws of nature, the same laws that enable us to know those objects. We achieve knowledge by ordering under concepts what we apprehend through our senses within space and time. We can thus identify what would otherwise be a 'blooming buzzing confusion' as individual things with specific characteristics.[1] This is Kant's epistemological project, which seeks to establish philosophically the validity of claims we make in everyday life, namely, that we know at least some of the things we encounter in the world. But, so far, Kant's transcendental philosophy offers no account of the possibility of moral agency. Indeed, it may look as if his epistemic theory entails that we are wholly determined through the laws of cause and effect and that our primary orientation is towards knowledge of objects. In the *Critique of Practical Reason* Kant goes on to establish that human agency is grounded in a distinctive principle that cannot be reduced to causality. Insofar as we are agents, we determine our actions in accordance with our free will, not through the laws of mechanical necessity. This capacity for self-determination is, at its highest level, the ability to act morally. Agency in general rests on a capacity for freedom; morality rests on the capacity for free self-determination in abstraction from any considerations other than the exercise of reason, a capacity that is, ultimately, moral. When we act morally, we obey the 'Categorical Imperative' that is, the principle that our actions are – or should be – conducive to the recognition of humanity in every human being as they, too, are free moral agents. Kant, thus, had established that we have two distinctive primary orientations, but gradually he came to the conclusion that a problem raised by his critics needed to be addressed. It appeared that he had established that we are both unfree (in the world of nature) and free (in the moral world). How could this be so without an existential rupture in our psyche?

The broad strokes of this picture should already be familiar from my discussion of the 'Context' for this *Reader's Guide*, where we saw that Kant hopes that *The Critique of Judgement* – the 'third' critique – will solve the dilemma that has arisen. An account of our ability to judge aesthetically will address the gap between our capacity to know things governed by strict mechanical laws in nature and our free moral agency. The key to the solution Kant has in mind is that aesthetic judgement is based on the power of judgement, in contrast to both epistemic judgements where the faculty of understanding is predominant and moral agency based on reason. The power of judgement makes possible a new mode of experience, namely, aesthetic appreciation, which stands in a systematic relation with both cognition and morality. This is why the third *Critique* is able to complete and, even, make possible the critical system as I suggested in 'Context'.

In judging aesthetically we respond to something given to our senses, an empirical object, yet our response to it is playful or exploratory. We are, at the same time, both of and beyond the empirical world, through the transfigurative power of imagination that takes up something we apprehend and finds in it much more than might initially be evident at the level of appearance. We are inspired by beautiful things to discover more about ourselves, that is, our capacity for attributing to an empirical given a significance beyond what is presented to us. Now, morality also requires that we transcend the empirical realm of cause and effect and beautiful things are symbolic for our capacity to do so. This is why the freedom of the mind in the aesthetic case is a precursor to the freedom characteristic of moral agency.

While beauty points towards our capacity for being moral, it also points towards the possibility of cognition or, more narrowly, knowledge. When we appreciate things as beautiful, we combine a capacity for taking them in as 'intuitions' through our senses with a capacity for seeking a concept for what we apprehend. This also happens in the synthesis of a sensory intuition under a concept characteristic of cognitive judgement, with a very important proviso: in that case we aim to achieve knowledge, whereas in the aesthetic case if we aim at anything at all, it is to remain in our contemplation of the thing, not to know it as such. But just because the same basic structure of mental activity is at work, the aesthetic judgement reveals something about the fundamental conditions of cognition, which, we will discover, Kant calls 'cognition in general'.

Aesthetic judgement thus looks towards morality and towards cognition, but remains distinct from both. It is arguable, although I can only point to it here, that taste is exemplary for both moral and epistemic judgement, just because it is based on the power of judgement that makes possible any judgement whatsoever.

2   SOME CENTRAL CHARACTERISTICS OF AESTHETIC JUDGEMENT

What does Kant mean when he speaks of beauty? To say that some thing or event is beautiful is not to say that it is pretty or merely 'easy on the eye'. Right at the beginning of the 'Analytic of the Beautiful' Kant remarks enigmatically that beauty has something to do with a 'feeling of life'. I will suggest that in his view, beauty reveals the activity of the mind in response to phenomena available to our senses, that is, seen and, perhaps, also heard by us.

Famously, Kant insists that beauty is not in the object. This has encouraged many of his readers to conclude that beauty is subjective in the sense that it is in the subject *rather* than in the object. If so, it sounds as if Kant's aesthetics signal a move to the interiority of the mind, in contrast to his previous concern, in the *Critique of Pure Reason,* with the way in which the mind is capable of determining an object given to the senses so as to achieve knowledge of it. But already at the outset of the first *Critique* he introduced a philosophical version of the 'Copernican Revolution', that is, a radical shift from the prevailing perspective, arguing that if we are to establish how knowledge can be achieved, we must stop thinking of objects as entities unconnected to our experience of them. We must recognize that an object that can be known by us necessarily appears to our senses and is determinable by our concepts. Some have thought that this theory makes knowledge entirely dependent on the internal workings of the mind, which has become the ultimate author of reality. However, Kant is committed to the position that objects are accessible to our senses and our thinking and does not deny their material, extra-mental status. The mind generates the formal dimension of objects, that is, their order or organization, but can only do so in response or relation to a given that is ultimately extra-mental. In other words, knowledge can only arise because we have certain subjective capacities that allow us to take up things in the world. In the reconstruction of the text in 'Reading the Text', I will suggest that it is not that Kant's account of aesthetic judgements aims to establish them as merely subjective in opposition to objective epistemic judgements. Rather, aesthetic judgements reveal the deeper structure of our claims to knowledge: beauty draws out the implications of the relation between subject and object that must be in place if we are to experience objects in such a way as to gain knowledge of them. This helps explain why at the very outset of the *Critique,* Kant says that aesthetic judgements do not give rise to cognition and yet at a later stage goes on to say that they are related to what he calls 'cognition in general'.

Beauty arises when some thing in the world inspires a response on the part of our minds. The thing incites us to explore it through our senses and in our thought. It is as though it were designed so as to stimulate our response and yet, Kant insists, there is no such design. The beautiful thing is peculiarly suited to us and to the kind of beings we are, combining a capacity for taking in things through our senses with a capacity for ordering this input under concepts. A virtuous circularity develops between this particular thing and our minds. The more we look at it, the more we are encouraged to look and alongside our looking, we find ourselves thinking about what we see. Kant talks about a play of the faculties, by which he means that our capacity for apprehension through the senses (reinforced and expanded in imagination) works in concert with our capacity for conceptualization, the understanding. This is the 'harmony of the faculties' characteristic of judgements of taste. But what is often missed is that this harmony within the mind could not arise were there not at the same time a harmony between thing and mind. Aesthetic judgement only arises when we come across some thing that gives rise to a free playfulness between our senses and thinking. Thus there is not only a harmony of the faculties, but a harmony between the beautiful thing as I perceive it and the activity of my mind in response to that thing. These two harmonies can be analytically distinguished from one another, yet neither is the cause of the other. Within experience they are always intertwined and are best thought of as a dual harmony.

If beauty signals a harmonious relation both within the mind and between it and the world, the sublime introduces disharmony. We judge something sublime when it defeats our capacity for sensory comprehension. We cannot simply take it in, because it is too large or too powerful. What we take in through our senses does not hold together or, at least, threatens to fall apart. In the case of beauty, our sensory intake harmonizes with a general capacity for understanding sensory phenomena. But now, we are stymied. The absolutely large or overwhelmingly powerful phenomenon defies our capacity to take it in through our senses and, as a result, it cannot be held together or 'comprehended' so that we might be capable of synthesizing what we apprehend and recognize it under a concept. It is thus, in principle, impossible to attain knowledge of the absolutely large as such and such a determinate object. Kant characterizes this as a disharmony of the faculties of imagination and understanding. (Later I will explain why he speaks here of imagination and not of intuition, which is the term he uses for the sensory dimension of experience in the *Critique of Pure Reason*.) The failure of our subjective cognitive powers in the face of a sublime phenomenon gives rise to displeasure, but Kant claims that there is a saving grace concealed in this break-down of experience. Our senses are defeated, but, at the same time, we discover an alternative power, the capacity as rational beings to think beyond the sphere of sensible experience. Although our senses and imagination are overwhelmed by the enormity of the phenomenon with which we are faced, in thought we can make sense of and even transcend it. In short, we discover ourselves as beings that are not only animal, but also rational insofar as we have a capacity to think the infinite and guide our actions by moral principles having their ground not in the world, but, rather, in ourselves. This is the positive result of the sublime and gives rise to an indirect pleasure.

So far, Kant has outlined the characteristics that identify the beautiful and the sublime. He believes, however, that he has to go further and finally prove that what he has described has a necessary basis, that is, that aesthetic judgement is not simply a variation on, but necessary for human experience. This involves establishing that aesthetic judgement, like epistemic judgement and moral principle, deserves a place in transcendental philosophy, the philosophical reconstruction of the fundamental structures of the human condition. In the *Critique of Pure Reason* he argued that we could not have any experience at all if we did not have the capacity to order sensory objects under a categorical framework of concepts arising from our power of understanding. In the *Critique of Practical Reason* he argued that our intervention in the world as agents requires that we are capable of directing our actions by a moral principle: the Categorical Imperative, ultimately traceable to our power of reason. There is no agency without the possibility of moral agency. In the third *Critique* Kant seeks to show that aesthetic judgement is also part of the primary framework that makes experience possible. (Here I use the term 'experience' in a wider sense than does Kant in his epistemology, where the term is equivalent to 'knowledge'.) If aesthetic judgement is to qualify as part of the system of transcendental critique, then he must show that it, too, stems from the most fundamental conditions that make our experience possible and these, for Kant, are the subjective conditions he calls 'faculties', the capacities that first make possible that we experience anything at all. Kant intends to argue in the 'Deduction of Taste' that aesthetic judgements of beauty have such a basis in the power of judgement. (He does not think that an explicit deduction of the sublime is necessary for reasons we will consider when looking at the details of the text.)

The task of the 'Deduction of Taste' is to establish that judgements of taste can be traced back to a subjectively universal and necessary principle. There is much debate about whether or not the 'Deduction' is wholly distinct from the 'Analytic', where Kant investigated the main characteristics of taste. It is broadly correct to look to the 'Analytic' to provide a description of judgements of taste and to the 'Deduction' to establish the validity of those judgements, but as we will see in 'Reading the Text' the second of these tasks already enters into the argument of the 'Analytic'. In my view, the distinctiveness of the official 'Deduction' is twofold. First, Kant introduces a precision in his characterization of the power of judgement, namely as the faculty that makes possible 'our very ability to judge', which is only exercised in an autonomous fashion in judgements of taste. Secondly, he clarifies the formal status of the relation in which the subject stands to the object in a judgement of taste. I suggest that the nature of this relation is best understood as 'pre-determinative', that is, prior to determination as knowledge.

As we saw in the first part of this 'Overview', if I am to appreciate something as beautiful, my mind must display the general mental activity that would be necessary if I were to know some thing as an object. And yet, insofar as I am judging aesthetically, I am not engaged in the pursuit of knowledge. In this case the activity is that of the power of judgement exercised in its own right, rather than subservient to the faculty of understanding as it is in the cognitive case. In the first *Critique* Kant established that judgement is necessary for the possibility of any knowledge whatsoever; while in the third *Critique* he reveals that it is only when judgement is exercised as a distinctive power under its own principle that aesthetic judgement becomes possible. In the 'Deduction of Taste' Kant argues that the power of judgement as 'our very ability to judge' founds the subjective universality and exemplary necessity of taste. The beautiful thing is not just pleasurable for me alone: I hold that it should also be so for all other judging subjects and I call on them to agree with me. (They may not do so, but we will see that this does not necessarily undermine the validity of judgements of taste.) As an aesthetic judge, I inhabit a community of taste because every other judging subject shares the ground of taste, that is, they also, as judging subjects, have recourse to the power of judgement, the exercise of which displays the subjective conditions of cognition. Aesthetic judgement is part of the fundamental repertoire of human experience because it is based on the capacities that make experience possible, the subjective conditions through which we encounter things in the world in concert with other judging and self-regulating human beings.

Kant's thinking about aesthetics emerges out of a concern with beautiful nature, but he was also responding to a tradition of evaluating artworks. It is sometimes suggested that Kant was concerned principally, at least, with beauty in nature and not with artworks. Hegel thought this was the case and designed his own aesthetics as a reversal of Kant's. Others have argued that Kant only turns his attention to artworks in the later sections of the *Critique* when he discusses genius. However, throughout the 'Analytic of the Beautiful', Kant's examples consistently are selected from the field of art. It is first in his account of the sublime that he suggests that natural objects alone qualify for aesthetic judgement and, even there, he begins his account with a discussion of human artefacts, while he concludes that the sublime is ultimately neither in art nor in nature, but rather in the mind. On occasion later in the text, Kant comes close to suggesting that artworks may not be worthy of pure aesthetic judgements, but I will argue that this development arises from a misapplication of his own theory. Throughout the *Critique* Kant considers the ways in which artworks give rise to aesthetic judgement, although, admittedly, he sees our response to nature as leading more unproblematically to judgements of taste. This, I would suggest, is a tendency that has a historical determination and was not necessary for his project. While it is important to understand Kant's position as an individual thinker at a specific point in history, it is also important to take up his project as a way of thinking relevant to another time, in particular, our own.

CHAPTER 3

READING THE TEXT

1 THE PLACE OF AESTHETIC JUDGEMENT WITHIN THE CRITICAL SYSTEM

Kant wrote two versions of the 'Introduction' to the *Critique of Judgement,* only one of which he published. (The unpublished version is referred to as the 'First Introduction'.) Both introductions are notoriously difficult and I will not attempt a continuous reading of them here. Addressing the detail of their arguments would not only take more space than we have, but also would introduce topics that are only indirectly related to aesthetic judgement. Nevertheless certain central themes of the introductions are necessary for laying out the role Kant apportions to aesthetic judgement within the critical system and for explaining why it is necessary for that system and for human experience in general. Here, drawing on the 'Preface' and only the published version of the 'Introduction', I will discuss two elements: the systematic place of judgement between nature and freedom; and Kant's notion of the purposiveness of nature for judgement, along with its significance for both aesthetic and teleological reflective judgement.

In the 'Preface' Kant asks if judgement, which he already casts as the mediating link between understanding and reason, has its own *a priori* principle, in other words one with its source in the peculiar activity of that faculty alone, just as do those other higher cognitive powers without which experience would not be possible. Understanding is the faculty that gives the law to nature, while reason operates under the laws of freedom. Judgement's principle would give a rule *a priori* to the feeling of pleasure and displeasure and establishing that there is such an *a priori* principle is the task of the *Critique of Judgement* [AA 168].[1] The problem initially posed in the 'Introduction' is that we inhabit a natural world, where causal laws hold sway and, at the same time, we are moral agents capable of self-determination in accordance with the law of freedom. This could result in existential fragmentation, where our embodied natural selves stand in no relation to our moral selves, and if this were the case it is difficult to see how morality could have any relevance for life as it is lived. Kant says that would be *as if* we inhabited two worlds, yet he clearly thinks this would not be a viable situation. Instead he insists that although the principles of nature and freedom are distinct from one another, it must be the case that we, as moral agents, are capable of having an influence within the natural world. Moral beings must be able to act in the natural world, that is, our moral intentions must be capable of having real effects otherwise we would not be free at all. The only way in which this can be insured is if there is a way of connecting nature and freedom ['Introduction', Section II, AA 175/6].

In Section III of the 'Introduction', judgement is firmly identified as mediating between understanding and reason [AA 177]. Judgement is, generally, the ability to think of the particular as falling under a universal, either determinatively when the rule is given or reflectively when only the particular is given [IV, AA 179]. Determining judgement gives rise to knowledge and is based on pre-established, although strictly formal, rules, supplied by understanding or reason. In contrast, reflective judgement operating without guidance from any other faculty, seeks out a rule that must remain indeterminate and in so doing opens up the possibility of an order emerging in the course of an exploration that can never be finalized. A prime example of this is when judgement operates reflectively in investigating empirical laws with a view to ordering them relative to still higher principles. Nature is primarily ordered or determined by the laws of understanding, such as the law of causality, as Kant argued in the *Critique of Pure Reason [C.Pu.R.]*. Yet laws of understanding operate at such a high level of formality that it is quite conceivable that nature, in its detail, is anarchic. Henry Allison calls this the threat of 'empirical chaos' [Allison, 2001, pp. 38–9.]. Only judgement can supply a rule that establishes order for the multiplicity of empirical laws. Kant calls the order that arises, the 'purposiveness of nature in its diversity' [P: IV, AA 180].[2] The principle on which such order is based is a transcendental principle of judgement [V, AA 181]. Only judgement operating as an autonomous power, as what in Section 35 will be called 'our very ability to judge', makes possible the presupposition of the purposiveness of nature for our cognition, an ability to presuppose that there is a unity among the diversity of empirical laws allowing us to have a coherent experience. To make such a presupposition is to assume that the detail or particularity of the natural world is accessible to our cognitive power and thus is knowable by us. The principle of judgement thus operates heuristically, facilitating our project of investigating the natural world in its empirical detail. This principle is subjective and cannot objectively give the law to nature, because it is entirely possible that the detail of empirical nature would not fit with our cognitive power. Nevertheless, the particular sense in which this principle is subjective allows for the investigation of the objective world. Indeed, Kant says that we would not make any progress in our cognition at the empirical level if we did not have such a capacity [V, AA 183–6].

In the 'Preface' we saw that judgement gives a rule to the feeling of pleasure and displeasure. Kant now says that the attainment of an aim is always connected with a feeling of pleasure [VI, AA 187]. He suggests that when we discover a way to trace one empirical law to another so as to explain the first, we feel pleasure. We once also found pleasure in ordering natural phenomena as species falling under genera, but at this stage of our cognitive history we no longer do so. The cognitive aim of seeing one empirical phenomenon as an instance of a larger group has become automatic: we have lost sight of the achievement it represents and of the activity of judgement necessary for it. For this reason, we need something further if we are to rediscover the activity of judgement hidden deep in our empirical investigation of the world. Otherwise, we might just accept that 'empirical chaos' is unavoidable [VI, AA 188]. In doing so, we would not only deny the existence of a capacity we possess, we would, in so doing, undermine its effectiveness.

So far we have learned that judgement's ability to make sense of the law-governed order of the empirical world arises from presupposing a purposiveness of nature for our cognitive power. Even though there is a wide diversity of empirical laws, it is possible to order those laws so as to make sense for us and facilitate our exploration of nature. In principle at least, empirical nature is not alien to our aim of achieving knowledge of it, an aim that would give rise to a pleasure if we attained it and even the anticipation of which pleases us. But it has also been established that we have great difficulty in being aware of the activity of judgement that makes sense of the empirical world. Kant now introduces two ways in which we can become aware of a power so central to our experience.

The first and most important point of access to our power of judgement arises in our aesthetic appreciation of beautiful objects. Aesthetic pleasure expresses an object's being fitted for our cognitive powers, which, in response, relate to one another in a free play [VII, AA 189/90]. This is what I call a dual harmony. Kant's point is that cognition requires the combination of a capacity for taking things in through our senses, which he calls 'intuition' in the first *Critique*, with a rule of the understanding. In the third *Critique* imagination stands in for intuition and this is broadly for two reasons. First, already in the cognitive case imagination is closely implicated with intuition and has the role of making possible the re-identification of an intuition over time [*C.Pu.R.*, A 98–102; See also B 150–2].[3] Secondly, in aesthetic judgement imagination transfigures the merely sensory given by directing to it a contemplative attention, as we will see in my discussion of the 'Analytic of the Beautiful'. In aesthetic judgement the same capacities that operate in cognition are combined, but understanding does not supply a rule for imagination. There is no rule for taste, or at least no explicit or determining one, and the faculties of imagination and understanding must co-operate freely in 'play' or 'harmony'. Our minds are open to the possibilities of a phenomenon without our trying to explain it. In this state of mind, we feel a pleasure simply in the fit between a given phenomenon and our mental activity.

Kant outlines some of the characteristics of aesthetic judgement, which will be discussed in more detail in the main body of the text. Judgements of taste should, properly, attend only to the form of an object and they involve, perhaps unconsciously, a comparison with our general ability to refer intuitions to concepts [AA 190]. Restricting our attention to the formal conditions of apprehension will ensure that aesthetic judgement can be traced back to the fundamental conditions of cognition

in general, referred to in this passage as the general possibility of synthesizing an intuition under a concept. It is also
crucial that the beautiful thing brings about a harmony of the
cognitive powers without there being any intent to do so. The
coincidence between a natural phenomenon and our mental
activity only bears a general significance if it is not based on
a purpose or specific goal [VII, AA 190–1]. Further, pleasure
arises in response to an empirical presentation [*Vorstellung*] or
sensory phenomenon, but this does not result in the pleasure
being merely empirical, resting as it does on the universal subjective conditions of the cognition of objects [AA 191].[4] As Kant
will develop in the body of the text, an aesthetic judgement
involves an awareness of the phenomenon's conduciveness to
the subjective conditions of judgement in general. Our feeling
of the play of the faculties, necessary in some proportion for
any cognition whatsoever, is the basis for our finding an object
beautiful. Thus it is not just our feeling of pleasure in the object,
but the feeling of pleasure in our mental activity in response to
the object that qualifies as the basis for aesthetic judgement.
Despite this important distinction, the object is the necessary
empirical condition of a reflective awareness of the relation
in which our mental activity stands to nature. Indeed, we can
understand the purposiveness of nature for our cognition in
general terms as resulting from our capacity to relate to the
world through varying the combination of our mental powers.
Finally, Kant very briefly suggests that in addition to purposiveness for cognition, he will also explore a purposiveness for
our freedom through an examination of the aesthetic judgements that respond to phenomena displaying a lack of form in
the 'Analytic of the Sublime' [AA 192].

Now we can explain why Kant sees aesthetic pleasure as giving
access to the purposiveness of empirical nature. The pleasure
we take in the fit between a particular object and the activity
of our cognitive powers is a microcosm of what is aimed at in
our reflective judging of empirical nature. The beautiful object
encourages the exercise of our cognitive powers and we become
aware of their harmonious cooperation with one another. Now
if nature as a whole were revealed as fitted for our cognition of
it, we would have achieved the aim of empirical cognition and
would feel a pleasure. But all we can do is adopt the cognition

of nature as a whole as a goal and seek to move closer and closer to achieving a coherent view of the empirical world. Our pleasure can only arise incrementally in the achievement of local solutions, never in a final match between nature and mind, for if this were the case, judgement would be exercised determinatively, not reflectively. Most importantly, this cannot happen because Kant is committed to the view that the natural world (in its detail at least) does not automatically conform to the mind. The mind is not master and has to seek out the order of nature at the empirical level. Nevertheless, something beautiful pleases us because of the fit or purposiveness between a particular object and our mental response and this singular instance opens up the possibility that nature in general may also be accessible to the ordering activity of our minds. We can thus hope – although we cannot know – that the aim of a fit between nature and mind may be achievable.

Teleological judgement is a further way of reflecting on the purposiveness of nature usually hidden from us in the course of our empirical exploration of the world. Teleological judgement does not, however, give insight into the activity of judgement operating independently from the other faculties [VIII, AA 193. See also IX, AA 197; 'Preface' AA 169/70]. Teleological judgement is the ability to consider certain natural phenomena as natural purposes, that is, either as internally organized so as to fulfil a purpose or as necessary for some further purpose. Such judgement requires a combination of judgement with reason, the faculty that introduces purposes into the field of nature [VIII, AA 193]. Whereas an aesthetic judgement addresses a particular phenomenon traced back to the subjective conditions of judgement, teleological judgement refers the phenomenon to a whole that is conceptually graspable, even though the concept is reflective, not determining. In other words, we cannot definitively establish teleological order, although we can explain it in an indeterminate and incomplete, or, 'regulative' fashion, that is, through reflective judgement.

The ability to see natural phenomena as guided by purposes is crucial for Kant's aim of bridging the gap between nature and freedom, so we may think that the second part of the *Critique of Judgement* is more important for his systematic aims. Moreover, Kant says that while we cannot throw a bridge from nature to freedom, our capacity to intervene as free agents within the natural world ('causality through freedom') arises from the ability to regard sensory objects as conducive to purposes and, eventually, to a final purpose [AA 195–6]. This is just what teleological judgement does. Yet Kant says that the ability to make the leap from nature to freedom rests in judgement's presupposition '*a priori* and without regard to the practical' of a transition between them [IX, AA 196]. As we have seen and will see in greater detail in what follows, it is in aesthetic judgement that the principle of judgement or, more precisely, the presupposition of the purposiveness of nature for our judgement is expressed purely as a reflection on the power and activity of judgement [Hughes, 2006b]. Teleological judgement could not even get started in fulfilling the systematic role of providing a transition from nature to freedom, if it did not rely on a principle that can be purely expressed only in an aesthetic judgement. [See also VIII, AA 193–4 where Kant speaks of formal purposiveness as a preparation for teleological judgement.]

The reason for writing a third *Critique* arises from the discovery that judgement is a cognitive power in its own right, distinguished by its own specific principle. Judgement's peculiar capacity is to presuppose a principle of the purposiveness of nature for our cognition (or judgement). This heuristic principle allows for the discovery of an order at the level of empirical nature, which when we judge aesthetically or teleologically is capable of giving us pleasure. Normally, though, we do not pay attention to the achievement this entails and consequently we feel no pleasure and are not even aware of the activity of judgement required. Aesthetic judgement provides an opportunity for focusing on a relation with a particular phenomenon given to us empirically and yet conducive to our mental activity. In appreciating this object we become aware of the activity of our judgement, which is necessary not only in this aesthetic case, but generally in all cognition. This fragile link opens up the possibility that nature is open to our intervention as rational beings. Teleological judgement builds on the initial stepping stone made by aesthetic judgement, seeking out ways in which purposes arise (although only for a subject) within the natural world. In this way it becomes at least conceivable that a transition between nature and freedom could be achieved: that is, that a self-determining moral agent could bring about her purposes within the natural world. Without the fit between mind and nature the purposiveness of nature for judgement makes possible, it would not just be as if we inhabited two worlds; we would indeed be in a condition of existential dichotomy.

Study questions

Do you think there is a gap between cognition and morality? If so, could judgement bridge it?

Is the 'purposiveness of nature for our judgement' to be found in nature or in our minds or is it simply a philosophical conceit?

Is aesthetic judgement a privileged species of judgement?

2   THE FOUR 'MOMENTS' OF A JUDGEMENT OF BEAUTY

2.1   Introduction to the 'Analytic of the Beautiful'

In the 'Analytic of the Beautiful' Kant sets out to present the principal characteristics of 'taste', that is, aesthetic judgements that express our liking for beauty. While there are other kinds of liking, aesthetic pleasure is distinctive, being marked by four defining aspects each of which is discussed in a 'Moment' or section of the 'Analytic'. Aesthetic judgement is disinterested; its subjective universality is expressed in our requiring that all other judging subjects also like this object; its 'purposiveness without purpose' [Zweckmäßigkeit ohne Zweck] means that something deemed beautiful gives rise to the purposive activity of the human mind, yet invites no actual cognitive, appetitive or moral purpose; and, finally, the necessity of the pleasure we have in the object is due to its resting on a common sense, that is, the mental activity necessary for any cognition whatsoever. At this stage of his account Kant is principally intent on laying out the main features of aesthetic judgements. While he offers arguments that clarify and even justify his account, he does not conclusively prove that there are such judgements nor does he present a systematic account of their place within the range of human mental activity in general. Instead, he starts by describing a phenomenon that should be identifiable – although perhaps only unclearly so – from our own experience. We may already have a view that aesthetic judgements are merely expressions of personal preference or, ultimately, are subsidiary to moral judgements, but whatever our view we have a sense of what it is to find something beautiful. Kant presupposes this acquaintance and seeks to clarify what is really going on when we respond aesthetically.

In what follows, I will highlight the contemplative attention characteristic of taste; the sense in which aesthetic judgements are 'subjective' and the way in which they involve and even reveal a relation to objects. We will also see that taste is 'sociable'; how it entails a feeling aware of itself as a feeling and in what sense it qualifies as indeterminate. I also examine the conflation of the grounds of cognition with those of taste that arises especially in Sections 9 and 21. I suggest a solution, which allows Section 21 to be recognized as central to Kant's account of aesthetic judgement, even though Kant does not provide a plausible account of his argument until later in the 'Deduction of Taste'.

2.2 Moment 1: the disinterestedness of taste

The first Moment is concerned with taste's characteristically disinterested character, although he does not directly discuss this until Section 2. He begins by situating taste relative to cognition and establishing its distinctively aesthetic or subjective status. Later in the Moment he distinguishes the pleasure that accompanies judgements of taste from moral and sensory pleasure.

In a note right at the outset of the first Moment and before the commencement of the first section, Kant announces that taste is the capacity to judge objects as beautiful. It is thus a receptive capacity arising in response to something given to us in experience, that is, something empirical. Kant also announces that he intends to analyse the fundamental features of taste following a strategy already established in the *Critique of Pure Reason* with regard to cognitive or epistemic judgement, which for my current purposes I will treat as equivalent. At times Kant suggests that moral judgement is also a form of (practical) cognition, but this is not crucial for our discussion at this stage. In his analysis of the faculty of understanding, central for our capacity to know an object, Kant first of all sets out a 'Table of Judgements', which expresses the range of forms of possible judgement. Only following this does Kant introduce the 'Table of Categories', laying out the forms of concepts through which we think of or know objects. The categories are always directed to the possible knowledge of an object, whereas the forms of judgement are not yet aimed at knowledge and operate at the level of the most general activity of judging which *could be* but has not yet been directed to achieving knowledge. In the first section of the 'Analytic of the Beautiful', Kant insists on the distinctiveness of taste from cognition. We might think that this means that taste has nothing to do with knowledge at all, but it will turn out later that aesthetic judgement stands in a relation to what Kant calls 'cognition in general'. Situating beauty in relation to the 'Table of Judgements' allows us to see how aesthetic judgement may be grounded in something that is prior to or broader than cognition, narrowly construed as epistemic. This would be judgement as the general capacity to combine different mental orientations as a necessary, but not sufficient condition of cognition; an ability that operates prior to knowing anything in a determinate fashion. But although Kant finds it useful to follow the general features of judgement already established in his epistemology, in the initial note he also insists that he will not follow the order of his previous account. While the analysis of a judgement aimed at knowing an object always starts with its 'quantity', aiming to establish if it is valid of every, a particular or only one instance (universal, particular and singular judgements), analysis of aesthetic judgements begins from their 'quality'. In the second section of the first Moment, we will discover that the quality Kant identifies is that of disinterestedness. He does not, at this point at least, adequately explain why he starts with the quality of aesthetic judgements.

In Section 1, Kant aims to establish that a judgement of taste is aesthetic, that is, that it is subjective and not objective or cognitive. The point of the 'Analytic' as a whole is to establish the distinctiveness of aesthetic judgement and this is crucial, for otherwise there would have been no justification for writing a third *Critique*. Each critique is an analysis of a fundamental or higher mental capacity. Whereas the *Critique of Pure Reason* is principally concerned with the understanding and its ability to give rise to knowledge of objects, the *Critique of Practical*

Reason aims to establish the way in which practical reason lies at the basis of all genuinely moral judgements and actions. Now Kant's task is to establish that there is a distinctive third higher faculty, the power of judgement, which makes possible distinctively *aesthetic* judgements. It is already clear that Kant has a certain agenda in writing his third *Critique*, for he believes it will bridge the gap between the other two.

However, Kant's motivation is not simply systematic, although it may sometimes seem so. He has the insight that there is a further fundamental structure of possibility within human experience; one that cannot simply be explained in terms of knowledge or morality, although it may well stand in relation to both of those. Judging something as beautiful allows us to see that not every way in which we experience the world is immediately epistemically or morally charged. We have a capacity to simply stand back and gaze appreciatively at something and when we do so we may well say that it is 'beautiful'. This is a distinctive response to the world and is characterized by a particular form of mental activity that counts as contemplative or reflective. Pointing out the disinterested quality of judgements of taste is a first step for establishing the way in which they differ from other judgements. Identifying 'disinterestedness' – the term is first introduced only in Section 2 – allows him to point to a distinctive phenomenology or style of being in the world and this is necessary if Kant's further analysis is to get going. The second and third Moments (and, to a lesser extent, the fourth) develop the phenomenology of aesthetic judgement, but they would have no foothold were Kant not able to first point to something and say 'taste is like this' or, at least, 'taste is something like this'. My suggestion, then, is that in the first Moment Kant initiates a description of experience offered as a tentative phenomenology of taste. He cannot say 'taste, definitively, is this' and, indeed, the whole critique is devoted to the attempt to establish whether or not such an elusive ability can be established. This is not, however, because Kant's powers of argument are weak, but rather because the topic under discussion is systematically resistant to definition. Taste's qualification as the subject of the third *Critique* is, first, that it counts as a distinctive form of responding to things. But this phenomenologically unique orientation has, at the same time, the task of mediating between cognition and morality and, as a result, taste is simultaneously distinctive and intermediary, making it difficult to establish exactly what it is and, even, whether it exists.

The aesthetic judgement, as we have seen, is contrasted to a cognitive one. Whereas the first is subjective, the second is objective. In a judgement of taste the subject 'feels herself', that is, she has a feeling of pleasure or displeasure that expresses being affected by the presentation of an object. Kant remarks at the same time that this feeling refers to 'nothing whatsoever in the object' [AA204]. This has led some readers to conclude that aesthetic judgement is subjective in a privative sense, that is, it amounts to a form of introspection. But although Kant clearly sees aesthetic judgement as a form of reflection experienced as a feeling of pleasure or displeasure, the feeling is in response to the presentation of an object and so there must be something to which we respond. Moreover, although Kant insists that our imagination is central and that we are not engaged in cognition, he also remarks in passing that there may be some role for the understanding, the cognitive faculty *par excellence,* suggesting that aesthetic judgement stands in *some* relation to cognition. We can thus conclude that an aesthetic judgement is marked by feeling pleasure in response to an awareness of an object, but this does not give rise to knowledge and is rather a self-awareness of being affected by something.

Looking at a building with a view to acquiring knowledge about it is quite different to viewing it with a feeling of pleasure. In the aesthetic case we experience a 'feeling of life' [*Lebensgefühl*], which Kant says is the basis for a specific capacity of discrimination or judgement [AA 204]. While in the first paragraph we found that the aesthetic subject becomes aware of herself, we now find that the specificity of this form of awareness makes possible a particular way of responding to things. This confirms that our self-awareness is not merely introspective, for it allows us to respond to an object in a specific way. What does aesthetic judgement discriminate between? Only some objects give rise to a feeling of pleasure and they, as a consequence, stand out in contrast to everything else. When we experience a feeling of pleasure in response to some such object we find ourselves in a quite different state of mind from that in which we would if the object were disagreeable or even merely neutral for us. The 'feeling of life' is a reflexive awareness of our mode of relating to things in the world. This is to say, that in being aware of feeling in a particular way about some thing, we are simultaneously aware of our response to that thing. So, I would suggest that aesthetic judgement is directed both to objects and to our feeling about them. The feeling of life operates primarily as a reflection on the affective relation in which we stand to the world and, although it is principally a feeling of mental activity, it is the response of an embodied mind aware of its own sensory being. This is because aesthetic self-awareness is necessarily mediated through a sensory awareness of external things.

This distinctive capacity for discrimination or judgement is not to be confused with cognition, where we would seek to identify the object as such and such in a determinate description, regardless of the relation in which it stands to any appreciation of it. In an aesthetic judgement there is a comparison of 'the given presentation in the subject with the entire presentational power' [P: AA 204]. What does this mean? The 'given presentation' is the object as it appears to us. The 'entire presentational power' is the complex mental activity that makes presentation of an object possible. In Kant's view the presentation of an object requires a combination of at least two different ways in which the mind responds to something given to the senses. We will discover in Section 9 that the particular orientations Kant has in mind are the faculties of imagination and understanding. There is something about the aesthetic object that affects the way in which these faculties relate to one another, even though they are not operating so as to make possible a presentation of an object that will give rise to knowledge. This is why a comparison between the object and our mental response to it arises. Kant's point is that there is something about this particular thing in the world that allows us to become aware of our ability to present objects in general.

Kant concludes Section 1 by emphasizing that he is not using the term 'aesthetic' in the way he did in the 'Transcendental Aesthetic' of the first *Critique* where he was referring to our ability to apprehend objects through our senses. The aesthetic, as opposed to the epistemic, sense of 'aesthetic' refers to an awareness that is only accessible as a feeling. It is worth remarking, though, that this new sense of the term does not rule out a role for sensory apprehension *within* the analysis of taste.

So far Kant has not even mentioned disinterestedness, the quality that supposedly distinguishes taste. In Section 2, he introduces the term that will anchor the phenomenological distinctiveness of aesthetic judgement. (In the title of this section he uses the phrase *ohne alles Interesse* or 'without all interest', while in the final paragraph he talks of a pleasure that is *uninteressiert*. It is clear from the context that Kant intends not that we are bored with something beautiful, but, rather that we are engaged with it in an unbiased way.) First he remarks that interest is a desire for the existence of an object. When we find something beautiful we judge it through 'mere contemplation' in intuition or reflection [AA 204]. Kant's point here is that I could either be looking at something or seeing it in my mind's eye, that is, in my imagination. We can now see that the positive connotation of disinterestedness is not so much that of detachment from the object but of a contemplative attention to it. It is the quality of our attention to the object that counts as disinterested, not our lack of interest in it. There are many ways in which we can miss the point about beauty. I can see a palace, for instance, as simply a display of pomp, or I can hold that I'd rather have something more useful or, again, I might focus on the inequality that allows some lucky few to own such a (worthless) thing. I might even say that I wouldn't be in the least concerned about such splendour if I was utterly isolated from society. All of this may well be true. But the issue is, rather, whether just in looking at the palace I feel a liking for it, even though I have no desire for its existence, nor any intent to possess it. The disinterestedness characteristic of the aesthetic orientation to the world is best described as contemplative attention and arises when my interests do not determine the relation in which I stand to what I see or imagine.

In Section 3 Kant considers another kind of liking, the agreeable, which *is* connected with an interest. The agreeable is liked simply at the level of sensory perception. Kant distinguishes between sensation and feeling, where the first is the sensory component of cognition and thus qualifies as objective, while the second can only be subjective. The green colour of meadows is a sensation, while the agreeableness of this colour is a feeling – though a merely entertaining, not a purely aesthetic one – and can only be subjective, that is, in the mind of the spectator and not something out there in the world. The agreeable evokes an inclination: I am gratified by it in such a way that I cannot be indifferent to its existence. I desire the agreeable and act in order to acquire it. As I am inclined towards the agreeable thing, I do not really make a judgement about it: I am propelled towards it. I can allow no contemplative distance between myself and it. Thus my enjoyment of chocolate does not involve my admiring it across a space of contemplative attention, but in guzzling it up.

Section 4 identifies a further kind of liking, which is for the morally good. This also involves an interest. To call something good is always to relate it to a purpose; something is good either as a means or as an end in itself. In the latter case, it is morally good. In both cases we like something because we have an interest in its existence and cannot simply take a position of contemplative attentiveness to it. It matters to me if my computer is reliable or if the immigration laws are fair and the way in which these things matter to me means that I demand that they are one way and not another. I do not stand back and appreciate them just as they are, I intervene or, at least, take a position if they are not as I think they should be. This means that I have an idea – or, as Kant puts it, a 'concept' – of what the good is supposed to be. I have, however, no such idea of what something beautiful should be. This is what leads Kant to introduce some examples that seem to resist regulation. 'Flowers, free designs, lines aimlessly intertwined and called foliage' are such that we like them without having any sense of their following a pre-established formula [P: AA 207]. Indeed we like them because they are free and seem to have no significance beyond being pleasing to the eye. But Kant also says that such liking is reflective and 'leads to some concept or other (but it is indeterminate which concept this is)' [P: AA 207]. Such free patterns give rise to a reflective activity of the mind, but we cannot resolve the multiplicity of different possibilities into an explanation. So now we see that the understanding, as the faculty of concepts, has a role to play in aesthetic judgement; Kant need only exclude the concept's determining what counts as beauty. At this stage of his account Kant suggests that aesthetic judgement is indeterminate in the sense that there is a multiplicity of different possible explications of (or concepts for) the pleasurable phenomenon. Later he suggests that the mental activity which makes taste possible is indeterminate. These two positions are not incompatible with one another, but they are distinct.

It has often been thought that Kant rules out any role for determinate concepts in aesthetic judgement and even that he rules out all concepts *tout court*. It is now clear that Kant leaves room for indeterminate conceptual activity within aesthetic judgement, but is there any place for determinate concepts in his account? Answering this question requires us to go beyond the letter of Kant's account, but I think we can see that determinate concepts, such as 'meadow' or 'palace', need not be excluded from aesthetic judgements and indeed it would be difficult to make aesthetic judgements were we not able to use concepts to identify and describe the phenomenon we appreciate. It is simply the case that the concept cannot produce, that is, define or explain beauty. If we are to experience beauty, we have to await the phenomenon and contemplate it without expecting explanation.

In Section 5 Kant compares the three kinds of liking that have been under discussion so far. Both the agreeable and the morally good are desired by us, even though one is liked just because we enjoy it, while the other is valued as good in itself. In contrast to both of these, the contemplation characteristic of aesthetic judgement arises from our 'holding up' the object to our feeling of pleasure and displeasure, that is, to the feeling that discriminates aesthetically [AA 209]. Kant's repeated references not only to pleasure but also to displeasure are often mentioned in the Kant literature. Beauty, which is under discussion at the moment, gives rise principally to pleasure, although Kant regularly refers to pleasure *and* displeasure. Meanwhile the sublime, which is the subject of the following section, gives rise to a complex mixture of pleasure and displeasure. From now on I will refer mostly only to pleasure in my reading of the 'Analytic of the Beautiful'. Aesthetic judgement, which is the source of judgements of both beauty and the sublime, provides an *a priori* principle for the feeling of pleasure and displeasure as we discovered in the 'Preface'. I suspect it is because he has the faculty of judgement in its full extension in mind, that Kant mentions the positive and negative variants of feeling. While investigating both this suggestion and how displeasure might be relevant to taste would be very interesting, I cannot do so here. [See Brandt 1998, Shier 1998, Hudson 1991, Fricke 1990, Grayck 1986] The beautiful object gives rise to a contemplative feeling of pleasure without our having any further agenda or desire for the object. As is already becoming clear, the aesthetic judgement 'holds up' the object in the sense that we reflect on the way in which it affects us, that is, gives rise to a pleasure in us. In what follows I will argue that the more general implication of this characterization of beauty is that aesthetic judgement is a reflection on the relation between an object and our subjective response to it. In this sense, corresponding to the dual harmony, there is a double reflection, first on the object and secondly on the relation in which we stand to it. The agreeable, the beautiful and the good are three different ways in which objects relate to our capacity for feeling pleasure, but only aesthetic contemplation is capable of achieving a reflection on the relation between subject and object, that is, our capacity for feeling in response to something given to us in experience. This, I will suggest, is because aesthetic liking is a feeling that is aware of itself as a feeling.

Kant now engages in the sort of distinctions that are much appreciated by 'ordinary language' philosophers, that is, he highlights different ways in which we use language. The agreeable is what gratifies us [*vergnügen*], the good is what we esteem [*schätzen*] or approve [*billigen*] and the beautiful is what we simply like [*bloß gefallen*] [AA 210]. But now Kant goes beyond the linguistic to a more existential level of philosophical analysis, saying that agreeableness is possible not only for human beings but for all other animals, while the good holds for all rational beings. As we are both animal and rational, human beings straddle this divide and only we are capable of a liking for beauty, which requires both an animal and a rational nature. The beautiful, which is the only pleasure that can count as disinterested and free, is thus distinctively linked with the human. I think it is clear from this passage that taste can only be free in the aesthetic sense if it is not determined by an interest. An interest, Kant says, gives rise to a need and this would make aesthetic freedom impossible. The morally good arises from an imperative, but it is nonetheless valued by us insofar as it is an exercise of the free will legislating for itself. Such willing is free in the moral sense, but it is not free in the aesthetic sense because it is determined by a pre-existing principle (or 'concept') and is not liked merely in our apprehension of it. If aesthetic judgement is a free liking, then it must also be disinterested in the sense I have established here, that is, it must be a contemplative appreciation of something we see or imagine. Returning to explication through linguistic differentiation, Kant contrasts the three likings as inclination [*Neigung*], respect [*Achtung*] and favour [*Gunst*], which correspond to the agreeable, the good and the aesthetic, respectively.

We can now recap what we have discovered so far in the first Moment. Finding something beautiful is not a form of knowing, but arises from a reflection on a feeling of pleasure in response to an object. Because aesthetic judgement is based on a feeling and not on a concept, it counts as subjective and qualifies as a distinctive way of judging the world. In the 'Introductions' to the *Critique of Judgement* Kant distinguished reflective judgement from the determining judgement that gives rise to knowledge. We also saw that aesthetic judgement allows us to be aware of our reflective capacity for introducing order into the range of empirical objects. Thus aesthetic judgement is a form of reflective judgement that has become aware of itself. We can now see that the account he gave of aesthetic judgement in the 'Introduction' combines what in Section 1 he calls a peculiar form of discrimination and what I have called a feeling that is aware of itself as a feeling. Aesthetic reflective judgement deploys concepts, as any judgement must, but it does not explain or determine phenomena through concepts. Any concepts that are employed seek to capture something that must always remain unexplained or indeterminate. The basis of such judgement has been traced back to feeling and the first step in a phenomenological description of aesthetic response is its identification as contemplative attention, which is what Kant means by talking about disinterestedness.

2.3 Second moment: the subjective universality of taste

Sections 6 through to 9 comprise the second Moment, which introduces the idea that taste is social or, better, sociable. When we make judgements about beauty, it is part of the logic, one might say, or as Wittgensteinian philosophers might say, the grammar of such statements that we call on others to agree with us. I would add that the introduction of a sociable dimension counts as a development of the phenomenology of taste. Although it is the individual who judges in a judgement of taste, she does not judge just for herself, but also for a community. The community in question is not the actual one within which she finds herself, nor indeed any other empirical community: in judging aesthetically she situates herself within the community of all judging subjects, that is, alongside anyone who shares the distinctively human make-up that combines sensory or animal with intellectual or rational capacities.

At the outset of Section 6 Kant claims that taste's appeal to universality 'can be inferred' [*gefolgert werden*] from its disinterestedness, for if something is not based on 'private' or personal considerations, then it must be valid for everyone [P: AA 211]. Although this derivation of the second from the first Moment has been challenged by interpreters of Kant, and especially by Paul Guyer in whose view Kant claims that the second Moment can be 'deduced' from the first, we can see what he means in general terms. [See Guyer, 1979, pp. 131–3 and a response in Allison, 2001, pp. 99–103.] The sort of contemplative attention that qualifies as 'disinterested' requires making a judgement not based on personal interests. We are highly engaged with the phenomenon under inspection, yet not with a view to self-gratification or from moral motivations. Although aesthetic judgement may seem detached, we only stand back from the usual commitments and interests of everyday life. Seen from this perspective, aesthetic judgement interrupts and suspends our dominant inclinations in order to open up a different sort of attention. The peculiarity of this alternative mode of relating to the world is that the individual must both judge for herself and, simultaneously, call on the judgement of others. The context or horizon of taste is always already sociable, not in the sense that we already agree about what is beautiful, but in that it is part of my considering something beautiful that I care what you think about it. Agreement may be what I aim for, but in no sense can it be guaranteed in advance. Kant will return to this tension within the dynamic of taste, but never explicitly explores what we could call the pathos of aesthetic judging.

Kant now specifically addresses the role of the object in aesthetic judgement. It is because we address the object without any additional agenda that it seems as if we were referring to it and thus, as if our judgement was logical (or cognitive). But, all we refer to is the object's presentation to the subject, that is, the object's appearing to us. So the object is in our sights, but not so as to gain knowledge of it or to make use of it. So far we know that in an aesthetic judgement we contemplate the object in such a way as to focus on its presentation to us. We will explore further what this means in what follows. For the moment, Kant says that aesthetic judgements are like cognitive judgements in that they claim to be valid for everyone. Subjective validity is necessary for any cognitive judgement, which must in addition claim objective validity by establishing something about the object. As we have seen, aesthetic judgements do not explain or determinately describe the object, although they do concern how the object appears to us.

We might interject here that surely, when we make aesthetic judgements, we do indeed describe the object. If I'm discussing a painting or some other visual work of art, I will usually start by saying what it looks like. If my subject is music, I will talk about what it sounds like. Such descriptions are necessary if those I am speaking to are to understand the features to which I intend to draw their attention or, indeed, if I am to develop my own appreciation of the work. However, as we saw in my discussion of the fourth section of the first Moment, there is a role for indeterminate concepts in judgements of taste and even for determinate concepts, as long as their use is merely preparatory for taste. My aesthetic judgement starts when I begin to make an evaluation of the phenomenon under consideration, that is, when I say 'this is beautiful', not just that there is a dominant use of red in the work. If I now begin to say how this use of red gives a particularly powerful aesthetic affect, then I have moved from determinate description to aesthetic evaluation. I am no longer treating the painting as an object and have moved to the level of considering it as a presentation that has a certain aesthetic affect on me and, I want to suggest, also on you. The evaluation characteristic of aesthetic judgement must be combined with description, because otherwise how could it be an evaluation of the object? However, the descriptions that enter into aesthetic appreciation are not explanatory in intent, but rather open up our ways of seeing in an exploratory way and, for this reason, they can only be indeterminate. While Kant does not investigate the combination of evaluative and descriptive elements within the phenomenology of taste, I think something like the sketch I have just given is a natural extension of his account.

Leaving aside this consideration of the place for description within aesthetic evaluation, the point Kant is making is that if I think I know something about an object, I will simply assume you will agree because the grounds of my claim are not private to me and are based on a state of affairs beyond both of us. But if I appreciate a painting, I call on you to judge likewise without being able to compel your agreement. This is the complex sociability that taste relies on and is that of an individual judge necessarily finding herself within a community to which she cannot be indifferent, yet with which she cannot simply coincide.

Kant has constructed an analogy between aesthetic and cognitive judgement, saying that it is *as if* taste gave rise to knowledge, when it is not really the case [AA 211]. The expression 'as if' [*als ob*] carves out the space of aesthetic judgement and establishes its role as mediating between cognitive and moral judgement. We have just discovered that aesthetic judgement's subjective universality qualifies it as analogous to cognitive judgement. Later we will find that aesthetic judgement also operates *as if* it were subject to rational principles.

Having compared and contrasted aesthetic judgement to knowledge, in Section 7 Kant returns to the distinctiveness of taste from the agreeable and the morally good, although in fact he says very little about the latter. He merely reiterates that judgements of taste are not based on a concept, whereas moral judgements are based on a moral concept, or more properly, a principle. The agreeable, like taste, is not based on a concept and yet these too are distinct from one another. When I like a certain sort of wine, a particular colour or one musical instrument rather than another, Kant suggests I am simply saying something is agreeable to me and cannot require that everyone else agrees. We would be wasting our energies if we argued about personal preferences. Yet when we consider something beautiful we cannot be indifferent to the views of others. Kant uses a range of expressions for the way in which we appeal to the agreement of others. He talks about 'requiring' (Pluhar's translation) or 'expecting' (Guyer and Matthew's version) agreement. The German verb *zumuten* could also have the sense of 'I ask of you (that you agree)'. Kant even says that we 'demand' [*fordern*] the same liking [AA 212–3]. We reproach others and deny they have taste for not agreeing. But we must also remember that aesthetic judgements carry only subjective universality and cannot presuppose agreement as do objective cognitive judgements. While we may require and even demand agreement from others, their compliance is not automatic when we are concerned with beauty. Kant concludes by conceding that even when we are engaged in agreeable activities we are concerned to reach agreement. Anyone organizing a party will want to please her guests, but the agreement that she aims at is general, that is, includes all the people she invites, not universal, that is, for all human judging subjects. Moreover, her aim is to entertain their senses and perhaps also their minds. The sociability of the agreeable is empirical, Kant says, and I would add that the sociability of the beautiful is transcendental in that it appeals to the fundamental capacity for judgement displayed by all human beings.

Kant begins Section 8 saying that the subjective universality of aesthetic judgements is remarkable for the transcendental philosopher, adding that the logician is unlikely to share this point of view. Validity for all judging subjects is relevant for the transcendental project of investigating the range of *a priori* synthetic judgements. The logician simply takes these for granted, whereas the transcendental philosopher's task is to uncover how they are possible. While Kant has already insisted that taste is distinct from cognition, he is now beginning to establish that an aspect of our cognitive power is uncovered only through the analysis of the subjective universality of aesthetic judgement. This is the sense in which aesthetic judgement is of great importance for the transcendental philosopher.

Judgements of taste 'ascribe' [*ansinnen*] to everyone or 'expect [*zumuten*] assent' from them about a liking for the object [G: AA 214]. In a note to his translation of both these verbs as 'to expect', Pluhar remarks that the expectation in question has no connotation of anticipation and so I call on you to agree and think you *should* do so, but I have no assurance that you will. Kant says that such judgements are 'public' [*publik*] and count as instances of the 'taste of reflection'. There is also a 'taste of sense' which concerns the merely agreeable and, like taste proper, arises from the relation of the presentation of the object to our capacity to feel pleasure and displeasure. However, generally, Kant uses 'taste' to refer only to aesthetic judgement. The strange thing, he says, is that aesthetic judgements make a claim for universal agreement despite the disagreement that frequently arises. This underlines that Kant in no way assumes that we will simply agree in our aesthetic judgements, but only that agreement is at issue for us when we so judge.

Kant now says that when we quarrel in matters of taste we assume that it is possible to make an aesthetic judgement, while we disagree as to whether or not the standard of taste has been properly applied [AA 214]. Kant's own considered view is much more radical than this, for he has left open the possibility that there may be no distinctive principle of taste, while later he will trace back our quarrelling on such matters to a disagreement about the character of the principle on which aesthetic judgements are grounded, rather than on the faulty application of that principle. [See 'Dialectic of Taste'.]

Kant goes on to state that if something is objectively universally valid, then it must also be subjectively universally valid, that is, if a judgement holds of an object then it must be valid for all judging subjects [AA 215]. But there are also judgements that have only subjective universal validity, without making any claim to objective validity. These are aesthetic judgements. Kant makes the rather misleading comment that they do not refer to objects at all. What he surely means is that they do not identify or determine anything in the object, yet the object must still in some sense be at issue, for it is its presentation that is worthy of aesthetic appreciation by all judging subjects.

The second Moment concerns the logical quantity of aesthetic judgements, which Kant now reveals is singular. Objectively universal judgements rest on concepts that are capable of sub-suming or explaining things given to our senses. Concepts are always general and only thus establish order in our sensory experience. But aesthetic judgements involve considering a sin-gular presentation of an object and the feeling of pleasure that it invokes [AA 215]. As such, they cannot make claim to general patterns and must count as singular, strictly asserting the beauty of a particular thing. It is possible, once a singular judgement has been expressed, to generalize from it, but such a general judgement will never qualify as aesthetic. So, I can say that a particular rose is beautiful on the basis of the pleasure it gives me in looking at it, but if I go on to say that *all* roses are beauti-ful I am no longer engaged in *aesthetic* judgement. Judgements about the agreeableness of a sensory phenomenon are also aes-thetic and singular, but they do not carry the additional status of universality, which Kant now says is the aesthetic quantity of aesthetic judgements. So the quantity of aesthetic judgements turns out to be that of singular judgements that are nonethe-less universal. A singular phenomenon has universal validity, not because it applies to *everything*, but because it evokes – or should evoke – the pleasure of *everyone*.

If we tried to judge objects entirely in terms of concepts we would be incapable of an aesthetic response and this is why there is no rule that establishes whether or not something is beautiful. No one can persuade us through argument that something is aesthetically pleasing, for we need to 'submit the object to our own eyes' [AA 216]. Yet, at the same time, we con-sider our judgement valid for everyone. This is the tension that structures Kant's account of taste from beginning to end. It is a tension that is generative of taste and thus is not capable of being wholly dissipated. But a tension is not necessarily a paradox and aesthetic judgement is not a self-contradictory position; rather it is one that marks out a sociability that does not dissolve the autonomy of the subject. The voice of the indi-vidual speaks for the broader community of all judging subjects in finding something beautiful.

Kant says that all that is postulated or claimed in a judgement of taste is a universal voice expressing a liking not dependent on concepts. The task in hand, as we have already seen, is to establish the possibility of aesthetic judgement based on a distinctive cognitive power and thus deserving a dedicated critique within transcendental philosophy. This is why Kant now says that all that is postulated is the *possibility* of an aesthetic judgement valid for everyone. Such a judgement does not claim that everyone actually agrees, but instead merely requires their agreement. Kant's point is that in adopting an aesthetic position I cannot simply assume that everyone will agree, but I must call on them to do so. For this reason, Kant remarks that the universal voice is simply an idea, by which he means that we aim at an ideal of agreement while not being able to assure it in reality. Kant emphasizes that he is not yet considering what this idea rests on. He will return to this question in the fourth Moment where he suggests that the ground of aesthetic judgement lies in our capacity for common sense and, ultimately, in the subjective conditions of judgement.

The priority for the transcendental philosopher is establishing whether there is or is not a distinctive capacity for taste, while the question of the success an aesthetic judge may have in any particular claim to taste is treated as subsidiary. Nevertheless, just the use of the word 'beauty' signals that in actual judgements of beauty we aim at the idea of subjective universality. This sounds very tentative and we might wonder if we could ever be confident we had made a judgement of taste. But Kant now says as long as 'he' – and here he means the aesthetic judge – distinguishes what is properly aesthetic from what is agreeable and good, he can be quite certain in having exercised aesthetic judgement [AA 216]. The result of this insistence on attending to the formal conditions of taste may make it seem that our exercise of the universal voice is the only thing for which we require universal assent, not our actual preference for a particular object. Even if that were the case, surely Kant is insufficiently concerned about the ease with which we might misidentify or, even, disguise from ourselves a motivation that is not purely aesthetic. He seems fairly cavalier about the ease with which mistakes about the relation in which we stand to phenomena can be eliminated from aesthetic judgement. And can he really separate out a claim about the activity of judgement from a claim about the instance that inspired that activity? In other forms of judgement this would be possible, but for a singular judgement that arises only from a singular presentation of a thing, there seems to be little scope for making such a distinction. My frame of mind when judging aesthetically can only be made sense of as arising from an encounter with a particular object. Is it plausible to claim that my exercise of judgement has universal validity and that this beautiful vista which gives me so much pleasure does not? I think it would be possible to develop Kant's position so that his distinction between personal aesthetic preference and the general transcendental ability to judge could be illuminating. This would involve highlighting the insecurity in making judgements of taste. Kant, however takes the opposite strategy at the end of Section 8, when he himself offers a version of the commonplace view, saying that certainty about taste can be secured if we apply the principle correctly.

Section 9 starts with the promise that it will present the 'key' to the critique of taste, that is, a question that will establish whether or not a distinctive faculty of taste can be identified and thus deserves a third *Critique* dedicated to its investigation. The question is the following: in a judgement of taste does the pleasure in the object precede our judgement of it or *vice versa*? Now there is something very odd in the way this question is initially set up, because judgement appears twice, first as the general phenomenon under inspection and secondly as a subdivision of it. I will come back to this. Most pressing is the need to establish what Kant means by 'preceding'. The crucial issue is whether the pleasure we take in an object grounds the judgement of taste or, alternatively, the judgement of taste grounds the pleasure we take in an object. Thus the precedence that is the key to the critique of taste is logical rather than temporal. We will consider later whether the contrast he draws here is adequate for identifying the activity of judging under consideration.

Kant begins by arguing that if the pleasure we take in the object preceded the judgement in the logical sense we have established, then our judgement would be based on the object. This would mean that judgement was merely an expression of a sensation and would signal that we find the object agreeable, not beautiful. The judgement – if it qualifies as such – would be empirical, describing a sensory liking. The object would be the cause of our pleasure, so the judgement could not be universal or *a priori*. It can hold only of this object and for me at the time I am deriving pleasure from it. It is, thus, neither objectively nor subjectively universal, as it refers to *this* object and only to *this* subject, namely, me. Moreover it is not *a priori* because it is not based directly on the exercise of a fundamental cognitive faculty, in this case, taste, and is merely an instance of my exercising my capacity for desire at an experiential or empirical level.

Now Kant introduces without explanation the notion of 'the universal communicability of the mental state' and says that this is what must be prior to the pleasure we take in an object [P: AA 217]. The oddity within the initial formulation of the question has been removed by substituting the second incidence of 'judgement' in the title of Section 9 with a specific aspect of aesthetic judgement, namely, its universal communicability. So it is not so much that judgement is prior to the feeling of pleasure about an object, but rather that the status of taste as capable of being communicated to everyone is the foundation for the pleasure we take in an object. It is *because* we can require everyone to agree with the pleasure we take in a particular object that this pleasure qualifies as aesthetic. This is the sense in which judgement or rather the defining element of aesthetic judgement – its universal validity for all judging subjects – precedes the pleasure we take in an object.

The way in which Kant expresses the 'key' is potentially misleading in another regard, for it sounds as if judgement has priority over feeling, whereas the specific characteristic of aesthetic judgement is of being expressed only in a feeling not a concept. If, however, we make another distinction that Kant does not make sufficiently clear, we begin to resolve this problem. We can speak of a feeling of pleasure in the object, but there is also a feeling of pleasure distinctive of the very act of judging in an aesthetic manner. (The necessary relation between a judgement of taste and a feeling of pleasure will be the subject of the fourth Moment.) While these two pleasures are intertwined with one another, because a judgement of taste can only occur if there is an object in which we find pleasure, Kant wants to establish that the activity of the mind supplies the ground for our response to the object and not *vice versa*.

So what is the universal communicability of a mental state? Kant says that only cognition can be communicated universally. What he means is that an objective state of affairs can be agreed on by everyone as it is the case regardless of differing personal perspectives. While taste is distinct from cognition, it, too, can call on the agreement of others insofar as its basis is the mental state necessary for 'cognition in general' [*Erkenntnis überhaupt*]. Kant says that this mental state is the relation between the 'presentational powers' [P:AA 217]. This means that taste counts as universally communicable insofar as its basis is a relation between the powers or faculties that first make cognition possible.

In the terms of the *Critique of Pure Reason,* both sensibility and understanding are necessary in order for knowledge to arise, that is, intuitions or sensory input must be combined with concepts, which are general rules for the organization of sensations. In the *Critique of Judgement* imagination stands in for intuition. Although a full explanation of this development would be too complex to go into here, in my account of the 'Introduction' I offered a provisional explanation. In aesthetic judgement imagination stands in for intuition by transfiguring a sensory input into something we respond to with contemplative attention. Our sensory apprehension is transformed into a reflective attention that does not merely follow the rhythm of our normal everyday 'seeing' of the world.

We now are in a position to textually establish what has already been hinted and what I have mentioned in a preparatory way: namely, aesthetic judgement stands in some relation to, even though it is also distinct from, cognition. Taste rests on the capacities that make cognition possible. In a cognitive judgement the relation between intuition and understanding would be governed by a cognitive concept or rule, but in this case there is no pre-given rule. From this Kant concludes that the faculties stand in a relationship of 'free play' with one another [AA 217]. He now identifies the presentational powers required as imagination, which combines the manifold or many aspects of intuition, as well as understanding, which finally achieves unity through the introduction of a concept. This free play of the faculties must be communicable, Kant argues, because it pertains to cognition which is necessarily valid for everyone. We learn at the outset of the third paragraph that communicability is the element within the judgement of taste that grounds our pleasure in the object. Anything that is subjectively universal must be communicable, for this is just what it is to say that it is valid for all. While communication is the empirical realization of a transcendental structure of possibility, namely, communicability, only a very close analysis of that structure would allow us to establish the relation between the latter and subjective universality. For the moment, it is sufficient to distinguish the possible, which is expressed as a principle (communicability and subjective universality) from its effect in an actual communication.

In reiterating what he has argued so far, Kant introduces another turn of phrase, saying that in aesthetic judgement the faculties 'harmonize with each other as required for cognition in general' [P: AA 217/8]. This is the famous 'harmony of the faculties' much discussed in interpretations of Kant's aesthetics. As is often remarked, a major difficulty now arises, for Kant appears to say that the free play of the faculties is necessary for cognition. First of all this would make cognition dependent on the state of mind distinctive of aesthetic judgement and thus, it would follow, make cognition dependent on aesthetic judgement. Secondly, this formulation flies in the face of Kant's recent insistence that cognition rests on a rule, making it distinct from aesthetic judgement where there is a free play of the faculties. But we might begin to wonder what exactly Kant means by 'cognition in general'. Does he mean any old cognition, that is, *all* knowledge or does he means something subtly different, for instance, the general conditions of cognition and yet not cognition proper, that is, knowledge? We must leave aside this issue for the moment, bearing in mind a potential solution, namely, that he should have said that cognition requires *some* relation between the faculties, which only stand in a specifically harmonious relation of free play when we judge aesthetically.

The ability to communicate one's mental state is pleasurable, even if all we are communicating is the relation in which our cognitive powers stand to one another and say nothing about anything outside our minds [AA 218]. Although this claim may seem to provide evidence for those who see Kant's aesthetics as signalling a turn to the interior mental life of the subject, it can, nevertheless, be situated within the relational reading I have been developing. As we have seen, there are two pleasures that arise when we judge aesthetically: first, there is a pleasure in an object, but there is also a pleasure in our capacity for judging the object in a distinctively aesthetic manner. So when Kant asked if judgement precedes the feeling of pleasure in an object or *vice versa* and even when he says that the answer is that the universal communicability of a mental state has priority over that feeling, he had not yet told the whole story. Universal communicability does indeed (logically) precede any pleasure we take in an object in that if the pleasure were not characterized by its validity for everyone, it would not qualify as aesthetic. However, universal communicability is itself expressed as a feeling of pleasure. So even the universal validity of the activity of our mental powers, regardless for the moment of which object may have prompted them, gives rise to a feeling of pleasure. This is one side of the dual harmony and, we can now see, the double pleasure characteristic of a judgement of beauty. Indeed, we may say that aesthetic judgement is shot through with feeling at every level. Ultimately, taste is based on feeling, though it is very important to emphasize that feeling is not emotive, that is, not something that happens to us but is, rather, a way in which we are aware of ourselves and the world. I have suggested that we can see this as a feeling that is aware of itself. Admittedly, though, the relation between the two ways in which feeling enters into aesthetic judgement is not clarified here or, other than indirectly, elsewhere.

Kant acknowledges that he owes an explanation of how it could be established that communicability is necessarily accompanied by a pleasure. While it would be possible to point to particular examples of such a coincidence within experience, these could never establish the necessary connection between communicability and pleasure that is required. Kant remarks that he cannot answer this question until he has addressed the prior issue of whether and how aesthetic judgements are possible *a priori*. In the fourth Moment of the 'Analytic of the Beautiful' he addresses this question, arguing that aesthetic judgements are necessarily accompanied by pleasure because of their basis in the fundamental apparatus of cognition, that is, the *a priori* cognitive faculties. He also goes on to give a further solution to the question of the very possibility of judgements of taste in the 'Deduction'. For now, he moves to address a question he considers less difficult.

Do we become aware of the free play of the faculties in an aesthetic judgement through our senses, that is, aesthetically, or through an awareness of a rational purpose that generates the relation in which they stand to one another, that is, intellectually? If we are engaged in knowing something, we guide our judgement by a concept and, when we are aware of the relation between our faculties, we experience an intellectual consciousness of it without making any reference to a feeling of pleasure or displeasure [AA 218/9]. Kant gives the example of the schemata of judgement, presented as necessary for synthesis of an intuition with a concept in the *Critique of Pure Reason*. His point seems to be that in cognitive synthesis we are in some sense intellectually aware of the cooperation of our faculties as the result of the operation of a conceptual rule or category. But a judgement of taste is not based on a concept and establishes, rather, the feeling with which I respond to an object, so the relation between the faculties can only be accessed in our sensory awareness of things. In a judgement of taste we have a 'sensation' [*Empfindung*] of a particularly easy exchange between imagination and understanding [AA 219]. (It would have been better if Kant had used the term 'feeling' [*Gefühl*] here, because although the awareness we have of our mental activity necessarily arises in response to sensory apprehension, it is reflective and does not occur as a sensation.) The relation of imagination and understanding is 'indeterminate', that is, knowledge is not attained, yet at the same time we become aware of the relation between the faculties necessary if we are to know anything at all. Whereas earlier Kant said that in a judgement of taste it is indeterminate which concept applies, he now characterizes as indeterminate the mental activity on which any such judgement is based. Indeterminacy has shifted from the surface to the ground of taste. When we use our faculties so as to establish knowledge of something, we are aware principally of the object and not of the mental activity that makes that knowledge possible. As we have seen, Kant raises the rather puzzling possibility that we can become aware of the subjective conditions of such an objective orientation to the world even in the schematizing necessary for knowledge, but he does not say what this would amount to. He may be suggesting that in addition to our awareness of the result of our mental activity, we are aware at some, perhaps pre-reflective, level of its process. What is clear is that he thinks that in the case of aesthetic judgement we can become aware of the relation between these subjective conditions or faculties in sensing – or, better, feeling – a reciprocal harmony between the faculties. This occurs when we encounter a singular phenomenon, that is, one that pleases us just for itself, and yet at the same time harmonizes with the mental relation necessary for any cognition whatsoever. The judgement arising from such a coincidence between a thing in the world and our mental powers is therefore valid for all human beings, who are just the sort of beings who combine intuitions with concepts in order to give rise to cognition.

We can elucidate this dense set of claims in the following fashion. I see something that makes me stop and look more and, at the same time, it makes me think about what I am looking at. What I take in through my eyes (my intuitions) invites more reflection (my concepts – although indeterminate ones as they don't give rise to knowledge) and what I think makes me see more. There is a virtuous circularity between my seeing and my thinking: this is what Kant means by a free play of the faculties. And in my awareness of an unusually good fit between this particular object and my ability to take it up through both looking at it and reflecting on it, I become aware of the mental apparatus that allows me to take in and think about anything I experience, even though I normally do not pay so much (contemplative) attention nor feel any particular pleasure when I do so. In this way, aesthetic judgement has illuminated the subjective conditions of any cognition whatsoever. It is for this reason that beauty is liked universally even though it does not qualify as cognition, being grounded not on a rule or concept and only on a feeling. Aesthetic feeling arises most obviously as a response to an object, but at a deeper level it gives us an indirect access to our cognitive ability and thus is a feeling aware of itself. It is because of the role played by feeling that judgements of taste qualify as distinctively aesthetic and are not solely the effects of a cause outside of us, in which case they would be merely empirical and not of particular interest for the transcendental philosopher who seeks to establish the framework of cognition in general.

2.4 Third moment: the relation in which taste stands to purposes

Kant now considers what, if any, role is played by rational purposes in judgements of taste. He suggests that it is *as if* they were guided by purposes and yet this cannot be the case, because of the free activity of the mind characteristic of them. Kant suggests there is a 'purposiveness without purpose' in the aesthetic way of presenting objects.

2.4.1 *Purposes and purposiveness; design and the role of the object*

In Section 10 Kant defines a purpose as the conceptual cause of something's existence. A purpose is the formal or intellectual cause of an object, while there is also a material cause that makes the idea real. When something is caused by a concept – strictly speaking he is referring to rational ideas, not concepts of the understanding – then it is the result of an intervention by our power of desire or will, that is, our practical power to organize the world in accordance with our motivations, moral or otherwise. (A concept of the understanding is a general term that can be applied to a given empirical object so as to give rise to knowledge, whereas a rational idea expresses an infinite standard that can never be grasped in determinate terms.) But there are also phenomena which, while not generated by concepts, it makes sense to think of *as if* they were dependent on purposes. We talk of them heuristically as if they resulted from purposes in order to explain and grasp phenomena that, otherwise, would be difficult to explain. In these cases, Kant says there is 'purposiveness without a purpose' or 'purposiveness as to form' [AA 220]. In other words, we attribute purposiveness to objects in our way (or form) of thinking of them.

Section 11 takes up this idea, saying that judgements of taste are based solely on our way of presenting an object as purposive, without its being the result of any purpose. Kant defends this characterization of taste, saying that any judgement based on a purpose displays an interest. If I bring about something because of an idea I have, then I must will to bring it about and have an interest in so doing. This could arise either as a subjective purpose in line with my own preferences or as an objective purpose when I want to bring about a state of affairs in accordance with the moral law. But a judgement of taste is not motivated by an interest in either of these ways, thus it cannot be directed by a purpose. All a judgement of taste requires is the relating of my faculties in response to the look of an object. The harmonious relation of the faculties that forms the basis of taste is connected with a feeling of pleasure in the object, which we require others also feel even though we cannot compel them to do so. This basis does not give rise to a liking that is either agreeable or moral in nature. Rehearsing a conclusion achieved in the previous Moment, Kant says that it is because we consider this liking to be universally communicable that it qualifies as the basis for the judgement of taste. Now, in Section 9 Kant said that the liking for the object cannot be the basis for the judgement or, indeed, for universal communicability. So the liking in question must be the feeling for the state of mind where the faculties of imagination and understanding are in free play with one another, as I suggested in my reading of Section 9. A feeling of pleasure in the activity of our cognitive faculties is the basis for taste. This liking, Kant now says, is just – we might add, 'for' – the subjective purposiveness in the presentation of an object. He goes on to say that the liking is the 'mere form of purposiveness, insofar as we are conscious of it, in the presentation by which an object is given us' [P: AA 221]. Our pleasure is in the way in which the mind takes up or presents the object. The activity of the mind is pleasurable in itself, although what pleases us is the presentation of an object, that is, its being taken up by our minds. Although we have seen that the aesthetic object implicitly played a role from the outset, the phenomenological description of taste has now been extended to explicitly include the object.

Section 12 begins with a reminder of something that was established in Kant's epistemology, namely that the relation between causes and effects must arise within experience. The relevance for the discussion here is that even if taste were motivated by a purpose lying beyond the range of experience, we could not establish such a concept as the cause of our pleasure in an object. However, all this comment rules out is that a purpose could be the empirical, not the rational or formal, cause of aesthetic pleasure. The argument against this alternative possibility comes elsewhere in Kant's insistence on the absence in judgements of taste of purposes, which are entailed by rational ideas.

In the second paragraph Kant clarifies that the pleasure associated with taste is, indeed, our consciousness of the play of our faculties that is purposive for cognition, but goes on to say that this is always accompanied by a presentation of an object. Kant has already suggested in Section 11 that the presentation of the object is purposive for our judgement of it. His point now is that the relation in which the faculties stand to one another in a judgement of taste is fit for the purpose of cognition. But as no actual knowledge is aimed at in this case, the relation of judgements of taste to purposes is that of displaying formal purposiveness or purposiveness without purpose. More precisely Kant speaks of the 'mere form of the subjective purposiveness of a presentation' [AA 222]. What he means is that the judgement of taste displays the formal conditions of the activity of the mind that are required if an object is to be available to us as something of which we can have knowledge. Thus even when emphasizing that aesthetic pleasure arises from the play of the faculties, taste's significance for the relation in which the subject stands to an object is evident.

Despite not displaying a purpose and thus not being caused by a concept nor by a rational idea, a judgement of taste nevertheless displays a certain causality in the peculiar sense that it makes us want to stay in the contemplative frame of mind that characterizes it. 'We linger over our contemplation of the beautiful' [AA 222]. This suggests that the temporality of taste is more extended, less rushed – or, at least, feels so – in comparison with the rate of time prevalent in our everyday projects. Aesthetic judgement tends to 'reinforce and reproduce itself', which sounds rather like taste is a *causa sui,* causing the continuation of its own existence, although only as a presentation of an object and, thus, presumably, only once triggered by that object.

In Section 13 Kant insists that if in finding something beautiful, we needed to be charmed or to feel emotion, we would not achieve taste. Charm and emotion arise when we find an object agreeable and both are associated with an interest in gratifying our senses. Kant says that such motivations pertain to the matter rather than the form of the liking. What he means is that such a response would not be concerned with the relation in which the presentation of the object stands to our cognitive faculties. We reflect on the formal purposiveness for our judgement of what we sense only when we attend to this relation. We are, in other words, only then aware of the subjective formal conditions of cognition. When we are charmed or emotionally moved by something, we are interested in its existence and thus are materially attached to it. As a result, our attitude is not one of formal reflection.

At the end of this section Kant rules out any role for charm in judgements of taste, although in Section 14, for instance, he suggests that charm may enliven and help sustain or even, in limited cases, increase our aesthetic pleasure. Surely all Kant needs to claim is that charm cannot be the ground of taste, which would explain his saying that should taste *need* charm, it would end up being merely agreeable. Charm may well be an impediment in distracting us from taste's purely formal basis, but although such agreeableness may make an appreciation of purposiveness without purpose difficult to achieve, there is no reason why it should make it impossible. An artwork may have some charming elements and yet at the same time lead us to a reflection that is much deeper than its surface elements. For instance, a student chose as an example of beauty for her class presentation the painting 'Lily Rose, Lily Rose' by Sargent. She wanted to show us that this painting is worthy of universal liking. As I admitted to her later, my first response was to find the painting too saccharine, too charming. Yet, once I took time to consider the painting I could see that there was more to it than its merely attractive surface. Good looks do not preclude reflective depth: they may just make it more difficult for us to recognize. Nevertheless, I think that, on consideration, Kant's point is that if a painting, for instance, charms us very immediately, the result may be that it is difficult to respond reflectively through a free play of the faculties. Put in this moderated way, his perspective, while contestable, is defensible.

Section 14 introduces two of the most contested aspects of Kant's account of taste and raises other problems besides. Whereas it is often thought that until now the basis of taste has been identified as lying exclusively in the formal purposiveness of our cognitive powers in their relation to one another, he now introduces the idea that there is a purposiveness in the form of the object [AA 225]. This may seem to go against his repeated insistence that taste has a subjective basis. However, as we have already seen, the formal purposiveness of the mind arises in response to the presentation of an object. We are to some degree conscious of the relation between the look of the object and our mental activity when we find something beautiful, even though we may simply think, mistakenly, that the beauty is *in* the object. Taste is subjective because this is not the case, but this is not to say that taste has nothing to do with the object. The subjective status of taste entails not that beauty is something merely in the subject, but rather that it is something merely in the presentation of an object for a subject and not in the object itself.

The object that we aim to know in the cognitive case is one that appears to us, not a pristine thing that stands in no relation whatsoever to our experience of it. It is not a 'thing in itself', but rather an 'appearance', in the terms Kant established in the *Critique of Pure Reason*, yet it is capable of being known in its own right. Even though it must appear to us if we are to have knowledge of it, our knowledge is of something other than us and not of a mere projection of our minds. It is just such an independent but accessible object that gives rise to aesthetic pleasure, but on this occasion we are not concerned to determine or know anything about the object and, as a result, can become aware of the way in which it enlivens our mental powers. In an aesthetic judgement the presentation of the object and our response to it are always dually at issue. Thus, the formal purposiveness of the object always stands in relation to the formally purposive activity of the mind. So the supposed shift in Section 14, and even already in the last words of Section 13, is not the slip that some have suspected [Guyer, 1977, p. 58 suggests that the problem arises from 'an inversion of terms']. Both sides of the relation between object and mind must be addressed if it is to be established that there is indeed a relation and that it provides the basis for taste.

The second and perhaps even more derided development is Kant's insistence that taste is directed only to the formal aspects of an object. [See Guyer, 1979, pp. 220–3, Allison, 2001, pp. 131–8.] We have already seen in Section 13 that liking for the material aspects of an object qualifies as agreeable and not purely aesthetic. Aesthetic liking, it now transpires, is a liking for the way in which the object is laid out in space and, I will suggest, also in time. Pluhar translates as 'design' Kant's term for the extension that qualifies for taste. The German word '*Zeichnung*' carries none of the connotation of purpose of the English term 'design' and is literally translated as 'drawing' (as in Guyer and Matthew's translation) or, we might say, 'tracing out in space and time'. Kant's point is that we find beautiful the way an object is elaborated or sketched in its spatial extension and, as it was established in the 'Transcendental Aesthetic' of the *Critique of Pure Reason* that every spatial intuition arises in time, we must conclude that the aesthetic object also has a temporal extension [*C.Pu.R.* A 31/ B 46]. Some readers have thought that Kant is insisting that beauty pertains only to primary qualities, rather than to the secondary qualities distinguished by Locke. [For a nuanced version of this position, see Crawford, 1974, pp. 101–10. For a more tentative account see Guyer, 1979, p. 228.] While this distinction, especially prevalent in the early modern philosophical tradition, is clearly in the background of the position Kant adopts, I do not think he simply equates taste with the appreciation of primary qualities. His point is, rather, that taste requires a response to the organization of the spatio-temporal qualities of an object: how the object is sketched out or appears in the world. Aesthetic liking is for the appearing of the appearance in space and time.

Colour and tone, Kant thinks, please us at the sensory or material level and do not give rise to a purely aesthetic or reflective pleasure [See Guyer, 1979, pp. 224–37]. His point is that if colour and tone affect only our senses and do not give rise to a reflective consciousness of a relation between presentation and mental activity, then they may affect one person in quite a different way from the way they affect another. As a result, neither carries the universal validity characteristic of taste. But Kant is hesitant about the conclusion he has just drawn, for in a footnote, following the lead of the Swiss physicist Euler, he concedes that it may be not only that colour and tone affect our senses, but that we also reflect on them. If this were the case, they would qualify as worthy of taste in that a relation between sensory perception and the reflective activity of mind would be discernible in our apprehension of both.

Kant now makes a further move that is very damaging for the plausibility of his account, insisting that if an aesthetic judgement is pure, this requires that the phenomenon is uniform and the exclusion of anything alien. [See Allison, 2001, p. 134; Guyer, 1979, pp. 248–55, on abstraction and judgements of taste.] This, he says, is what it means to restrict taste to form. He concludes that, even if colour and taste may qualify as beautiful, only what he calls 'simple' colours will make the grade. In contrast, mixed colours do not achieve the standard of purity [AA 224–5]. Having insisted on the priority of spatial – or, as I have suggested, spatio-temporal – organization over the qualitative elements of things, it might now seem that if something beautiful is to be coloured, it must be monochrome. [For a persuasive account of why this would be a bad argument, see Guyer, 1979, pp. 230–3.] But, it is possible that Kant is thinking of the colour spectrum here, so when he speaks of simple colours he means those primary colours that are included in the spectrum, in contrast to those mixed colours which, supposedly, are artificially blended. Kant's view of purity here seems to arise from using the concept 'pure' as if it were a definition, instead of investigating its meaning in relation to the role it plays within his argument. In this case, at least, he appears to follow an analogical link with primary qualities, suggesting that primary colours may be worthy of purely aesthetic appreciation, whereas hybrid shades are not. Up until this point in the argument the purely aesthetic status of taste requires only that we detach ourselves from all external interests, be they personal or moral, adopting a position of contemplative appreciation in response to the presentation of the object. This is the only form of 'purity' or abstraction that is required. There is no reason so far why such a disinterested relation can only arise in response to an object that is uncoloured, monochrome or, indeed, displaying only the colours of the spectrum. Kant here falls into a tendency that is one of the risks of philosophy, namely, to suppose that rigour can be achieved through definitions. Kant has explicitly excluded that there is a rule for what will qualify for taste. The implication of this is that we can only wait for something beautiful to arise within our field of vision.

Spatio-temporal extension cannot be established as the sole basis for taste in advance of an aesthetic encounter, any more than colour and tone can be ruled out. Kant's definitional use of the term 'pure' leads him astray, perhaps in the direction of his own preferences and, if this is so, his critique of taste risks being tainted by what is merely agreeable (for him). It may be that Kant is influenced by the link he is in the course of establishing between cognition and taste. Perhaps he thinks that, as only the spatio-temporal elements of an object are capable of giving rise to knowledge, a judgement based on the subjective conditions of cognition and, thus, pertaining to 'cognition in general' must take up the same elements of the objective world. I think it would be plausible were Kant to say that the spatio-temporal elaboration of objects is necessary both for our knowledge of them and for our potential aesthetic appreciation of them. It would be odd, even nonsensical, if I claimed I knew an object and yet confessed I had no sense of its spatio-temporal dimensions. For Kant, in particular, an object just is an appearance in space and time. If we now consider the aesthetic appreciation we may have for a phenomenon primarily appealing to us through its colour, we find that there is an initial plausibility for a moderated version of Kant's stance. Rothko's series of paintings, the Seagram Murals, arrest us through their use of colour – red and maroon, predominantly – but it is also the case that their colour appears over the spatial surface of the canvases and would not be perceivable were it not extended in space.[5] However, to say that spatio-temporal layout is a necessary condition of my experience and even of my appreciation of it is not to say that this is a sufficient condition. The world is not monochrome and no more is it painted solely in primary colours.

Yet another problem arises for commentators from the way in which Kant links perceptual form with aesthetic judgement. His insistence in Section 14 on spatial (or, better, spatio-temporal) form as giving rise to taste is difficult now for another reason. Every perceived object has some shape in space. If what we appreciate when we like something aesthetically is spatio-temporal form, then why do we not just like everything? If spatio-temporal form is what we find beautiful, then is not everything beautiful? [Allison, 2001, pp. 184–92;

Meerbote, 1982, p. 81. See also Allison, 2001, p. 136 on the distinctiveness of aesthetic and perceptual form.] The arguments for and against this conclusion are very complex and we cannot go into them here. However, despite the subtlety of critics' arguments, I think the specific nature of the link Kant makes between perception and taste is often missed. Aesthetic liking is a response to something that is given to our senses and everything that can be given has a spatio-temporal form. But that is not to say that everything that has a perceptual form is worthy of aesthetic liking. All objects have perceptual form and only thus are they candidates for aesthetic liking: however, only some such objects will give rise to aesthetic liking, on the basis of the particularity – or singularity – of their formal qualities [Hughes, 2007, pp. 284–90.].

Design or form is essential, Kant says, for all visual arts, for instance painting and sculpture, but also architecture and horticulture. Colour, if it is permitted, is now limited to making the artwork vivid, not beautiful. What would Kant have made of the colours of a Poussin or a Raphael, had he seen an original? And surely even if his aesthetic education was limited by his reliance on reproductions for his familiarity with great artworks, he must have visited some colourful gardens around Königsberg, at least in the summer time! Even though his theory does not need the conclusion he comes to, at this point Kant's mind seems to be set on a rather barren distinction between form and what he sees as the merely material aspects of the world. What he needs is an appreciation of Merleau-Ponty's insight when, drawing on the painter and writer Paul Klee and on Matisse, he insists that colour allows the line to be seen, and *vice versa* [Merleau-Ponty, 1964/1993, 'Eye and Mind' pp. 142–3]. We do not need to choose between colour and form, nor is there any necessity that colour be restricted to the spectrum, which is a particular determination of the range of perceivable colours.

Nevertheless, I have suggested that what Kant means by design [*Zeichnung*] may not be as restrictive as we might imagine and there is encouragement for this view at the end of Section 14. The form of objects of the senses, both spatial and temporal, is, he says, either shape or play. Play is further subdivided into the play of shapes in space (theatre and dance) and the play of sensations in time. We should note that it is now clear that aesthetic form is temporal, as well as spatial. Moreover, the spatio-temporal form to which Kant is alluding, insofar as it is playful, is not merely static: it is mobile and even fluid. Perhaps if Kant had developed this thought further he could have come to the conclusion that aesthetic form is a particular modulation of perceptual form, where the line becomes free and what it is for something to have spatio-temporal extension becomes open for reflection. He could, as I have suggested, have gone even further and explored the way in which form and matter stand in a dynamic relation to one another: this is an insight his perspective invites and, perhaps, even requires. But even if we restrict ourselves to the letter of his position, without drawing out its further potential, it seems that the playfulness of some aesthetic forms, at least, means that they amount to rather more than the merely primary qualities of an object marking out a definable position in space. Although this clarification applies directly only to playful aesthetic forms rather than to aesthetic shapes, I think the argument could be extended to the latter as all judgements of beauty rely on a playfulness of the faculties unconducive to a liking for rigid form. This is the perspective Kant takes later, when he insists that regular forms are not conducive to taste. [See 'General Comment on the First Division of the Analytic'.]

At the end of the main discussion of purposiveness without purpose, Kant remarks that even ornamentation [*parerga*] can contribute to taste. Ornamental features operate by charming our senses, yet they are not excluded from taste, so long as only their formal features are taken into consideration. A frame may enhance a painting if it is well chosen, but distracts from the beauty of the artwork if it is gaudy. Derrida has elaborated a reading of Kant's aesthetics, focusing on the role of the *parergon* as marginal to the artistic object [See Derrida, 1978/1987]. While picture frames, drapery on statues or colonnades around a building can add to our taste, Kant announces rather dogmatically that emotion is not at all compatible with taste, although he concedes that it plays a role in aesthetic judgements of the sublime, which we will discuss later. Kant's final word is to stress that taste can have neither charm nor emotion as its determining basis. As I have argued, this need not rule out that charm can be part of the wider story of taste and there is no reason why the same argument could not be applied to emotion.

2.4.2 *Perfection, adherent beauty and the ideal of beauty*

The remaining sections of the third Moment concern ways in which a rational idea may potentially play a role in aesthetic judgement. For this reason the discussion in Sections 15 to 17 falls under the general topic of the relation in which taste stands to purposes, which we learned in Section 10 are rational ideas that formally cause an object to exist.

Beauty has often been understood as perfection and in Section 15 Kant denies this common view. Perfection is measured relative to a concept of what the thing should be, either as to its utility or as to its moral goodness. But, as we already know, taste is not dependent on any concept, thus there is no measure by which perfection could be aesthetically judged. Finding something beautiful does not imply even a confused concept of the perfection of an object and concerns only our engagement with the object. What determines taste is not a concept, but a feeling of a harmony in the play of the faculties in the presentation of an object. Crucially, we can only feel this mental accord, yet if perfection were in question we would have to refer to a concept of what the thing should be. If this involved a confused concept of perception accessed by sense – as a Leibnizian might argue – we would need an understanding that also senses or a sense that uses concepts. Both of these are contradictory ideas from the perspective of Kantian dualism, which insists on the distinctiveness – though necessary cooperation – of two faculties, understanding and sensibility.

Understanding, the faculty of rules or concepts, has a role to play in aesthetic judgements, but, Kant says, it determines not the object in order to give rise to knowledge, but the judgement. What he seems to mean is that understanding establishes that aesthetic judgements are determined by an accord between a presentation and the mental activity characteristic of taste and hence establishes *judgement's* rule in an appeal to universal subjective validity. The claim is, however, still rather opaque. Why would understanding be needed to establish the rule-giving capacity of the distinct power of judgement? It has already been established that understanding has a role to play in aesthetic judgement insofar as only an indeterminate, not a determinate concept of beauty is aimed at. Moreover, we have also seen that aesthetic judgements require the activity of the faculties necessary for 'cognition in general', which we would naturally assume stands in some relation – yet to be determined – to the faculty of cognition, the understanding. Kant's additional suggestion that understanding establishes the rule-giving capacity of judgement is neither illuminating nor, it would seem, necessary.

Despite Kant's insistence that perfection has no role to play in beauty, he now moderates his position. In Section 16 he introduces the notion of accessory or adherent beauty, which is directed by a concept of how something should be and thus allows for consideration of how perfect it may be with regard to this standard. Free beauty rests on no such conceptual basis and is, as we have just seen, derived only from a feeling that can be traced back to the relation between a presentation and our mental powers. Kant now offers some further examples of free beauty, which as we have seen, is identified principally through its spatial form: flowers, many tropical birds, crustaceans, designs *à la grecque,* patterns of foliage used in interior decoration and musical fantasia. (This final example emphasizes that design is elaboration not only in space, but also in time, as Kant already suggested at the end of Section 14 in talking of the play of sensations in time.) These are beautiful and yet they represent nothing: the beauty is in the presentation to the eye or ear and in our reflective response to what we see or hear. Such judgements count as pure judgements of taste, where our imagination is contemplative and at play.

Examples of adherent beauty include a human being, a horse or a building such as a church, a palace, an armoury or a summerhouse. All of these, even a human being, imply a concept of purpose or a standard of taste. We do not simply look at the singular instance and find it beautiful: we already have an idea of how it should look. When we exercise our taste according to a principle of how something should be, we are, Kant says making a rational judgement rather than a pure judgement of taste. But it is important to add that a judgement about a beautiful church, for instance, would not be a pure rational judgement and is rather still one of taste, even though reason plays a role not compatible with free beauty. When we judge something as displaying adherent beauty, our activity of judging is mixed with a concept of reason alongside the play of understanding and imagination, which in this case is not entirely free. Aesthetic judgement here takes a lead from reason, yet is still directed to what is presented to the eye.

Such judgements are not strictly universal because they are fixed to a pre-established standard, but they are useful for promoting moral rational ends. Adherent beauty prepares the way for morality. But Kant also suggests that this requires a relation of the mental powers that encourages us to stay in that state and is subjectively valid. These are two prime characteristics of taste, so why does adherent beauty not qualify? I would suggest that, although adherent beauty involves some harmony between the presentation of the object and our mental activity, which to a certain extent counts as in play, the harmony between the object and the subject is not entirely free and nor is the play of our faculties. What we see does not spontaneously fit with our mental reaction to it, because we have introduced a standard – an idea of what this thing should be like – into the equation. A free beauty arises when, for no reason, something given to us in experience fits harmoniously with the activity of our mental powers. This is why we can require that such a convergence is worthy of universal approval. In the case of adherent beauty the 'fit' is partly due to our having something in mind about the nature of the phenomenon. Yet Kant is not suggesting that the concept of this object is private to me, which would result in the liking I have for it being merely agreeable. The concept that guides our appreciation is a rational idea, which is both objectively and subjectively universal.

In summary, adherent beauty cannot be universal in a purely aesthetic sense and yet it can be universally significant for the way in which we combine rational ideas with our appreciation of sensory appearances. I have just suggested that adherent beauty fails to be aesthetically universal because it does not display a free convergence between what is given to us through our senses and the response of our mental powers. Such a harmony between subject and object is, ultimately, the basis for aesthetic judgement. In the 'Analytic of the Beautiful' we have seen that Kant describes this as a relation between the presentation of an object and the play of our faculties. In the 'Introductions' to the third *Critique* he talks of a purposiveness of nature for our power of judgement, which is characteristic of all reflective judgement including the aesthetic variety. Although it would not be possible to go into such a tricky topic in any depth here, it is arguable that the relation between subject and object that is the pervasive topic of the 'Analytic' is an instance of the purposiveness of nature for our judgement, explicitly discussed only in the Introductions, but, as we will see, mentioned in the 'Analytic of the Sublime', lying behind the assessment of artistic beauty and reintroduced in the 'Dialectic'. What we can conclude is that judgements of adherent beauty call on the agreement of others, although they are not so deeply rooted in the cognitive relation we stand in to the world as is the call to agreement evoked by beauty.

We have seen that taste is not determined by a rational concept, while adherent beauty, if it is to be useful for morality, must refer to reason. We should bear this in mind, because later it may look as if taste itself is an instrument for moral reason. Kant now rules out such an instrumentalist reading, even in the case of adherent beauty. He says that it is not so much that either beauty or moral perfection gain in being allied to one another, rather, the 'complete power of presentation' benefits [P: AA 231]. His point, I would argue, is that we should not see the faculties as competitors for domination of the mind, but rather that they work together for its expansion through the complex inter-relationship of several distinct mental orientations. When I associate the kind of contemplative attention characteristic of taste with a rational idea of perfection, I turn my attention away from free beauty but I also turn towards a whole new vista of moral implications.

Section 17 delves deeper into the elements of adherent beauty. A pure judgement of taste considers its object as 'vague' [*vage*], that is, undetermined by any concept, although we have seen that it is not necessarily inconsistent with Kant's position that indeterminate concepts will serve as part of the description of such beauty and even that determinate concepts can be preparatory for this. Adherent beauty is 'fixed' in that it relies on a concept of objective, not formal, purposiveness [AA 232–3]. We have an idea in mind about how the thing should be and this determines our appreciation of this instance of a general class of things. In our imagination we generate an 'ideal' – Kant writes 'idea' [*Idee*] – or archetype [*Urbild*], that is, a sensory presentation of a rational idea [AA 232]. We never quite achieve such an ideal, even in our own minds, though we continually strive towards it. The nearest we come to encountering such an imaginative goal within experience is in finding an individual phenomenon that appears to express the ideal. When we do so, Kant says that there is an 'individual exhibition' [*einzelne Darstellung*] of the ideal and this is achieved by the imagination [P: AA 232]. His point is that some beautiful phenomenon – be it natural or artistic – embodies an aesthetic ideal we have in mind. Both the standard for our appreciation of fixed or adherent beauty and our response to an empirical phenomenon that expresses that ideal are ultimately traced back to imagination. Imagination is the vehicle through which we aspire to a rational idea, yet our standard is the sensory expression of that idea. Rational ideas are not capable of sensory expression, but aesthetic ideals *are* and indeed can only be exhibited through our senses. The imagination generates a standard – perhaps, even, a rule – by finding a particular instance that it takes up and explores so as to release its potentiality for taste. (Taste, here, is not *pure* taste.) The phenomenon is discovered through our senses and transfigured by imagination so that this individual thing or event can serve as an aesthetic ideal.

When an ideal enters into taste the resulting judgement is partially intellectual, that is, imagination is oriented towards an idea of reason. Flowers, furnishing and views can count as free beauties, and even mansions, trees and gardens almost qualify as vague beauties just because it is not clear what they are for. In contrast, human beings [*Mensch*] determine their own purposes through the exercise of reason and, therefore, we have an idea of what their purpose may be. The sensory appearance of a human being must be judged relative to the ideal of achieving our highest purpose. This is an ideal of moral perfection and we are the only beings on earth who qualify for such a standard of taste. What Kant means is that the beauty of a human individual in some way displays his or her rational and moral being. Human beings are not like other beings in the world because they are rational agents and this must be taken into consideration in our appreciation of any beauty they display. In insisting that human beauty must be adherent, Kant distances himself from the classical view that the human figure is the pinnacle of beauty. Kant agrees that human bodily perfection counts as an archetype, but insists that it is distinct from pure aesthetic judgement where the only criterion is pure form, informed by no idea or purpose of how it should be.

The ideal of beauty, which as we have seen is restricted to human beauty, has two elements, an 'aesthetic standard idea' and a rational idea [P: AA 233]. The second of these takes as a standard for human beauty the (rational) purposes that, we have just seen, motivate our lives and provide a standard of perfection for adherent beauty. In contrast to this rational standard, the standard idea of any being – and not just humans – starts from experience and generates a model that captures the range of instances of that particular type. Kant seems to be suggesting that in the case of a human figure we take into consideration our distinctively rational orientation in generating such a 'type'. An aesthetic ideal arises from the combination of the empirically oriented scanning process that gives rise to an aesthetic standard idea with the identification of the particular characteristic of human beings in their orientation towards rational purposes. The standard idea alone cannot give rise to pleasure and merely supplies a rule by which the correctness of a judgement of beauty can be checked [AA 235]. The aesthetic ideal thus combines the rational idea of the moral purpose of humankind with a rule of empirical uniformity.

After this long diversion about adherent beauty, Kant concludes the third Moment saying that he has established that (pure, free or vague) beauty is the 'object's form of purposiveness' [AA 236]. Beauty is not in the object in the sense that it is something out there in the world irrespective of what we think of it. However, the object must display beauty for us and it does so when its form [design or *Zeichnung*] corresponds to the purposive play of our faculties of imagination and understanding. In such instances, our minds display formal purposiveness for the activity of cognition in general, but so too does the object that prompts such appreciation. As we already learned from the first two Moments, the judgement that arises will be free from personal or moral motivation, displaying a contemplative attention and will call on the agreement of all other judging subjects. The third Moment has developed the idea of a contemplative attention that is subjectively universal by explaining the relation in which the object or phenomenon stands to the mind in such cases. Aesthetic contemplation arises when the form of the object encourages a harmonious play between the faculties and when we call on all other judging subjects to share our pleasure in the object. In the fourth Moment Kant tries to show why pleasure necessarily accompanies aesthetic judgements.

Kant's characterization of beauty as purposiveness without purpose in the third Moment entails that aesthetic appreciation makes sense in its own terms and is not merely an instrument for other ways in which our lives are meaningful, such as seeking out knowledge, aspiring to moral ends or satisfying personal preferences. But the autonomy of aesthetics that is opened up does not amount to a detachment from other aspects of our lives. Taste, as we have already seen, stands in a necessary relation to the possibility of cognition. In his account of adherent beauty Kant shows how certain beautiful things are indexed to an idea of reason. Admittedly, in this case they do not count as pure instances of taste, strictly understood, but we will see later on that aesthetic judgement in general must stand in some relation to rational ideas. The autonomy of taste is a complex one as its elements are borrowed from other domains. Imagination and understanding have been transposed from their normal habitat which formerly appeared to be exclusively epistemic. Taste occupies the middle ground between knowledge and morality and can only do so by sharing elements with them, while also opening up new ways in which those elements – or faculties – stand in relation to each other. This is essential if the systematic aim of the third *Critique* is to be possible, that is, if the gap between knowledge and morality is to be bridged. Aesthetic judgement can only be the link between the two extremes insofar as it is both distinct from and yet related to both: the autonomy of taste is not absolute but, rather, relational.

2.5 Moment 4: aesthetic judgement is necessarily connected with pleasure

Having established the subjective sense in which aesthetic judgements count as universal in Moment 2, Kant moves on to establish the specific sense in which they are also necessary. But if he is to show that they do indeed display the 'exemplary' necessity he attributes to them in Section 18, he needs to establish that they have a foundation in the fundamental structures of cognition. Consequently, in Section 21 he traces taste to a 'common sense'. We will see, however, that he encounters a fundamental problem, with the result that the necessary status of taste is not yet established.

Section 18 begins with the remark that we can feel pleasure about any aspect of our experience, but usually the connection between our knowing or evaluating something and the pleasure associated with it is merely contingent. There is no necessity that knowing something, for instance, gives rise to a pleasure, although it may do so. The situation is very different when we make an aesthetic judgement, for taste is expressed *as* a feeling of pleasure. The connection between liking an object and judging it aesthetically is a necessary one and it is the task of the fourth Moment to establish this. Now, there are a variety of different types of necessity. Theoretical objective necessity arises when I report a state of affairs and, consequently, am in a position to predict that everyone will make the same observation. Practical objective necessity is based on the moral law, which commands us to act in a certain way. Aesthetic necessity holds for a universal rule that cannot be stated and thus is 'exemplary' for all judging subjects [AA 237]. Appreciating something as beautiful is the only case where there is a necessary connection between judging and liking. In this case the rule cannot be derived from experience, nor is it cognitive or moral in status.

Having established the sense of the necessity he will attempt to establish between aesthetic judgement and pleasure, in Section 19 Kant insists that such exemplary necessity is always conditional, that is, we can only 'solicit' [*werben*] it. Thus far we are familiar with this proviso from the second Moment. Now Kant goes a step further in clarifying the nature of the validity of aesthetic judgements, saying we can claim such conditional necessity because aesthetic judgement is based on something 'that is common to all' [AA 237]. While there was already some anticipation of this claim in the second Moment's themes of a universal voice and of 'cognition in general', Kant now intends not only to describe the sociability of taste but also to establish the validity of this description by tracing it to a ground within all judging subjects. In Section 8 Kant said that if we restrict our judgement to formal conditions we will succeed in making a pure aesthetic judgement; he now says that if we always subsumed any particular instance under the common basis of aesthetic judgement, we could be confident that others would agree in the way we say they ought. His position in Section 19 is a logical extension of his earlier position, as a pure aesthetic judgement bearing subjective universality must be one that calls on the agreement of others. In this respect the fourth Moment makes explicit something already implicit in the second. An advance made in this section and in the Moment as a whole is the focus on a plurality of judging subjects, who share a common capacity that is the basis for aesthetic judgements.

Section 20 reveals that this basis is 'common sense' [*Gemeinsinn*] or, more strictly, the idea of one. Kant is not here concerned with practical good sense, which we often refer to as common sense and for which he prefers the title 'common understanding', because it judges by concepts. Common sense or *sensus communis* is, rather, a subjective principle that determines through feeling what is liked. Judgements of taste are possible only if there is such a common sense, by which he says he means the 'activity [*Wirkung*] of the free play of our cognitive powers' [AA 238 *Wirkung* is usually translated as 'effect', but common sense might then appear to follow on from the harmonizing of the faculties and I do not think this fits with Kant's position overall or with the argument he will present in Section 21]. While at this point Kant's account is difficult to construe, common sense is either identical to or a result of the play of the faculties already introduced in Section 9.

But all Kant has established so far is that *if* judgements of taste are based on common sense *then* they appeal to the necessary agreement of others in finding this particular object beautiful. Before moving on it is worth remarking on a point that will be significant for our later discussion. In Section 20 he generally refers to aesthetic judgements in the plural. We must conclude that he is concerned here with the validity of our aesthetic evaluations of particular objects whereas, in the 'Dialectic' we will see that the validity he seeks to establish is not principally that of particular aesthetic judgements but rather of the principle of taste.

In Section 21 Kant sets out to establish whether or not judgements of taste are in fact based on a subjectively universal principle. In pursuing this line of questioning, he aims to establish not only whether there is such a principle, but what it is. The argument he now provides is one of the most complex arguments of the *Critique of Aesthetic Judgement* and has been the subject of a number of quite different interpretations. The reason why it has been read in such different ways is that, once again, Kant gives an unclear account of the relation in which the 'harmony of the faculties' stands to cognitive judgements. At the end of Section 21 he seems to suggest that a harmonious play of imagination and understanding is necessary not only for taste, but for any cognition whatsoever. The (implausible) conclusion would be that knowledge is based on an essentially aesthetic frame of mind. This has led Henry Allison to argue that the section is not concerned with taste at all and is, instead, a deviation from the main body of Kant's discussion, focusing on a common sense necessary only for cognition. [Allison, 2001, pp. 149–55. See Guyer, 1979, pp. 279–307 for the view that Section 21 is a first attempt at a deduction. Crawford believes that it counts as the fourth stage of the deduction. Crawford, 1974, pp. 125–33.] In contrast to Allison's epistemic reading, I hope to show that there is a viable aesthetic reading that allows us to see how Section 21 leads on from previous sections and concerns the relation between taste and 'cognition in general', first raised in Section 9. [See Hughes, 2007, pp. 177–89.]

The contents of any judgement – whether it gives rise to knowledge or not – and the belief that we have about that judgement must be capable of being communicated to all other judging subjects, otherwise we would be merely expressing our subjective point of view and would not establish anything about the object. Kant says that otherwise the judgement would not achieve a harmony [*Übereinstimmung*] with the object [AA 238]. But, he adds, for objective communication to be possible, even the mental activity necessary for any cognition must be capable of being communicated. Kant goes on to clarify that he is referring to the attunement [*Stimmung*] of our cognitive powers necessary for 'cognition in general', namely, the proportion [*Proportion*] in which the faculties stand to one another if an object is to become available to us as a presentation, that is, as cognizable. (Here the terms 'attunement' and 'proportion' reinforce one another. At this stage the distinction between these terms is not yet important.) Kant's point is that the cognitive powers must stand in some reciprocal relation so that cognition can arise. As we have already seen in discussion of Section 9 above, in the first *Critique* it was established that knowledge only arises from a combination of sensory input (intuition) with conceptual organization (understanding). If these two faculties worked against one another, knowledge would never arise. They must, instead, cooperate or be attuned to one another as the subjective condition of cognition. This status explains why the mental activity can, along with its objective content, be communicated to all judging subjects. Kant refers directly to his epistemology, saying that the necessary attunement of the faculties takes place when an object taken in by the senses in collaboration with imagination 'prompts' [*in Tätigkeit bringt,* literally, 'brings into activity'] the understanding to find for it an explanatory concept [AA 238].

So far, the account can be read entirely in epistemic terms. Kant now introduces the idea that there is not just one, but a variety of ways or proportions in which the attunement of the cognitive powers arises and that this can be traced back to the variety of objects we encounter. The first point to note here is that the object is not an idle wheel and plays a role in prompting the specific proportion of the faculties that arises. Secondly, the term 'proportion' now expresses a particular modality within the 'attunement' of the faculties, necessary for cognition in general. What I think he means is that distinguishable judgements characterized by distinctive relations between the cognitive powers arise in response to different objects or states of affairs. If we are to successfully take up an object, there must be some cooperation or attunement between our faculties, but there is a different style of relation or proportion between the faculties according to the way in which we respond to the object. He goes on to say that there is one particular type of judgement in which the attunement of the faculties is determined only by a feeling and yet is highly conducive to cognition. Although

Kant does not identify this particular relation of the cognitive powers, drawing on his wider account we can infer that he is alluding to taste. The harmony of the faculties distinctive of taste is necessary for 'cognition in general' and, yet, is communicable by feeling alone in that the subject 'feels himself' [AA 218; AA 204]. This is a proportion of the faculties that is highly conducive to cognition without giving rise to any cognitive result and so communicates only through a feeling. While it is arguable that the judgement arising from feeling and highly conducive to cognition *may* not be identical to taste, surely it is highly likely that it is.

Kant now states that the only way such a feeling could be universally communicable would be if there was a common sense. I would suggest that by 'common sense' he here means the ability to coordinate our mental faculties as is required for any cognition whatsoever. The communicability of an objective judgement is due, at least in part, to the existence of a state of affairs in principle available to all. But an aesthetic judgement is subjective and cannot rest on facts, so the only way such a judgement qualifies as communicable is if it displays the subjective condition for validity, the coordination of the faculties. Indeed, this subjective condition is also a necessary condition for the possibility of grasping states of affairs. So this particular (aesthetic) proportion of the faculties can only count as valid because it is based on an attunement of the faculties necessary for all cognition. Thus Kant thinks he has established that there is a basis for judgements of taste by showing that they rest on common sense, the attunement of the faculties necessary for any cognition whatsoever. We might add that they count as a special case or 'proportion'.

The general aim of the fourth Moment was to establish the necessity of aesthetic judgements, that is, to show that they are necessarily associated with a feeling of pleasure. Judgements of taste have now been shown to bear necessity insofar as they rest on the universal conditions of all cognition and, unlike objective judgements, we are aware of the universally valid viewpoint they express only in an exemplary or indeterminate fashion as a feeling. Judgements of taste call on the necessary agreement of others *as* a feeling of pleasure. Thus Section 21 completes the task of the fourth Moment and of the 'Analytic of the Beautiful' as a whole and yet Allison's epistemic reading would make it a diversion from the main argument. As Section 22 will not so much further the achievement of Kant's goal as assume it, Kant's argument would have to end in Section 20, which we have seen establishes only the possibility that there may be a common sense and not that there in fact is one. Read as Allison reads it, the 'Analytic of the Beautiful' would end on a highly hypothetical note. While Kant is still hesitant about the status of taste and even its possibility, I do not think it is plausible to conclude that his account is quite so up in the air as the epistemic reading of Section 21 would force us to conclude.

But there is, undeniably, an element of Kant's argument that undermines his claim that he has offered a riposte to scepticism. In the final sentence of Section 21 he suggests that common sense is the necessary condition of any cognition whatsoever, yet, he has already claimed that it is the basis for judgements of taste [AA 239]. The lack of a distinction between the different roles played by common sense in cognition and taste seriously undermines his argument. The failure of this section as a deduction of taste leads Allison to deny that the communicability arising as a feeling belongs to aesthetic judgement. My suggestion is that Kant should have said that any cognition whatsoever rests on an attunement of the faculties, but taste rests on a peculiarly harmonious relation or 'proportion' between the cognitive powers, which makes apparent the general activity of our mental powers in cognition. In response to the sceptic, for whom it cannot be proven that the contents of the mind grasp objects in the world, the aesthetic judgement can be held up as demonstrating an instance where there is a harmony between the object and the play of our minds [AA 238/9]. Knowledge is, in principle, possible because this object prompts me to find it beautiful. As Kant repeatedly insists, beauty is not something we discover *in* the object. Beauty uncovers the relation in which an object must stand to the mind if knowledge is to be possible, even though in this case the proportion of the faculties is distinct from that necessary if knowledge is to be achieved. None of this is clarified by Kant, leaving his account open to the charge of inconsistency and in need of a radical reconstruction such as Allison's.

In Section 20 Kant introduced the *idea* of a common sense and in Section 22 he emphasizes that the exemplary validity of taste is merely ideal. We cannot predict that everyone will agree with us and can only say that they ought to do so. Kant now declares that the problem raised in the title of Section 21 – whether we can, in fact, presuppose a common sense – has been answered in the affirmative, just because we make judgements of taste. Surely, we must now conclude that Kant believes such judgements display the particular attunement determined by feeling introduced in Section 21. This would explain why he begins the following section so confidently.

It may seem, however, that Kant is arguing in a circular fashion for in Section 21 he claims that the necessity pertaining to judgements of taste can only be established if it can be shown that such judgements are based on common sense. And if our liking for certain objects did not bear necessity, then there would be no distinctively aesthetic judgements and only subjective preferences which would not require a third *Critique* for their analysis. So, in Section 21 Kant argues, in short, that judgements of taste are only possible if there is a common sense, whereas in Section 22 he says that common sense is established because we do in fact make judgements of taste. However, this second statement is a very simplified version of his position and rests on the argument given in the previous section. Kant starts from the position that we do in fact make judgements of taste and then seeks to establish the validity of such judgements. Indeed, in general, his transcendental philosophy set out to investigate the validity of our claims, epistemic, moral and aesthetic. [Thus in the *Critique of Pure Reason* he distinguished between the fact of our judgement – *quid facti* – and the validation of such judgements – *quid juris*. A 84/ B 116. See Allison, 2001, pp. 67–84]. So both Sections 21 and 22 start from the fact that we make judgements of taste, but only Section 21 aims to establish that there are distinctively aesthetic judgements. The fact that we make judgements we consider expressions of taste is not sufficient to prove that common sense has been established. The proof that it is possible to make a valid claim for aesthetic subjective universal validity is only established when it is shown that those judgements are based on common sense. *Then* it is possible to say that judgements of taste display the existence of common sense. This reinforces the view that Section 21 is supposed to be the core of the fourth Moment and that Section 22 cannot be.

To complicate things further, Kant now poses the question: Is there any such common sense at all? The specific twist to a recurrent theme is that judgements of taste may turn out to be disguised rational judgements based on a principle of reason and thus taste may only be an 'artificial' ability reason aims to bring about for its own purposes, rather than an 'original' and 'natural' one [AA 240]. But if taste were merely operating in the interests of reason, then a critique should not have been devoted to it. Kant has opened a can of worms, just when we might have expected him to have come to a firm – even if partial – conclusion. The difficulty of establishing the distinctiveness and even the possibility of taste is, however, not avoidable, just because of its mediating status which blurs the boundaries between it and other faculties. [See Hughes, 2006a.][6]

Disappointingly, Kant does not develop this theme, nor does justice to the radical nature of the problem he has introduced, saying that all that is necessary is to analyse the elements of the power of taste – which he now seems to assume is an original and natural one – and to unite them in the idea of a common sense. This strongly suggests that the relation between the four Moments is progressive. Common sense, as the harmonious cooperation of the faculties, is the basis of judgements that are contemplative and thus valid for all judging subjects and arises when an object gives rise to a play of the faculties. In such cases we necessarily experience a pleasure because the subjective conditions of cognition are displayed, albeit in a harmonious relation not required for cognition in its everyday form.

2.6 The conclusion to the 'Analytic':
the 'General Comment' and 'free lawfulness'

Taste is the ability to judge an object in relation to the 'free lawfulness' [*freie Gesetzmäßigkeit*] of the imagination [AA 240]. In order to understand this characterization we need to appreciate that imagination is either reproductive or productive. When imagination is reproductive it follows the laws of the understanding so as to give rise to knowledge. This is the use of the imagination that was discussed in the epistemic argument of the *Critique of Pure Reason*, where it served as the condition of the possibility of synthesizing intuitions with concepts. But even this epistemic use of imagination was ultimately traced back to a productive ability without which reproduction could not arise [*C. Pu. R.* A 101–02; A 118; A 123; B 152]. In the context of the first *Critique*, however, the distinctive cognitive capacity of imagination, even as productive, is ultimately exercised under the influence of understanding's project of synthesizing intuitions with concepts so as to give rise to knowledge. (I have argued elsewhere that understanding requires the cooperation of productive imagination and cannot merely coerce it. See Hughes, 2007, pp. 120–51.)

Kant now announces that productive imagination is free insofar as it is the capacity to introduce forms for intuitions so that they can be taken up by concepts. Now in the epistemic case imagination makes synthesis possible precisely by supplying forms for intuition so that they can be synthesized under concepts. Something is given to us in intuition, but if it did not have a form we could apprehend, it would not be possible to determine the intuition under a concept. This is why the 'synthesis of imagination' is the necessary intermediary step between apprehension and conceptualization in the first edition of the 'Transcendental Deduction' and figurative synthesis is the key to the application of a concept to an intuition in the second part of the second edition version of the same argument. However, as I have just remarked, in the epistemic case imagination, even when productive, is not free because it generates forms in accordance with the laws of understanding, that is, with a view to making an intuition fit for a concept and *vice versa.*

Contrastively, in the aesthetic case the imagination must find a form for an intuition without following a law of understanding, even though that form would, under other circumstances, be the necessary condition for our achieving knowledge of it. In this case we are faced with an intuition of an object – either a natural beauty or a visual artwork – that we are aware of through our senses and to that extent our imagination must, as in the epistemic case, follow the form of something that was not simply dreamed up by the mind, at least not that of the aesthetic spectator. Yet, despite the constraint posed by something given to us in experience, the form of the thing seems to echo just the sort of form our imagination would create were it left to its own devices. It is *as if* the object that stands before us was dreamed up by our imagination, for our minds play freely as if they were the authors of what we apprehend. Kant's point is that when the imagination produces a form in the epistemic case, it does so according to two constraints: it has to find a form for the given object and the form it finds must be capable of being taken up by the understanding. In the aesthetic case, the imagination produces a form for the given object even when there is no rule of the understanding at issue. The imagination produces a form that fits with the intuition, but also fits with the general conditions or 'lawfulness' of the exercise of understanding, even though no specific knowledge is aimed at or arises. Imagination is free because it is not subject to a rule, yet it is lawful because it is conducive to the general possibility of cognition. This combination qualifies as the 'free lawfulness' of the imagination in relation to the understanding, which is just another way of expressing 'purposiveness without purpose' [AA 241]. And this freedom of the imagination is prompted by the form of the object we find beautiful.

Kant now tries to illustrate what he means by 'free lawfulness'. Geometrically regular figures give rise to determinate judgements where our imagination follows a rule. Radically irregular figures, such as a one-eyed animal or an irregularly shaped room or flowerbed displease us, he says, because they are contra-purposive for our judging of them in that they seem to defeat the very conditions of judging, preventing us from explaining them through concepts. The highly regular phenomenon does not qualify for an aesthetic judgement because it is governed by a purpose and thus immediately invites cognition of it, while the wildly irregular fails because it is incompatible with cognition. Kant now offers some examples of objects suitable for aesthetic liking, namely, English gardens and baroque furniture. In these cases the forms we are looking at do not appear to be constrained by a rule and yet these (artistic) phenomena are not contra-purposive for judgement. They tantalize us with the intricacy of their forms, while at the same time inviting our attention in such a way that the mental activity that would be required for achieving knowledge of them is in play, yet no conclusion is reached. An English garden could be so far from the constraint of a formal French garden (such as that at Versailles) that it is almost as if it had no form at all. However, such a garden comes very close to the grotesque but cannot actually be so because a beautiful form must not be contra-purposive for cognition [AA 242]. Beauty occupies a balancing point between constrained form and no form at all. Kant develops this point with a discussion of the competing attractions of wild natural beauty and human creations, such as a pepper garden, concluding that natural beauty trumps artifice. Yet all he needed to argue is that for us to find something beautiful, it must have a discernible form but not follow a rule. Artworks and natural beauties can both qualify – and fail – by this standard.

The purposiveness without purpose that distinguishes judgements of taste arises when our mental activity is led by the imagination. But this is not to say that aesthetic judgement arises from an exercise of imagination in absolute detachment from other mental powers. The specific character of aesthetic freedom is that of being conducive to the general capacity for knowledge and yet not submitting to the laws of cognition. Imagination is conducive to cognition without giving rise to it. The aesthetic object, which is a condition of aesthetic judgement, opens up an array of possibilities that the imagination organizes so as to make a sense that is exploratory and yet does not establish *what* the object is, nor in which relations it stands to other objects. When we judge aesthetically we use our cognitive faculties so as to expand our experience of an object, not to discover the concept that would explain it.

Kant's concluding remarks on the distinction between beautiful objects and beautiful views reinforce my insistence that taste arises in response to our apprehension of an object. Beautiful views constitute a form of fiction [*dichten*] and encourage the play of the imagination. Kant suggests, although only by analogy, that beautiful views charm us, rather than giving rise to pure aesthetic judgement because they do not engage with something beyond the mind. Charm cannot suggest the purposiveness of nature for judgement, just because it does not display free lawfulness or purposiveness without purpose in response to the presentation of an object. For this reason it merely gratifies us and does not belong to a pure judgement of taste. In this passage, Kant reverts to excluding and not merely limiting the role of charm.

Study questions

In what sense is a judgement of taste 'subjective'?

How do you think an aesthetic judgement might evoke a feeling of life?

What, according to Kant, can aesthetic judgements 'require' and even 'demand'? What can they not do and why is this so?

Is Section 21 a first attempt at a deduction of taste?

Has Kant identified a distinctive phenomenology of taste?

3 JUDGEMENTS OF THE SUBLIME AND THE DEFEAT OF THE SENSES

Kant now turns his attention to aesthetic judgements of the sublime, which are distinctively linked with a feeling of disharmony. The sublime overwhelms us either by its size or its power, but at the same time reveals a source of resistance within ourselves, namely, our power of reason. I will draw out how the sublime qualifies as an encounter with the limits of comprehension, rather than as simply chaotic. We will look at Kant's suggestion that the sublime displays an 'aesthetic measure' prior to any mathematical measurement and I will suggest this has a wider significance for experience in general. And while Kant says that his discussion of the sublime counts as an appendix, we will see that this is only insofar as it cannot contribute to the 'purposiveness of nature for our judgement' discussed in the 'Introduction' and, it is now stated retrospectively, implicitly at issue in the 'Analytic of the Beautiful'. Moreover, I suggest that the sublime has a negative implication even for the purposiveness of nature and cannot be regarded as a mere appendix to the third Critique's systematic role of establishing the possibility of moral intervention in the empirical world. Finally, we will see that the power to judge the sublime is a peculiar capacity that arises only through the incapacity of one of its constituent elements.

3.1 The characteristics of the sublime and the organization of its analysis

In Section 23 we discover that the judging of the beautiful and the sublime share some very important features.

The sublime:

1. is liked for its own sake (or, is not based on an interest)
2. is judged reflectively, not empirically or logically (i.e., is not determined so that we can know it as such and such a thing)
3. is grounded on neither an agreeable sensation nor a determining concept
4. nevertheless refers to an indeterminate concept (or, more strictly, an idea)
5. stems from our power of exhibition, the imagination
6. is based on a harmony between an intuition and 'the power of concepts' (It will turn out that the power in question is reason, not understanding with which intuition harmonized in judgements of beauty. Moreover, the harmony is a complex one, the dominant first stage of which is a disharmony.)
7. is singular, as it is dependent on an intuition and yet lays claim to being universally valid for all subjects (There are no general judgements of the sublime, just as there are no genuinely aesthetic judgements about the beauty of roses in general.)
8. claims only the necessity of a feeling of pleasure and does not give rise to cognition (as was also argued with regard to taste in Moment 4 of the 'Analytic of the Beautiful').

So, we already know quite a lot about our capacity to make judgements about the sublime before we examine them directly. There is a good reason for this. Reflective aesthetic judgement, which made possible the judgements of beauty analysed in the 'Analytic of the Beautiful', is also the source of judgements of the sublime, although it operates differently in this case. The significant differences are the following:

• While a judgement of beauty is directed to the form of an object – the purposiveness of its form – judgements of the sublime typically arise in response to (relatively) formless objects.
• Consequently, we consider something sublime to be an exhibition of an indeterminate concept of reason, not understanding.
• While beauty was a presentation of quality, the analysis of the sublime is most focused on quantity.

- Whereas the pleasure arising from beauty opens up a feeling of life, the feeling that accompanies judgements of the sublime is one of constraint, followed by an indirect pleasure.
- While a beautiful object is purposive for our judgement of it, the sublime is contra-purposive in that it defeats our ability to take it in through the senses. (This is the most important distinction in Kant's view.)

The sublime defies our power of imagination in its role of taking in what is given in intuition and finding for it a form that makes possible explanation or cognition under a concept. Our power of imagination is defeated and along with it our ability to make sense of the world through our senses, but, just because of this defeat of the senses, we are forced onto a different plain, that of reason with its ideas of the infinite, the empirical correlate of which is the indeterminately large. Phenomenologically speaking, the quantity pertaining to the sublime is overwhelming size, although, more strictly, Kant focuses on logical quantity, that is, the status of judgements of the sublime as subjectively universal. The frustration of our attempt to relate to the world is translated into a pleasure in our ability to transcend the world through our power of ideas (not concepts), that is, our capacity to think what cannot be presented to the senses. Judgements of the sublime are purposive for our power of reason, even though they are not purposive for our power of judgement.

Objects of nature are not, strictly speaking, sublime: only the mind displays the sublime. Retrospectively clarifying something that was far from clearly established in the 'Analytic of the Beautiful', Kant now announces that it is quite correct to call very many natural objects beautiful. (I have suggested that Kant's insistence that judgements of beauty are 'subjective' means not that they have nothing to do with the object, but rather that they are not founded on a determination or predicate of the object and, rather, on the relation between subject and object.) Kant insists that only our ideas transform, for instance, a turbulent ocean into something sublime. While the activity of our minds clearly has a role to play in judgements of beauty, the sublime is even more directly referenced to the mind and, correlatively, less to the object. This contrast is reinforced when Kant now says that natural beauty reveals a purposiveness of nature for our judgement [AA 246]. Singular beautiful phenomena harmonize with our activity of judgement and, in so doing, reveal the possibility of a more general relation between mind and world. This is the sense of the anti-sceptical force of the 'Analytic of the Beautiful', claimed in Section 21. The sublime displays the absence of harmony between object and subject. Whereas in judging the beautiful we must 'seek a basis outside of ourselves', the sublime turns us towards the inner life of the mind [AA 246].

The 'Analytic of the Sublime' counts as an appendix to Kant's project of investigating 'our aesthetic judging of the purposiveness of nature' [AA 246]. Nevertheless, the sublime has implications for reflective judgement's epiphany of the relation between mind and world. Judgements of the sublime cannot directly illuminate the purposive relation (and potential harmony) revealed by beauty. But even if the sublime is not conducive to our ability to cognize or know something in the world, it is purposive for our thinking activity and for the moral capacity associated with it. Thus the sublime does not facilitate the life of the senses, but it does encourage the life of the mind of a being that is both rational and sensory and we saw in the 'Analytic' that this is just the sort of beings we are. So while the sublime counts as an appendix to the analysis of the purposiveness of nature for judgement, it is a necessary part of the account of the relation between our moral and cognitive dispositions. As this is a major motivation for the third *Critique*, the 'Analytic of the Sublime' cannot entirely qualify as an appendix. Moreover, the sublime strikes a dissonant note which negatively illuminates the purposiveness of nature for our judgement, placing the possible fit between mind and world within a broader context of possible relations in which I may stand to my material environment. Kant does not draw out the complex picture of mental life that underpins his critical philosophy, but we should not take too literally or quickly his demotion of the sublime.

Finally, it is worth remarking that even in judgements of the sublime we must be faced with something, however ill-formed it may be. Such judgements stem from the imagination, that is, the ability to hold together under a form what is given by the senses. In this case, no well-designed order is available, but we need *something* to defeat our senses if we are to derive an indirect pleasure from our capacity to go beyond them. Reflective aesthetic judgement of the sublime is oriented towards ideas of reason, but it operates through the imagination. We are still in the world when we judge sublimely: it is just that we have a glimpse of something beyond.

In Section 24 Kant says that the judgement of the sublime, just like the judgement of beauty, can be analysed into four moments, although he does not divide the text into separate discussions of each of these as he did in the 'Analytic of the Beautiful'. The quantity of the sublime is that of universal validity, its quality of disinterestedness, its relation of subjective purposiveness and its modality of a necessary subjective purposiveness. He now says that the 'Analytic of the Beautiful' began with quality because of its concern with the object's form, thus suggesting that in his account of taste the form of the object was at issue right from the outset. Restricting our attention to the formal features of the object, we stand in a state of contemplative attention to it. As the sublime is (relatively) formless, its analysis will begin with the moment of quantity, that is, its subjective universal validity. While there is no explanation of the primacy of the quantitative over the qualitative, it will turn out that what characterizes the sublime is its measure, that is, its absolute largeness for our senses, a size that threatens to defeat our senses in trying to take it in. The sublime defeats our capacity for measuring it relative to other phenomena, but, as we will see, this frustration coincides with a revelation about the basis of our capacity for measurement.

Following on from this architectonically motivated comment, Kant makes a much more illuminating distinction. While the beautiful invokes restful contemplation, the sublime incites an agitation of the mind that is, nevertheless, purposive either for our cognitive power or for our power of desire. In the first case, the sublime is mathematical, while in the second it is dynamic. This is the distinction around which the 'Analytic of the Sublime' is organized. I have already remarked that in the sublime reason takes the place of understanding, so it may seem odd that Kant refers to the cognitive power. However, cognition is broader than knowledge and includes both morality and speculative rational thinking aimed at the infinite, investigated by Kant in the 'Dialectic' of the first *Critique* and, importantly, in 'The Regulative Use of Ideas'. The mathematically sublime is purposive, not for our capacity to determine objects but rather for our ability to think the infinite and this (regulative) exercise of speculative reason counts as part of our cognitive capacity, considered in a wider sense.

3.2 The mathematical sublime

We call something sublime when it is absolutely large, that is, large beyond all comparison. Understanding is no help here because its exercise allows us only to judge the size of things comparatively, using one thing as the measure for another; while if we were to use reason as our guide we would start from an already established principle and there is none available here. Kant concludes that only our power of judgement can be the source of an evaluation of absolute largeness. He next claims that when we say something is absolutely large we call on the universal agreement of all other judging subjects, just as in the case of the judgement of beauty. Towards the end of Section 25 we discover that the sublime arises from the combination of imagination's striving for an infinity it can never achieve with reason's ideas of totality or completion. Within experience there is just one thing after another: this is the level at which imagination operates when it follows the rules of understanding. There is no completeness in the sensory world and only an open infinity that goes on indefinitely. As rational thinking beings, however, we introduce ideas of how things are systematically related to one another within a whole. Such a whole cannot be given to us in experience, at least not in such a way that we could achieve knowledge of it. In ordinary experience imagination holds together portions of the infinitely large range of things, so as to make sense of a subset of reality and potentially achieve knowledge of it. The sublime phenomenon is something so large that we cannot take it in: it stands in for the infinite, even though it is not strictly speaking infinite and only seems so. And just in defeating our senses, this absolutely large thing makes us aware that we have a capacity to go beyond the senses through our supersensible power of reason. The sublime phenomenon counts as such because it makes us aware of a sublime capacity within ourselves.

Section 26 concerns the aesthetic estimation necessary for an appreciation of the sublime. While mathematical estimation takes already established measures as its standard, aesthetic estimation operates 'by the measure of the eye', that is, just in looking at something [AA 251]. Kant's radical claim is that mathematical estimation finally rests on aesthetic estimation. Mathematical estimation is always comparative, taking its measure from some other act of measurement; yet in measuring, we have to start somewhere, which means we must have taken in the size of something without comparing it to anything else. This prior measure required us taking in something through our senses and holding it together as a unit that can then be used as the standard for other things. Kant surely does not mean that our ordinary, comparative (or mathematical) perception of things in the world is ultimately based on finding them sublime, so he must have a more general understanding of aesthetic measure for which the sublime plays a significant role.

Kant need not mean that our capacity for measurement can be traced back to an originary perception in our infancy. What he may mean is that if we are to see the size of things in relation to one another, then we must first be able to see, by the eye alone, the thing as a thing, that is, as having a not-yet determined extension in space and time. Comparative judgements can be traced back to an original capacity for seeing a thing in the world, even though any thing must also stand in relation to other things. The thing presents a standard for judgement not simply derivative from our experience of other things.

Theoretically speaking, there is no limit to what we can estimate mathematically. The series of numbers progresses to infinity. But what we can take in through our imagination reaches a limit. Thus, something that is absolutely large to our senses, while it may still be quite puny from a mathematical perspective, counts as sublime. (Mont Blanc is sublime if you're climbing it, even though it is dwarfed by higher mountains outside of Europe.) Absolute magnitude arises when something is absolutely large and yet we can hold it together in one intuition, that is, in our sensory awareness of something at one (perhaps extended) point in time. In general, intuiting something requires not only apprehension, but also comprehension.

In the 'Transcendental Deduction' of the first edition of the *Critique of Pure Reason,* it was established that apprehension arises from our power of intuition, which takes something in through the senses, but Kant also says that what we take in must be 'run through and held together' [*C.Pu.R.,* A 99]. What we take in through our senses must be capable of qualifying *as* a thing. Building on a requirement for comprehension ('holding together') already apparent at the level of intuition, imagination is the power that allows something taken in by our senses to be identifiable as one thing over time, that is, only thus does our intuition take on a form that could be determined by a concept so as to give rise to knowledge. 'But if I were always to drop out of thought the preceding representations (the first parts of the line, the antecedent parts of the time period, or the units in the order represented), and did not reproduce them while advancing to those that follow, a complete representation would never be obtained . . .' [*C.Pu.R.,* A 102].[7] Thus the comprehension of sensory apprehension is necessary if conceptual determination is to be possible and knowledge is to arise. But in the case of judgements of the sublime, no such conclusion or completeness arises. Instead, all we achieve is a level of comprehension (or 'holding together') compatible with a disinterested, though agitated, contemplation of the phenomenon. Although the thing is absolutely large and defies our sensory and cognitive powers, it must at least strike us as *something* that is absolutely large. So although the object we deem sublime is formless, it is not incoherent: it simply does not have the sort of well-formed appearance conducive to judgement and, ultimately, to knowledge. It has an identifiable, but not a cognizable, form.

As I have interpreted aesthetic measure, it has significance beyond the account of the sublime and illuminates not only the life of the mind but also our perception of things in the world. Kant does not explain what the wider ramifications of his account might be and we are not able to do so here, other than in suggesting a general way in which this idea might be developed. My suggestion is that the sublime reveals our general capacity for taking in and holding together a thing through the combination of intuition and imagination and does so at the limits of that capacity, where sense is in danger of breaking down.

The sublime, it seems, is a limit case, where if form were any more indeterminate it would defy our judgement altogether. As we will presently see, the examples Kant gives tend to support my suggestion that the sublime is not to be confused with the chaotic or the senseless and is, rather, the defiance of sense at its limits (and not beyond them). Were this not the case, Kant could not have said that aesthetic judgement exhibits absolute magnitude in one intuition [AA 251]. The sublime is as far as we can go without wholly losing a sense of measure – it is 'the aesthetically largest basic measure for estimation of magnitude' [AA 252]. While the absolutely large is not within our control, we are still – just about and very uneasily – capable of taking it in.

The two examples Kant gives of the sublime are the Egyptian pyramids and St Peter's Basilica in Rome. He says that if we are to find the pyramids sublime, we cannot stand too far away from them, for they would then have no effect on our aesthetic judgement, being too obscure. He means that even a huge architectural structure can look puny if seen from a sufficiently great distance. On the other hand, if we stand too close up, as we take in one portion of the pyramid, we will lose sight of the rest. Finding something sublime requires that we hold it together in one intuition, as a measure of a particular thing in a singular judgement. Any experience of an object requires that we hold together our impressions of it, only thus is it identifiable. The pyramids and the Basilica offer an immensity that cannot be fully grasped as a whole and yet they encourage our imagination to aspire to an idea of completion. What we see and take in with our imagination teeters on the limit of being comprehensible and ultimately evades our grasp as a totality. The sublime is almost beyond our capacity for estimating magnitude and it is because of this marginal status that it reveals the activity of aesthetic estimation 'by the eye' normally unnoticed in everyday experience. The evocation of a whole, simultaneously with the incapacity of our senses to deliver one, is constitutive of the sublime. Did we not feel we were on the brink of seeing the infinite, there would be no aesthetic measure of the absolutely great. The sublime hovers at the limit of our sensory power, serving as a measure that threatens to fall into the immeasurable and yet never quite does so. While the imagination is 'inadequate' and the experience counts as a *lack* of harmony, we nevertheless experience the sublime as a tentative whole, albeit one we cannot grasp [AA 253].

Any phenomena that arouse judgements of the sublime, despite the examples Kant has just supplied, come from 'raw nature' [*rohe Natur*] rather than art [G: AA 253]. This is because Kant assumes that artworks rest on determinate concepts that shape our perception of them. It is the intention of the artist that ultimately disqualifies artworks from achieving pure aesthetic status, be it beauty or sublimity. Kant is not entirely consistent on this point, as he often presents artworks as examples of aesthetic judgement. Moreover, it is arguable that he is mistaken in the exclusion of artworks and that it is unnecessary for his wider account. Just because an artist has intentions that are necessary for the creation of an artwork, does not mean that the aesthetic affect of the artwork is determined by these intentions. Admittedly, a clumsy artwork will show traces of the process of its production, but a successful artwork takes on a life of its own beyond any authorial intent. We will come back to this. With particular regard to the sublime, it is important to note that an artist can offer a presentation for our apprehension that intimates something that is not seen, being beyond either mathematical measure or human control. Goya's 'Disasters of War', for instance, present horrors that are almost unimaginable and indescribable. The artwork is, in such cases, capable of suggesting something it cannot show.

In Kant's view, the sublimity of 'raw nature' reveals a crucial aspect of the relation in which we stand to the objective world. In everyday apprehension of things in the world, we simply attend to one thing after another. We have to hold together the elements of any sensory intuition, but this does not tax our imagination unduly and we usually do not notice the mental activity that is necessary. However, because we are also rational beings we are motivated by the idea of infinity and, Kant suggests, even attempt to think infinity as a totality. Our ability to think the infinite as a whole reveals that we have a power that goes beyond the senses, that is, a supersensible power of reason. The recognition of this is experienced as a feeling of an expansion of the mind beyond the everyday world of objects.

Even when we go beyond particular natural phenomena and consider increasingly larger natural systems, such as the earth and even the planetary system of which our planet is only an element, nature does not qualify as sublime. The sublime is the 'mental attunement' between the imagination and the ideas of reason [AA 256]. In the mathematical sublime reason is a speculative capacity that extends the field of cognition. In the end, what is absolutely large is our mental power rather than anything in nature, which in contrast ends up looking 'vanishingly small' [P: AA 257].

In Section 27 Kant introduces an idea familiar to readers of his moral philosophy. In judging something in nature sublime, we are in fact displaying respect for our own supersensible 'vocation', that is, our rational ability to go beyond the mechanical order of nature. The imagination has shown its obedience to law by displaying its own abortive attempt to follow the mechanical laws of nature, while, at the same time, revealing an alternative law, that of reason. The complexity of the role played by imagination is an intricate one, suggesting that a power is exercised through defeat; a capacity arises from incapacity and a pleasure is generated from displeasure. The mental attunement of imagination and reason is one of conflict, not harmony. Kant even speaks of a violence done to the subject by the imagination. The sublime gives us a sense of the supersensible side of our being: it does so not by giving a direct prospect on rationality, but rather by allowing us to see reason indirectly through the lens of imagination. Something sublime in nature allows us a form of self-reflection on our rational powers, just as the beautiful made us aware of the relation in which we stand to nature, without which no knowledge would be possible. The indirectness of the self-awareness that emerges from aesthetic judgement is necessary just because of the depth and opaqueness of what is revealed. In Kant's view the two forms of aesthetic judgement reveal different dimensions of the supersensible. While the sublime reveals the supersensible within us, the beautiful makes visible the supersensible ground of the relation between mind and world. [This is discussed in the 'Dialectic'.] In both cases, we become aware of the supersensible, that is, a fundamental power of the mind, through the specific attunement (or 'proportion') of the faculties characteristic of aesthetic judgements. What is already apparent at this stage of the text is that what we can call the 'supersensible within' is reason and its ability to think the infinite. The feeling of the sublime is respect for this capacity.

3.3 The dynamically sublime

The dynamically sublime arises when a phenomenon disturbs our imagination, but in so doing opens up a moral perspective within the sensory field. In Section 28 we discover that an aesthetic judgement of the dynamic sublime arises in the recognition of the 'might' or 'dominance' of nature, yet we do not feel crushed because of an awareness of our capacity for moral self-determination [P: AA 260].

Not everything that gives rise to fear is sublime, but all natural phenomena that arouse a feeling of the dynamical sublime could, under other circumstances, cause fear. We have to be aware of the possibility of being fearful because it is only thus that we can assess the magnitude of the force with which we are faced. While in judgements of the mathematical sublime we were overwhelmed by the sheer size of something, now we are struck by the strength we would require if we were to resist a natural force. Yet when we are judging aesthetically, we are not in fact afraid of nature nor are we trying to resist it, we are merely *thinking* about doing so. Fear cannot be accompanied by the indirect liking characteristic of the sublime. Yet fearful phenomena such as thunderstorms, volcanoes, hurricanes and a stormy ocean can give rise to a pleasure, if we are in a safe place while viewing them. We think about what it would be like to be caught in such a situation and imagine how we might cope. Kant suggests that we can rise to the challenge in our imagination and find resources for resisting the force of nature. It is important to note here that such experiences of the sublime involve thinking about resisting nature, but we must be in some contact with what we are contemplating resisting. The feeling of the sublime requires a direct sensory encounter with nature, admittedly from a safe vantage point.

The first stage of the dynamical sublime is the overwhelming of our imagination, which is incapable of finding a standard for estimating the force of nature. The phenomenon with which we are faced is simply too great for us to be able to calibrate it within the normal range of natural forces. This particular force lies at the limit of our ability to measure the obstacles posed by nature to our free will. Yet in the face of this failure and even prompted by it, we discover an alternative standard that stems from our power of reason. As rational beings, we have the power to resist any external force even if it physically crushes us. The victim of torture may die, but she can still resist external forces that aim to make her take on alien values. In the aesthetic case, the situation is much less extreme and lies at the limits of our capacity for self-determination, rather than in its annihilation. Here the threat and our resistance to it arise only in imagining them, yet our imaginative reflection on a phys- ically overwhelming phenomenon allows us to become aware of a capacity for resistance that could be exercised in other situations where we encounter a real danger. From a morally rational perspective every risk posed by nature is small, while our power for self-determination is limitless. In feeling the sub- lime we realize that, were it necessary, we could raise ourselves above our normal concerns for property, health and even life itself, if our highest moral principles were at stake.

Kant insists that even though the situation that gives rise to a feeling of the sublime is not an actual threat, the awareness of our rational capacity (or 'vocation') is not simply imagin- ary. We have a capacity for moral self-determination, though it must be worked on and developed if it is to become strong. Feelings of the dynamic sublime encourage us in our convic- tion that we are moral beings and thus indirectly contribute to our taking a moral stance in everyday situations. Kant insists that both civilized and earlier societies have greatly admired the capacity for self-determination in the face of terrible occur- rences. He now makes the infamous claim that war can be sublime, whereas prolonged peace tends to debase the courage of a people. The point he is making is that war can be waged for moral principles and that peace may simply be a way of foster- ing commercial interests. I do not think Kant is aggrandizing war, but only suggesting that there are occasions when evasion of conflict would amount to submission to a force contrary to our power of self-determination. The recognition that war may be necessary and that there are dangers associated with peace does not undermine Kant's commitment to the political ideal of 'perpetual peace', which is the topic of one of his most important essays in political philosophy. [See 'Perpetual Peace'] Ultimately, politics should aim at a society in which all individuals mutually respect the worth of every other individual. Harmonious and mutually respectful peace is thus the aim of political life, but it may not be achievable through wholly peaceful ends. Just wars, not appeasement, may be necessary, on occasion, for achieving lasting peace.

Kant considers a possible objection to his analysis of the dynamically sublime, namely that, surely, we consider God sublime and yet it would be wrong to consider our capacity for self-determination superior either to the natural world, which is his creation, or to his intentions that lie behind natural phenomena. The key to answering this challenge is the realization that religion should not be seen as requiring the subjection of the will. The religious person should be capable of feeling reverence and admiration for God and not merely worship in order to ward against an overwhelming threat. True religion requires both quiet contemplation and the free judgement that marks it out from all external determination. Religion should be moral religion, as Kant argues in his *Religion with the Bounds of Reason Alone.* In finding the sublime in our own moral capacity, we reinforce our understanding of ourselves as freely willing to obey God and not just obeying him due to fear. The sublime pleasure we take in discovering our power of resistance to nature is, finally, conducive to a religion where God is genuinely respected.

In Section 29 Kant turns his attention to the necessity of the pleasure we take in the sublime. It is more difficult to require that others agree with our judgements of the sublime, than with our judgements of beauty. A feeling of the sublime, although based on the rational capacity for principled action present in all human beings whether civilized or not, requires a certain cultivation of both our aesthetic and cognitive powers. Culture helps us develop our rational capacity for ideas and to recognize that it is possible to resist nature. Only once we have been educated to develop this capacity are we in a position to fully appreciate the sublime within us. However, we are still justified in requiring and even demanding that everyone recognizes the dynamic sublime in nature, because such feelings are not conventional but deeply rooted in our identity as human beings. Indeed, were we not able to claim necessity for judgements of the sublime, they would not be based on an *a priori* principle and, hence, would not be part of transcendental philosophy and warrant inclusion in this third part of the critical system. The principle in question is the power of judgement, which in this case is oriented towards another power, namely, the rational capacity for self-determination [AA 266].

3.4 General comment on beauty and the sublime

At the end of the 'Analytic of the Sublime' Kant makes some general comments about the position he has developed so far, with regard to both the beautiful and the sublime. Much of what he says here re-emphasizes what has gone before. Nevertheless, he develops his position in some respects, which I will touch on selectively here.

He now says that the liking we have for something agreeable is quantitative in that it is only distinguishable insofar as we can measure how much pleasure we obtain. The beautiful is qualitative in that we are concerned with a certain quality of the object that suggests it is conceptually explicable, although in fact it is not. (The role given to the object here is, once again, more explicit than in his account in the 'Analytic of the Beautiful', although it is not inconsistent with his argument as I have reconstructed it.) The sublime consists, he says merely in the relation in which our imaginative activity stands to our supersensible power of reason. The absolutely good, at which we aim in our moral actions, is distinguished by its modality, that is, the necessity with which it commands us. This identification of each type of liking with quantity, quality, relation and necessity, respectively, is a simplification of Kant's position, because as we have seen each of these are attributable to both beauty and the sublime. However, we can make sense of this, saying he is now identifying the dominant characteristic of each of the types of liking distinguished in Section 5.

The relationship between imagination and reason in judgements of the sublime is one where imagination stands in for reason. Kant says that imagination is the 'instrument' of reason, but we should not read this as necessarily implying that imagination is simply an outpost of reason [AA 269]. Although we discover our power of reason when imagination fails, the sublime requires that we pass through the sensory in aiming at reason. Imagination is not a ladder that can simply be thrown away, for the characteristically negative pleasure of the sublime means that reason is only approached through the senses. The capacity for imagination, which in this case reveals itself as incapacity, is the necessary conduit to feeling reason's superiority to nature. The sublime is a complex feeling in which we hold together sensory disappointment with a rational alternative. However, Kant did not sufficiently develop his account of the continuing role of the sensory alongside the rational. Imagination has a dual role. First, as the representative of the senses, it seeks to hold together what is given to us in intuition and, secondly, it deprives itself of its own freedom in taking on a role as representative of reason. This is a particular and discordant version of the mediating role we have already attributed to imagination in the 'Analytic of the Beautiful'. In aesthetic judgements of both beauty and the sublime, the imagination moves beyond a merely reproductive or associative status, as we saw in the General Note at the end of the 'Analytic of the Beautiful', and follows 'principles of the schematism of judgement' [AA 269]. This idea is developed more fully in Section 35 in the 'Deduction'. At this stage I think Kant is already implying that even the sublime requires an exercise of judgement as a distinctive power and not merely as an adjunct of understanding or of reason. (This precision about the status of reflective judgement is expressed by the phrase 'our very ability to judge' in the 'Deduction'.) In judgements of beauty, aesthetic judgement arises from the free harmony of imagination and understanding; whereas, in judgements of the sublime imagination aspires to the ideas of reason, taking its standard from morality. In this case imagination is not as free as it was in the case of beauty, but it is not so much that imagination is determined by morality as that it *discovers* the possibility of morality through an aesthetic route. Just as the human agent must be free in order to be genuinely moral and even religious, so must we have a capacity for autonomous judgement if we are to be capable of sublime feeling as opposed to fear.

Latterly, Kant seems to concede that even judgements of the sublime refer to a presentation of the object, for he talks of our liking for the sublime in nature and gives some examples, such as 'mountains nearly reaching the heavens, deep gorges with raging torrents and deeply overshadowed wastelands' [AA 269]. The sublime begins with a presentation to the senses, even though one that ultimately defeats them. Both types of aesthetic judgement are based on 'how we see' something [*wie man ihn sieht*] and not just on how we think about it [AA 270].

Kant says that aesthetic judgements either of the beautiful or the sublime must not be based on covert teleological standards concerning a supposed purpose of the object. As imagination and judgement must be free in both cases, it cannot be that our pleasure arises from awareness of a goal for which the object was created. If we were purely intellectual beings we would think simply in terms of purposes, but we would not experience beauty or the sublime. Similarly, an aesthetic judgement cannot be determined by an emotion or 'affect', otherwise free judgement would not arise. Nevertheless, correcting a rather dogmatic comment at the end of Section 14, certain emotions are compatible with beauty and the sublime as long as they are not too powerful. Vigorous emotions, which make us aware of our capacity to overcome resistance, are conducive to the sublime, while relaxed or languid emotions are compatible with beauty. Kant suggests that the most sublime element of Judaism and Islam is the prohibition of images of heavenly or earthly things. His point is that the human capacity for rational freedom always stands beyond the visible realm. At this point, as elsewhere, he does not adequately focus on the aspect of his own account that requires that thinking the sublime can only arise out of an encounter with the sensory.

A remark near the end of this addendum to the analysis of aesthetic judgement in both its forms builds on the discussions of communicability in Sections 9 and 21 and is preparatory for Kant's discussion of this theme in the 'Deduction'. Both judgements of beauty and the sublime are universally communicable and for this reason they take on an importance in society where communication takes place. Nevertheless, solitude that does not arise from a dislike or fear of other people can genuinely count as sublime. Although we have already learned that communicability is characteristic of aesthetic judgement, this is one of the few occasions when Kant mentions communication.

Kant concludes the 'General Comment' with an assessment of Edmund Burke's contribution to the analysis of the beautiful and the sublime. Burke established a rich anthropological account of the psychology of aesthetic judgements, but he did not offer a satisfactory account of their status as valid for every judging subject. Judgements of taste are not 'egoistic' or private, but, rather, 'pluralistic' and are based on *a priori* principles [AA 278]. Kant clearly holds this not only for judgements of beauty but also for the sublime. Only as based on *a priori* principles, that is, on our most fundamental capacities, are aesthetic judgements capable of claiming universality. In the 'Deduction of Taste' that follows, Kant will investigate more deeply the *a priori* principle on which aesthetic judgements are grounded. The pluralist status of judgements of taste will be established through a more successful argument for their being based on a capacity 'common to all' than was provided in Section 21.

Study questions

Do you think the sublime overwhelms us or, rather, that it takes us to the limits of possible experience?

Does the 'Analytic of the Sublime' advance our understanding of purposiveness?

What is aesthetic measure and what is its significance?

What might be considered sublime?

Is the feeling of the sublime, finally, one of control or of its loss?

4   THE 'DEDUCTION' OF JUDGEMENTS OF BEAUTY

Judgements require a deduction when they make claim to universal validity: in effect, it is necessary to establish that they are based on an *a priori* principle. In addition to laying out the essential elements of the judgement of beauty, as he did in the 'Analytic', Kant now intends to offer a deduction of aesthetic judgement. Yet isn't this exactly what he did when, in Section 21, he argued that aesthetic judgements are based on an idea of common sense? If we read that section as a discussion of aesthetic judgement, as I think we must, then we have to conclude that Kant now thinks he did not achieve the goal of his deduction of taste at the end of the 'Analytic of the Beautiful'. In what follows, I will draw out how his argument progresses in the sections leading up to and including Section 38.

Judgements of beauty concern 'the mere apprehension' of the form of the object [*bloß die Auffassung dieser Form*] and the way in which it fits [*sich gemäß zeigt*] with our mental powers of understanding and imagination [Section 30, AA 279]. Kant goes on to say that in judgements of the sublime we are not really referring to, but, instead, making use of an object, which in its formlessness is subjectively purposive for the discovery of a supersensible power within us. In this case there is no need for a deduction distinct from an exposition because tracing the relation in which imagination stands to the supersensible power of reason, already carried out in the 'Analytic of the Sublime', is sufficient for establishing the validity of such judgements for all judging subjects. The clear implication is that the absence of reference to an object removes the need for an explicit deduction.

The indirect implication is that judgements of beauty require a separate deduction because of the relation in which they stand to beautiful objects. This means that at this stage of his argument, Kant suggests an analogy between the 'Deduction' of judgements of taste and the 'Transcendental Deduction' of the categories in the *Critique of Pure Reason*. The categories of the understanding are only ultimately shown to bear universal validity when it is proved that they are necessary conditions for the experience of objects [*C.Pu.R.* A 93/ B 126]. These conditions are the basis of any valid claim to knowledge and, while knowledge is not aimed at in aesthetic judgements, the conditions of cognition are in operation in a general way, as we have seen. Although Kant does not spell out his point, I think we have to conclude that the 'Deduction' of aesthetic judgement must, in establishing the universal validity of taste, also establish the relation in which judgements of taste stand to their objects. I will suggest that the advance of the 'Deduction' over Section 21 is twofold: on the one hand, it is established that the power of judgement as 'our very ability to judge' is exercised in an autonomous way only in aesthetic judgement; while, on the other, the pre-determinative relation in which the subject stands to the object when we find something beautiful comes into view. These two developments allow Kant finally to deduce the subjective universality and necessity of taste.

Even though Kant had already given a role to the object, especially in the third Moment, and had traced the necessity of universal approval to the subject's capacity for common sense in the fourth, he has not yet systematically accounted for the nature of the relation between subject and object that lies at the basis of aesthetic judgement. This would involve a working through of elements that were already introduced in the 'Analytic', namely the relation between the form of beautiful objects and the formal powers of the mind required for judging them. Although the object-directed trajectory of the 'Deduction' can be uncovered throughout, Kant does not always sufficiently emphasize it, sometimes falling back into a presentation of the deduction that emphasizes the aesthetic life of the mind, at the expense of clarifying the way in which the latter is a response to objects. Nevertheless, the attempt to establish the subject–object relation in judgements of taste is inextricably linked with the project of the 'Deduction', that is, establishing the subjective, yet necessary, universal validity of judgements of taste. I will attempt to trace the development of the two trajectories and show how they finally converge in Section 38 where Kant examines the relation in which the form of an object stands to the formal activity of the mind.

In Section 31 Kant reiterates that the deduction he is about to provide will establish the subjective universality of a singular judgement expressing the subjective purposiveness for judgement of the 'empirical presentation of the form of an object': that is, of the way in which the form of a particular object appears to us [AA 281]. When we apprehend something beautiful its sensory form appears particularly well fitted for our judgement of it. It is striking that, whereas it sometimes seemed in the 'Analytic' that there was nothing about the object that qualified a judgement as beautiful, it is now clear that the form – or design – of the object has an irreducible role to play. There are two peculiarities to the judgement of taste: it is both universal, though singular and necessary, yet not capable of compelling assent. Both features are by now very familiar to us, yet Kant devotes the two following sections to investigating each of them in turn. Kant says that if he can (finally) clarify the peculiar universality and necessity of judgements of taste, he will, in effect, have produced their deduction. This is the 'method' he intends to apply in the sections that follow.

Section 32 takes up the task of further investigating the peculiar universality of taste. Judgements of taste make claim to everyone's assent, just like objective judgements. It is 'as if' we were claiming knowledge about some characteristic of the object and yet all we are saying is that it 'directs itself' to our apprehension of it [AA 282]. The little phrase 'as if' will, once again, turn out to be crucial for the point Kant is making. Just as we cannot find the grounds for universality by taking a profile of the qualities of objects we find beautiful, no more will we succeed by taking a straw poll of other people's judgements. Thus the young poet must judge for himself even when he is not yet sufficiently experienced to come to a good aesthetic judgement. Our taste can be educated by following a model, but never by passive imitation [AA 283]. (Kant will take up this distinction again with respect to artistic creation in Section 49.) As taste cannot be taught, its universality must count as 'singular'. This section provides an elaboration of the way in which a judgement of taste claims universality, even though it is made by an individual judging subject. Kant emphasizes the first person singular origin of taste, while insisting that an aesthetic judgement is not particular to any one person.

We now expect that in Section 33 Kant will turn to the other peculiarity of taste, a necessity that cannot compel agreement. He begins by saying that taste operates 'as if' it were subjective because the judgements of others do not provide us with a valid proof for judging something beautiful. (He already introduced this characteristic of taste in the previous section in the course of establishing that it is as if taste were objective.) Secondly, judgements of beauty cannot be proven by finding rules that determine them. This alludes, indirectly at least, to Section 18's characterization of the distinctive necessity of taste as exemplary and not determining. A judgement of beauty is always about the universal validity of a singular instance, for example, a beautiful tulip.

In these sections Kant has elaborated the sense in which one judging subject can speak with a universal voice, but he has not yet provided a deduction of the principle of taste. While Kant addresses the subjective universality of aesthetic judgements directly and their necessity indirectly, the main achievement of these two sections is to situate taste in the median ground between the subjectively private and the objective. An objective judgement would compel the agreement of others just because it establishes a state of affairs accessible to all. It is *as if* the judgement of taste were objective because it claims the agreement of others, but is *as if* it were subjective because it cannot compel agreement. I have suggested that clarification of the respect in which a judgement of taste reveals a pre-determinative relation between subject and object is necessary for the completion of the task of the deduction. Kant's solution will be to establish a subjectivity that is not merely private and, indeed, is necessary for our knowledge of objects. In developing the middle ground between subjectivity and objectivity, these two sections contribute to the work of the 'Deduction'.

Section 34 announces that there is no objective principle of taste from which we can prove the correctness of a particular aesthetic judgement. But this is not to say that the task of deduction is hopeless. Kant now offers two injunctions. First, critics should investigate our cognitive powers and the work they do in aesthetic judgements. Secondly, they should clarify through examples the 'reciprocal subjective purposiveness', the form of which in a given presentation qualifies as the beauty of the object [AA 286]. As Kant goes on to discuss the reciprocal relation between the faculties of understanding and imagination we may conclude that this is what he means by 'reciprocal purposiveness'. Yet, it is also clear from this passage that mental harmony arises in response to the presentation of an object. Taken alone, the first injunction seems to restrict the task of the deduction to an examination of the internal life of the mind; however, the second injunction expresses the dual axis of taste, as a relation between subject and object.

We are now told that when a critique of taste works through examples it counts as an art, whereas scientific critique investigates the possibility of judging through an investigation of the cognitive powers. Critique, be it theoretical, practical or aesthetic in scope, traces our judgement back to certain primary cognitive powers. It is only if our judgements are based on this initial mental apparatus that they are worthy of inclusion in a transcendental critique of the fundamental elements of the human condition. In the case of knowledge it is possible to directly trace judgements back to their source in the faculties – principally, understanding and sensibility – through a theoretical investigation. This is what counted as a deduction in the first *Critique*. The question now is whether or not the same sort of proof is available for judgements of beauty. It is arguable that Kant should have taken the art of taste more seriously, especially given his insistence that taste has no objective principle, such as would be required for a science. While it is clear that he wants to establish that taste is not merely subjective opinion, perhaps he could have said that the critique of taste hovers between art and science, as it does between subjectivity and objectivity. This would be because in an aesthetic judgement, which can only be a singular response to a singular object, we can discern the activity of the cognitive powers indirectly, while our overt concern is for the direct liking we feel for an object. In other words, awareness of our cognitive faculties arises through engagement with an example. However, Kant insists that the critique that is an art would be merely physiological or psychological and restricts his project to the scientific one of a transcendental critique concerning our cognitive ability to judge objects of taste. In drawing this conclusion he underestimates the role that singular examples play in a transcendental critique of aesthetic judgement. The preference for critique as science, additionally, emphasizes the subjective side of aesthetic judgements and underplays – though does not, as we have seen, omit – the way in which our cognitive faculties respond to objects.

Section 35 continues the task of determining the peculiarity of taste. Taste does not rest on a concept, but only on the subjective formal condition of any judgement whatsoever, the power of judgement [AA 287]. This insistence on a third principal power in addition to understanding and reason is the result of the critical turn to examine the powers of the mind, announced in the previous section. Now, it has been clear from the outset of the *Critique* that taste arises from judgement, the third of the higher powers. The distinctiveness of Kant's account at this stage is that he now develops the idea, first sketched in the 'Introduction', that 'the power of judgement' is only exercised autonomously in aesthetic judgements, even though it is necessary for all our judgements. He writes that the basis of aesthetic judgements is 'the subjective formal condition of a judgement as such' and that this condition is 'our very ability to judge' [*das Vermögen zu urteilen selbst*] [P: AA 287].[8] The faculty of judgement is the source of any judgements we might make, be they cognitive, moral or aesthetic, yet it is only in the last of these cases that judgement is exercised without the direction of understanding or reason.

The distinction between the general role of the power of judgement in all judgements and its autonomous exercise in judgements of taste is crucial for making an advance beyond Section 21, where a lack of precision led to the impression that cognition rests on an aesthetic condition, namely, the harmony of the faculties. It is now clear that this is not Kant's intention and that, rather, he aims to establish that the universal validity of aesthetic judgements arises from their having as their ground the power of judgement which, in epistemic and moral contexts, is exercised in subordination to another faculty and, thus, is not characterized by a 'harmony of the faculties'. Even so, he now says that the power of judgement requires a harmony between imagination and understanding and we may think that the familiar problem has arisen once again. Although there have been difficulties in this regard previously, Kant's position now is that the power of judgement entails a harmony only when it is expressed in a pure form in aesthetic judgements. In order to clarify this, Kant could, however, have provided a further specification also missing in Section 21. The proportion of the faculties distinctive of a judgement of taste counts as a heightened example of the cooperation of the faculties necessary for judgement (and cognition) in general.

The next move in Kant's argument is to claim that whereas cognitive judgement entails the subsumption of an intuition (held together, as we've seen by imagination) under a concept, in a judgement of taste, imagination itself is subsumed under the general condition for understanding's subsumption of intuitions under concepts. This constitutes a very sharp shift of gear in Kant's account, but I think we can make sense of it as his attempt to supply the missing step, an alternative version of which I have just suggested. The judgement of taste rests on a relation between the faculties conducive to the schematization necessary for any cognition whatsoever. But in the case of beauty a subsumption does not take place; it is rather that the activity of the faculties that would be necessary for subsumption is displayed in a particularly lively fashion. This is described as the imagination's 'schematising without a concept' and arises as a feeling that allows us to judge the object in terms of its purposiveness for our power of judgement [AA 287]. In other words, the basis of a judgement of taste is a feeling about the harmonious relating of a particular object to our cognitive powers, which, in response to this object, harmoniously cooperate with one another.

Section 36 readdresses what Kant presents as the problem of taste, namely, how a judgement based on a merely subjective principle can claim the necessary agreement of all other judging subjects. An empirical judgement that connects a perception with a concept so as to give rise to knowledge can claim necessity, because cognitive judgements are based on a transcendental principle, as established by the 'Transcendental Deduction' of the *Critique of Pure Reason*. In other words, the deduction of the categories in the first *Critique* established the *a priori* framework that makes possible the application of the most basic concepts to empirical experiences. As a result it is at least possible that an empirical perception gives rise to knowledge.

But it is also possible that an empirical perception is linked not with a concept, but directly with a feeling of pleasure or displeasure. If such judgements are to be capable of requiring the liking of everyone, then they too require a transcendental principle. In aesthetic judgements, judgement is no longer a subsidiary power and is instead 'subjectively speaking, both object and law to itself' [AA 288]. [See Allison, 2001, p. 173.] This turn of phrase puts further emphasis on the specific way in which aesthetic judgements rest on the power of judgement. In cognition, judgement's task is to establish the applicability of concepts to intuitions. This is achieved through the intermediary role of imagination, which provides a schema, allowing for a concept to be figured or traced out in time and in space so that its synthesis with a sensory intuition is possible. In such cases judgement and imagination operate in the interest, finally, of cognition. However, in the aesthetic case judgement provides its own measure and is capable of reflecting on its role just because it is based on a principle peculiar to itself. Judgement has become reflective judgement and is no longer operating as determining judgement under the authority of the understanding. This is what is meant by the claim that judgement is object and law to itself.

An alternative way of raising the problem of the peculiarity of taste is now offered, no longer in terms of the status of the faculty directing taste, but rather through asking what goes on when we judge aesthetically. How is it that when I am judging something beautiful I judge on the basis of my own feeling and yet at the same time require that others agree, without trying to find out whether in fact they do so? In this phenomenological expression of the question of the status of taste, which has just been answered in structural terms, the convergence of subjective universality with exemplary necessity is apparent. A judgement of taste is enunciated by an individual subject and yet calls on the necessary agreement of all other judging subjects. How can this be the case? As yet, the only progress made in answering the question is structural, not phenomenological and rests on the identification of reflective aesthetic judgements as instances of the autonomous exercise of the power of judgement.

Kant concludes this section saying that it is clear that judgements of taste are synthetic. He even says that the *Critique of Judgement* contributes to the general problem of transcendental philosophy: How are synthetic *a priori* judgements possible? [AA 289]. This is a highly contested claim, for most readers of Kant hold that only determining cognitive judgements, which subsume an intuition under a concept, count as synthetic [Makkreel, 1990, pp. 47–51 and 1992; Hughes, 2007, pp. 156–60]. But Kant claims that judgements of taste are synthetic because they go beyond an initial sensory input, combining it with a feeling. The distinctive synthetic status of taste entails that an empirical feeling makes a claim to universal validity [AA 288/9]. This is puzzling, because Kant has suggested that the subjectively universal basis or principle of aesthetic judgement is a feeling, yet it can hardly be empirical. And, in any case, how could something empirical also be universally valid? What Kant must mean is that when I find something beautiful I experience a pleasure and have a feeling about some thing in the world. This is an empirical expression of taste's principle, which is an indeterminate idea of a common sense, that is, the attunement of the cognitive faculties, shared by all judging subjects. Taste's principle operates as a feeling of pleasure in the activity of the mind, as I argued in my discussion of Section 9. In this case we can say that the feeling is transcendental. [See, also, Section 20 where Kant says that common sense is a subjective principle 'which determines only by feeling' [AA 238].] He immediately goes on to say that common understanding, *unlike taste,* does not judge by feeling. In Section 36, Kant's point is that the synthetic status of aesthetic judgement arises from the combination of an empirical feeling (arising from an empirical perception) with the idea that everyone will assent. Such a feeling is empirical and yet takes on transcendental significance by appealing to 'our very ability to judge', which is common to all judging subjects.

Cognitive synthetic judgement achieves knowledge by going beyond a concept and synthesizing it with an intuition. Taste goes beyond not only a concept, but also an intuition and links the latter with a necessary feeling of liking and thus is part of the range of synthetic *a priori* judgements in general. Synthesis in its cognitive guise as 'Schematism' is the capacity to establish the 'significance' (*Bedeutung*) of concepts by transcending a merely logical thinking about things and grasping the content of an intuition under a concept [*C.Pu.R.*, A 146/ B 185]. Judgements of taste qualify as synthetic by reaching out not only beyond a merely logical grasp of things through concepts, but also beyond an empirical grasp of objects in conceptually determined intuitions.

All Kant states here is that a further species of *a priori* synthetic judgements has been discovered. He does not go on to investigate the specificity of their nature nor suggest they have a special role to play within the system of synthetic *a priori* judgements. We can, however, infer from what has been said so far that synthesis in this case will have no end, that is, no determination and will rather have the open-ended structure of purposiveness without purpose. I think it makes sense to go further and see this as a synthesis *in process* rather than synthesis as a result. [I argue this in detail in Hughes, 2007, pp. 151–6.]

We become aware of the way in which our faculties harmonize with one another in response to an object. While any cognition requires the process of synthesis if knowledge is to be achieved, only in an aesthetic judgement are we aware of this process, because the cognitive goal has been suspended and basing our judgement solely on that power alone, as was claimed in Section 35, we are free to exercise it not only as law, but also as object to itself. This would be the systematic significance of aesthetic judgements for the transcendental project.

In Section 37 Kant makes a distinction that has raised further interpretative problems. [See Allison, 2001, pp. 173–4, Guyer, 1979, pp. 258–9, Crawford, 1974, pp. 126–30.] He says that it is not our pleasure, but 'the universal validity of this pleasure' connected with 'the mere judging of the object', which counts as valid for everyone, that is, as a universal rule [AA 289]. What exactly is the point he is making here? Indeed we might conclude that he is arguing in a circular fashion: the universal validity of an aesthetic pleasure is taken as the universal rule (or validity) of taste. Alternatively, his position could be interpreted as inferring that, as the pleasure is not the rule, there is a rule prior to the feeling of the power of judgement as the very ability to judge discussed in Section 35. The problem with this interpretative resolution is that it would undermine the link between feeling and taste that has emerged so far, as well as Kant's insistence that taste cannot be based on a (determinate) rule. Allison's solution is to distinguish between the first-order aesthetic judgements we in fact make and the second-order principle on which they are founded, which alone is asserted *a priori* [Allison, 2001, p. 174.]. This distinction is an important one, while it is also important not to suggest too great a break between our actual judgements and the principle on which they are based. The principle of taste is, indeed, the proper subject of the 'Deduction', but its role is to validate particular judgements of taste. I think what Kant is saying here is that my merely feeling (aesthetic) pleasure when faced with an object is an empirical fact. But when I consider an object beautiful, I necessarily call on others to agree with me. This call to universal validity is a universal rule for the power of judgement. So the distinction Kant makes is between an empirical feeling of pleasure in an object and the universal validity claimed for it, allowing the feeling to operate as an exemplary universal rule. Put in this way, Kant's claim need not be circular and is defensible. The feeling that all others should agree in the pleasure I take in this particular object operates as a rule in that I call on all of them to share my feeling of pleasure.

Section 38 is the culmination of the deduction of judgements of taste, which aims to establish the subjective universality and necessity of taste through, I have claimed, establishing the relation in which a beautiful object stands to the activity of our minds, operating in response to that object or, at least, to the presentation of it. [See discussion of Section 30 above.] The argument of the 'Deduction' proper starts by reminding us that a pure judgement of taste arises from the pleasure we take in judging the form of an object. Having restricted our liking to the merely formal features of an object, we can conclude that the basis of this liking is the form's purposiveness for our power of judgement, which we are aware of responding to the presentation of the object. That is, if we are merely considering the form of the object, the power of judgement can only be directed to the subjective conditions for the employment of that faculty, which are shared by all judging subjects and are necessary for 'the power of judgement as such' (*die Urteilskraft überhaupt*) [P: AA 290].[9] Kant concludes that the harmony in which the presentation stands with the power of judgement must be valid for everyone and we can expect everyone to share our pleasure, establishing taste's subjective universality and exemplary necessity, respectively. In the 'Comment' that follows, Kant says that even though we may sometimes make mistakes in applying the principle of taste, the latter is not invalidated. This is a move already familiar to us.

What is the structure of this argument? Judging so that I am focused only on the formal qualities of an object, which adapt to or are purposive for the power of judgement, means that I base my judgement on the purely formal conditions of judging. If this is the case, then I have the right to call on your agreement, because I base my judgement on conditions that are shared by all judging subjects and am, in effect, judging for all of us, even though it is me who is judging and I am concerned only with a particular empirical object.

The clarification of the relation between object and subject that I have suggested is necessary for a successful deduction has now been supplied. If we attend to the purely formal characteristics of (the presentation of) an object that gives us pleasure, we are justified in claiming that it is beautiful and calling on everyone else to agree. The validity of the judgement of beauty has been deduced by showing that it rests on the conditions of judging *per se*, an attunement or cooperation of the mental powers. Uncovering how judgements of taste rest on the power of judgement as 'our very ability to judge' and operating as reflective judgement has been key, because only judgement so exercised attains a play of the formal subjective conditions of cognition. This is the return to the cognitive powers that was required if a critique was to count as scientific. Yet, in an aesthetic judgement, where there is a harmony of the faculties and no cognitive result, the power of judgement is only in view insofar as the form of a particular object stands in accord with it. A pure judgement of taste is subjectively universally valid and necessarily connected with pleasure because it rests solely on the formal judgemental apparatus shared by all and exercised in response to those aspects of an object that are accessible to all, its form or elaboration in space (and time). The dual harmony required by the two injunctions for a successful deduction introduced in Section 34 has finally been established through the critical clarification that aesthetic judgement is directly based on the power of judgement as 'our very ability to judge', exercised in response to the formal features of the object.

I have, additionally, suggested that the precise nature of the relation in which the subject stands to the object in aesthetic judgements counts as 'pre-determinative'. If taste displays the subjective conditions of cognition, while not giving rise to knowledge, then it follows that aesthetic judgements are characterized by a pre-determinative relation to objects. Knowledge is the determination of something as such and such a thing: in aesthetic judging I identify something in order to be able to appreciate it, but I do not aim to determine it as such and such a thing. As my mind makes use of the same powers of imagination and understanding, which would, in other circumstances, allow me to know that object, the relationship in which I stand to it cannot be characterized as non-determinative or even anti-determinative. My frame of mind is preparatory for – although

I have currently no interest in achieving – knowledge. Thus the relation in which I stand to the object is pre-determinative.

Section 39 returns to the theme of communicability which was so central in Section 21. Communicability [*Mitteilbarkeit*] is the basis that makes communication [*mitteilen*, i.e., to communicate] possible. The effects of the senses are not universally communicable because different persons may have quite different sensations in response to the same object. There is no way of objectively comparing your experience of the colour blue with mine or of establishing what blue looks like to you. We can devise a colour chart or provide a chemical formula, but that is not the same as establishing the sensory quality of blue. I can be sure what it looks like to me, but I cannot require that everyone else agrees, not only because there would be no way of checking for correctness but also because it is not clear what such a requirement would mean. Kant says that the diversity of liking for merely sensory qualities – a liking that can only count as agreeable – is even greater than is the range of our sensations of them. Communication of both sensory content and of our liking for sensation, is thus, ridden with difficulty. In contrast, the uniformity of moral feelings of pleasure can be established and even demanded, for in this case the communication of agreement is rational and rests on determining moral principles. Meanwhile, the sublime ultimately appeals to our moral or supersensible vocation and this is why we can call on others to agree with us.

The pleasure in the beautiful is distinctive in that it counts as one of 'mere reflection' which arises in response to 'the most ordinary apprehension of an object' [AA 292]. In apprehending an object, just as we would in having the most ordinary experience of it, we focus on what is, in this particular case, a harmonious activity of the cognitive powers, rather than on the outcome of their activity. The universal communicability of a judgement of taste stems from the judgement being based on the 'subjective conditions for the possibility of cognition as such [*Erkenntnis überhaupt*]' [P: AA 292]. Taste is communicable insofar as it rests on the subjectively universal principle of all cognition. A problem arises, however, when Kant says that the 'proportion' between the faculties necessary for taste is also necessary for the sound and common understanding, the basis of ordinary experience. This claim falls back into the confusion we have seen on several occasions, for Kant seems to be saying that empirical cognition rests on the harmony distinctive of taste. If he had said that taste rests on the same 'attunement' as ordinary experience, displayed in a peculiar 'proportion', in other words as a heightened or peculiarly harmonious relation of the faculties, he would have avoided this problem.

We have as yet heard very little about communication as an empirical event, although we have heard a lot about communicability as its condition of possibility. In Section 40 there is a development in Kant's account of communicability, which although still a formal condition of judgement takes on a more dynamic character. A distinction Kant first introduced in Section 20 is preparatory for this development and would, had Kant attended to it in Section 39, have helped him avoid the problem we have just been discussing.

The common human understanding by which we move beyond sensations so as to make sense of them through the application of concepts is often incorrectly called common sense. Common sense or *sensus communis* is, rather, the power to judge reflectively in such a way that we take into account everyone else's way of seeing matters. When we exercise 'mere judgement' in this way, we compare our personal judgement with human reason in general and move beyond a private perspective, adopting an inter-subjective one. In doing so, we liberate our judgement from prejudice. This is not achieved by taking a *vox populi* of the actual judgements of others, but, rather, we compare our judgement with the possible judgements of others. In doing so, one 'puts oneself in the position of everyone else' [AA 294]. Kant suggests that this can be achieved by limiting one's judgement to merely formal conditions, which we have seen means focusing on the form of the object in relation to the formal activity of judgement. When I judge aesthetically, I take on the broadened perspective of all judging subjects and abstract from any purely private interests and motivations. Admittedly, the way in which I invoke the judgement of others does not require that I actually communicate with them, but I open up my way of thinking so as to anticipate communication with other judging subjects. While this is still a very formal conception of social interaction, there is at least a requirement that I see myself as standing in relation to a community of judging subjects. This is why aesthetic judgement counts as pluralist and not egoist [AA 278]. While the sociability of taste was established as early as the second Moment and is part of the logic of the exemplary necessity of the fourth, it is only now that Kant suggests that making a judgement of taste requires me to put myself in someone else's position and not just that I require that they put themselves in mine.

It might well be objected that taste is not genuinely pluralist, as all I need do is judge for myself in response to the form of the object and then I can *assume* that I am judging in accord with the general conditions for all judging subjects. But in Section 40 Kant introduces a stronger requirement, namely, that we compare our putative judgements of taste with the possible ones of others: 'Now we do this as follows: we compare our judgement not so much with the actual as rather with the merely possible judgements of others' [P: AA 294]. Admittedly, he goes on to say that we achieve this by abstracting any material content from our own judgements. His account hovers between the beginnings of a more dynamically sociable account of aesthetic judging and one that rests on an analysis of the internal reflection of an individual. He could have said that abstracting from personal preference requires putting ourselves in the position of others, but he does not go this far.

Kant now offers an analysis of common human understanding, uncovering for it maxims which indirectly throw light on *sensus communis*. Common human understanding (*gemeinen Menschenverstand*) is a hybrid made up of a variety of powers and thus is much broader than the pure understanding, the prime actor in the first *Critique*. We could say that common human understanding is the understanding used in a pragmatic way, but now applied not only to cognitive but also moral situations.

The three maxims of the common human understanding are: One should think for oneself, think from the standpoint of everyone else and think consistently. The first of these is a maxim of understanding (in the narrow or epistemic sense of the first *Critique*), calling on us to liberate ourselves from prejudice and strive for enlightenment. The second maxim calls on us to develop a broadened way of thinking. This involves reflecting on our judgements from a universal standpoint and clearly refers to aesthetic judgement. The third maxim is, he says, the most difficult of all and requires that we make use of our power of reason. We can only achieve consistency in our thinking once we have developed our capacity for thinking autonomously, while, at the same time, we broaden our way of thinking. The consistency Kant has in mind is not simply that of avoiding contradiction, for this could be achieved without incorporating the goals of the first two maxims. The third maxim suggests that we develop a systematically meaningful way of thinking in which we are capable of both judging for ourselves and of taking into consideration the possible judgements of others. The result would be an exercise of reason as a capacity for self-determination based on *a priori*, not private, conditions. While only the second maxim directly relates to *sensus communis,* that is, to aesthetic judgement, the interrelation between the three maxims illuminates how judgement stands within a system of reason, understood in a broader sense including all the higher faculties, namely understanding, judgement *and* reason. Judgement has the specific task of broadening the mind in preparation for the highest task of rational self-determination. This insight will be important for his later discussion of beauty's role as symbol of morality and of the supersensible dimension of taste.

Ordinary communication requires the cooperation (Kant again, and problematically, says the 'harmony') of the mental powers, yet is governed by a law of the understanding. [AA 295]. It is only when the imagination is free in arousing the understanding, which in response encourages the play of the imagination, that not a thought, but a feeling is communicated. Taste is the ability to judge the communicability of feelings, by determining which feelings are capable of being communicated universally without a concept. When I say something is beautiful I claim that my feeling of pleasure in this object is communicable to everyone else. I thus require that you too feel this pleasure.

Kant now moves on to discuss genius, a talent for heightened communication through feeling alone. Communicability is necessary for any cognitive experience whatsoever and is exercised in an exemplary and free fashion in taste: genius is the ability to produce examples that communicate powerfully through employing those general conditions of communicability in an artwork.

Study questions

What is 'our very ability to judge' and in what sense is it 'object and law to itself'?

Is the aesthetic object more than incidental to the 'Deduction' of taste?

What role do you think is played by feeling in aesthetic judgement?

How does *sensus communis* come into Kant's account of taste?

Does the official 'Deduction' count as an advance over the argument of Section 21?

5   GENIUS, AESTHETIC IDEAS AND ART

Kant now turns his attention explicitly to artistic creativity and artworks. Central to his examination of art is his discussion of the creative genius's mental activity or 'attunement'. We are already familiar with this theme from his discussion of taste, although we will find that the creation of art requires a distinctive proportion of the cognitive powers. Kant expresses a reservation about the pleasure we derive from artworks in comparison with that arising from natural beauty. He maintains, however, that artworks give rise to taste and that their only shortcoming is that they give no insight into the relation in which nature stands to our cognitive powers, with the result that art cannot contribute to the hope that moral intentions are realizable. We will also find that, despite the distinctiveness of taste and genius and even a possible competition between them, taste is necessary for the development of genius and that aesthetic creativity and receptivity share certain features.

Despite the exclusion of any interest from a judgement of taste, in Section 41 Kant reveals that, once we appreciate something on the grounds of purposiveness without purpose alone, we can then take an interest in its existence on empirical or intellectual (i.e., moral) grounds. The beautiful gives rise to an empirical interest only in society. The communication of feeling characteristic of taste is conducive to our natural propensity for sociability. An isolated individual would not engage in the self-adornment that Kant sees as the most primitive level of aesthetic expression, the pinnacle of which is a liking for beautiful forms. Some interpreters hold that it is only now that Kant introduces art into his account, although we have seen that he often used works of art as examples of taste. [See Guyer's rejection of Gotshalk's view that 'Kant holds a *formalist* theory of Natural Beauty and an *expressionist* theory of Fine Art'. Guyer (1977) p. 48; Gotshalk (1967) p. 260] Instead, this is the first time he mentions the activity rather than the results of aesthetic creativity. The interest we take in creating beautiful forms within society is not properly part of the critique of taste. And an interest based on a pure judgement of taste may be confused with other inclinations so as to lead us to conclude taste is a consequence of such interests. If this were the case, we would have lost sight of the distinctive power of judgement and its expression in taste. Thus, despite conceding that beauty can give rise to an interest, Kant denies that it is founded on any. His principal task is to establish only the pure form of a judgement of taste and to show how our ability to judge might serve as 'a transition from sensory enjoyment to moral feeling'. Judgement, he says, is a 'mediating link in the chain' of the higher faculties [AA 297/8]. This is the systematic positioning of judgement with which Kant is concerned in his investigation of taste.

Even though Kant insists that the investigation of formal purposiveness is the main goal of his inquiry, taking a moral interest in the beautiful is the topic of Section 42. This is not, on reflection, so surprising, as the moral interest in the beautiful reinforces his systematic project of bridging the gap between cognition and morality. He insists, as he already did in his account of adherent beauty, that the beautiful is quite distinct from the moral, that is, it has a distinctive basis in the free exercise of the power of judgement. Moreover, artistic *virtuosi* are often anything but moral, while Kant holds that taking a direct interest in natural beauty is a sign of a good soul and conducive to morality. Now we might conclude that, retrospectively, Kant is saying that only natural, not artistic beauty is worthy of taste. But this is not the case – or at least, not yet – for he is presently discussing the moral interest that can follow from a judgement of taste and not the pure judgement itself. Indeed

Kant makes clear that from the perspective of pure taste natural and artistic beauties are on a par [AA 300].

But why should the interest accompanying a liking for the beautiful in nature have a moral significance? As so often at crucial stages of his argument, Kant turns to an analysis of the cognitive powers. Aesthetic judgement is an ability to judge and take a pleasure in the forms of objects from the perspective of mere judging, that is, as we have seen, on the basis of the formal conditions of judging. Moral judgement is the capacity to determine our actions according to the mere form of the moral law, the Categorical Imperative, which gives us the condition for any action that will count as moral. This too, Kant says, is associated with a pleasure although not a free one as it is derived from a moral principle. Thus there is an analogy between taste and morality in their both having a formal basis. Now, insofar as we are rational beings we are not satisfied to simply motivate our actions by moral principles and want our intentions to be fulfilled in reality. We thus take an interest in whether or not nature reveals a trace of its conduciveness to this possibility and beauty supplies just the hint we are looking for. Kant is suggesting that beauties in nature are conducive to the realization of moral intentions by showing that the latter are at least in principle realizable. His implied solution, at a very general level, seems to be that the harmony between mind and world displayed by natural beauty encourages the hope that even moral principles might finally come to harmonize with, and perhaps prevail within, the natural world. This suggestion is deeply indebted to his accounts in both versions of the 'Introduction' of the purposiveness of nature for our judgement. As artworks are not natural phenomena and, thus, he thinks, cannot suggest a harmony between mind and nature, they do not give rise to a moral interest.

Although Kant concedes that such an account may seem excessively complex, he insists that it is valid, arguing that the ability to take a moral interest in natural beauty is quite rare and only arises when the person is already trained in thinking in a moral way. Additionally, as aesthetic and moral liking are structurally similar, both being subjectively valid for all human beings, we need not be consciously aware of the systematic connection between them in order to see the first as propitious for the second. We instinctively make the analogy without undertaking the difficult transcendental argument that would show our association to be valid. Finally, the very appearance of beautiful nature as displaying a purposive order and yet lacking a purpose external to us, leads us to look for the purpose within ourselves, namely, in our moral vocation. Here, as on other occasions, it might seem that Kant suggests taste can be traced back to morality, despite his recent insistence on their distinctiveness. And yet his account only justifies him in saying that beauty in nature is suggestive of the possibility of morality, not that beauty can be founded on moral purpose. However, he is careful to stress that any such introduction of purpose into the account of taste can only be addressed from a teleological, not an aesthetic perspective. Thus we can see that the account of aesthetic interest falls outside of the account of the exercise of judgement exercised as object and law for itself.

Artistic beauty qualifies for a pure judgement of taste, but fails to give rise to a direct interest because it arises from the artist's purpose of pleasing us, which the artwork either conceals [*Taüschung* – literally, it deceives us] or displays [AA 301]. Kant's point seems to be that we cannot help being aware of the artist's intention and, for this reason, our liking for the artwork is necessarily referenced to a purpose. Yet, if this is right, artworks would fail to qualify for pure judgements of taste, while Kant has suggested earlier in this section that this is not the case and it is only that we cannot take a direct moral interest in them.

Kant's argument about the aesthetic status of artworks is seriously underdeveloped here. Even though an artist must have an intention in order to create an artwork, there is no necessity that her intention is the subject of our attention as viewers. The artist's genius is in concealing the mechanics, both material and psychological, of creation or, alternatively, transforming those mechanics into a distinctive artistic theme, as is the case in many modern artworks such as the Pompidou Centre's display of the elements of its engineering or, even, Tracey Emin's use of events drawn from her personal life. Kant could not have anticipated the scepticism with which we now view the 'intentional fallacy', that is, the attempt to explain an artwork from the intentions of the artist. We are inclined to view the meaning of the artwork as transcending the artist's intentions. Kant himself concedes that the artwork may conceal its intentions, though he expresses this negatively as deception or illusion. Nevertheless, Kant does not conclude that it is impossible to make pure judgements of taste about artworks and only that we cannot take a direct interest in them.

Kant finishes this section with an amusing scenario. The poet may be inspired by the sound of a nightingale's song on a moon-lit night, but, on discovering that the beautiful tones were made not by a bird but by 'a rogue of a youth' hidden in a bush, the creative urge to wax lyrical passes [M: AA 302]. Interestingly, this example, meant to assert that only natural beauty gives rise to a direct interest, suggests that true artistic creativity arises from receptivity to nature, a view shared by artists such as Goya. For Goya, this view in no way precluded art's taking on a moral significance. As we will see from what follows, Kant would have agreed with this: all he has ruled out is that art can give rise to a hope that nature is congenial to our moral purposes. Art is not sufficiently external to mind to achieve this.

While art cannot give rise to a moral interest, the charming effects of colour and tone, which were previously excluded from judgements of taste, are now partially rehabilitated. Colour and tone, unlike other sensations, are open to formal reflection, as was already suggested in the footnote on Euler in Section 14. For this reason, charm, although it cannot give rise to pure judgements of taste, is compatible with beautiful form. Kant does not go further and attain the insight of Klee and Merleau-Ponty into the mutual relation in which colour stands to form. For these thinkers, line helps us see colour, and *vice versa.*

In Section 43 Kant sets out to establish the nature of art, regardless for the moment of any interest to which it might give rise. He first distinguishes artworks, which arise from human activity, from natural objects, which are causal effects. Art arises from rational deliberation, not from instinct alone. Art is also distinct from science in that it is not possible to create a work simply by knowing the rules for its production. Knowing is contrasted to action and art is a species of the latter. Finally, art is distinguished from craft, which counts as mercenary art. While free art is agreeable in the very making, mercenary art is laborious and is only undertaken because artisans are paid to create something desired by society. However, even in free art there is constraint, that is, some guideline or 'mechanism' that gives guidance to the artist. Art, Kant suggests, must have not only a free spirit, but also a 'body' [*Körper*] without which it would be nothing at all [AA 304]. For this reason even the activity of art requires labour.

From what we have just heard, it comes as no surprise when in Section 44 Kant insists that there is no science, no book of rules, for the beautiful. There is only a critique of taste, that is, an analysis of the subjective powers on which it is based. Kant now applies these conclusions to art. Although some have been tempted to invent a category of 'fine sciences' to explain art's need for various sorts of knowledge such as ancient languages, classical culture and history, Kant insists that all we need say is that fine art often needs rigorous knowledge as a background condition, even though such learning cannot properly count as part of art.

Mechanical art sets about creating something for which there is a plan (or 'concept'), whereas aesthetic art intends nothing other than to please the viewer, either formally as fine art or by charming her senses as do the agreeable arts. Whereas in mechanical artworks cognition gives the rule to art, aesthetic artworks themselves count as 'ways of cognising' [AA 305]. This unexplained comment can be traced back to the general connection between aesthetic judgement and 'cognition in general', although here Kant goes further, suggesting not just that art is based on the same conditions as cognition, but even that artworks open up new ways of experiencing the world. [On the expansive role of aesthetic judgements in enlivening the mind, see Makkreel, 1990, pp. 90–9. See, also, Ameriks, 1992.]

Agreeable arts include story telling, table decoration, background music and diverting games. All of these aim to facilitate social interaction. Fine art also fosters sociability, although it does so without any agenda. The pleasure in such art is one of reflection, not sensation, and its standard is the reflective power of judgement [AA 306]. Judgement exercised without the laws of understanding or reason is the reflective power of judgement. Thus the power of judgement as object and law to itself is the basis for any judgement that counts as aesthetic, be it in response to natural or artistic beauty.

Section 45 addresses the intricate relationship in which art stands to nature and *vice versa*. We must see an artwork as distinct from a natural phenomenon and yet similarly free from rules arising from purposes. In short, we should not simply be fooled into thinking that an artwork is a natural phenomenon, as was the poet fooled by the 'rogue of a youth'! Kant goes on to say that if an artwork is to count as beautiful, we must take pleasure in the activity of judging it [AA 306]. If, however, the artist invites liking through the evocation of mere sensations only mechanical art will result. Paraphrasing expressions Kant used to refer to beauty in Section 8 and to the sublime in Section 26, fine art is liked by the eye alone and not through charming or emotional triggers. The clear implication of Section 45 is that fine art arouses a free play of the cognitive powers, just as beautiful nature does. This free play is purposive and yet must not seem intentional [AA 306/7]. The mental powers are purposive for one another insofar as they freely harmonize, so fine art is worthy of taste. And we have seen that the mental cooperation distinctive of taste only arises when an object prompts our response. This surely must also be the case for our aesthetic liking of artworks: there must be a harmony between object and mind in response to art.

The point Kant is making is that there is a mutual implication between beautiful art and beautiful nature in the way they appear to the viewer. Beautiful nature must look as if it is art, because it must be purposive and not just purposeless, as is nature generally. Beautiful nature looks as if it were produced for our pleasure and yet the harmony between the object and our cognitive faculties arises without there being any intention behind it. On the other hand, fine art must look as if it is nature because it, too, occupies the middle ground of purposiveness without purpose between purpose and purposelessness. As a result, although art arises from the purposes of an artist, it must look as if it does not. Kant says that the academic form of the artwork must not show, even though rules will, necessarily, have been exercised in its production [AA 307]. The artwork has to take on a life of its own, beyond the intentionality of the artist. This development of Kant's account shows much greater sophistication and avoids the intentional fallacy.

After the preceding discussion of our responsiveness to beauty both in nature and in artworks, in Section 46 Kant turns specifically to the question of aesthetic productivity, which he identifies as arising from genius as the natural talent to legislate in artistic matters. Just as the autonomous moral agent legislates for her own actions in accordance with the moral law, the genius gives the rule to fine, rather than mechanical, works of art. Art, as a form of human production, is a purposive activity. Any purposive activity follows rules, although in this case they cannot be conceptual. A genius gives a rule, based on the way in which her mind naturally works, or, as Kant puts it, the 'attunement' of the artist's cognitive powers.

Kant now lists four characteristic traits of genius. As genius does not rely on determining rules, it counts as original. Genius is exemplary in that, while not arising from imitation, it serves as a rule for others. (This distinguishes genius from nonsense, which is also free from rules.) Genius cannot be explained scientifically and is, rather, a natural disposition. Finally, it gives laws only to fine art and not to science.

In Section 47 Kant develops the idea that genius cannot be imitative. A great mind might still fail to qualify as a genius if his or her achievement is based on learning. Kant believes that the scientific followers of Newton are all imitators, however brilliant they may be. In contrast, one cannot simply learn to write great poetry: even if a poet studied closely the works of Homer or Wieland, she would not be able to learn how to write with their genius. Genius is necessary for art, but is not possible in science. Kant's point is that science arises out of a process of cognitive labour and not from inspiration and in this general contrast, he has a valid point. However, in giving no place to inspiration or original insight in science he makes too stark a distinction between art and science. While in science the predominant model for progress must be one of cumulative work, where it is necessary for one scientist to build on the work of others and indeed on her own work, there are also moments when the great scientist sees things differently for no other reason than because of the way her mind works. This is the moment of genius within the labour of science. Surely this was the case for Newton and for Einstein, as well as for those who open up major new perspectives in their wake.

Despite this limitation in Kant's account, it does not detract from his main point that genius is transmitted through examples. One genius communicates with another, not by giving formulae that can be spelled out, but, rather, by producing artworks that encapsulate a way of seeing things. The rule must be drawn out from the example and cannot be merely copied. A developing artist has the ability to 'follow' a work of fine art if her mind operates with the same intuitive insight as the great master or mistress. In Kant's words, there is a 'similar proportion' in the mental powers of the apprentice and the master. Genius creates the rich material necessary for a work of fine art, while giving it form requires academic training. It seems likely that Kant has in mind the 'mechanism' of art he mentioned earlier and which is distinct from the rule produced by the artist.

Section 48 addresses the relation between, on the one hand, taste, the judgement of natural or artistic beautiful objects, and, on the other, genius, the production of fine artworks. 'A natural beauty is a beautiful thing; artistic beauty is a beautiful presentation [*Vorstellung*] of a thing' [P: AA 311]. When he was directly concerned with taste, Kant spoke of our pleasure in the object, although he also often said that aesthetic judgements arise in response to the presentation of an object. This precision has led some readers to think that taste is not directed to an object, so much as to the mere appearance of the object. While it is true that Kant denies that there is anything *in* the object that determines a judgement of taste, I have argued that beauty arises from the way in which the object appears to us. For Kant, empirical objects are not things-in-themselves, independent from any possible perception of them but, rather, appearances or presentations, that is, they stand in a necessary relation to our sensory apprehension of them. An aesthetic judgement focuses on the 'way of presenting' [*Vorstellungsart*] an object. [See, for instance, AA 221.] What this means is that in such a judgement the way in which an object appears to us becomes accessible, in that the formal subjective conditions of cognition can be reflected on. The 'appearing of the appearance' is part of the content of an aesthetic judgement, although we only have access to this through the contemplation of an object that gives us pleasure.

So in what sense is the work of art distinct from natural beauty in this regard? We have seen that the object must be capable of being presented to our senses and thus can only be known insofar as it is presented. Whereas Berkeley held that to be a thing is to be perceived, Kant holds that to be a thing is to be perceivable. This means that the thing's existence is not dependent on our perception of it, even though every thing must in principle be accessible to our faculties. While a natural thing, beautiful or otherwise, exists whether or not we present or regard it *as* an object, an artwork is dependent on someone creating and, thus, presenting it. This would be the sense in which the artwork is not simply a thing, but a presentation of a thing. Despite this distinction between a beautiful thing and a beautiful presentation, our apprehension of the artwork, just as that of a natural beauty, lingers at the level of the appearing of the object and is not interested in further explanation of its being or genesis. In this regard taste and art focus on the way in which something is presented to our minds.

But at this point Kant says that, while a natural beauty is free from any conceptual determination, a judgement of an artwork has to be based on the purpose for which it is created. And if this is so, Kant says, judging an artwork necessarily means assessing its perfection relative to the purpose that motivated it. By making this move, Kant implies, although doesn't state, that artistic beauty cannot qualify for taste proper and only for adherent beauty. But this implied conclusion is unnecessary, as he has established in Section 45 that a product of genius, fine art must be viewed as if it were natural, in that we must abstract from any purposes that were necessary for its production. Indeed his insistence on art's reliance on purposes does not sit well with the account of genius he is about to provide.

Despite the limitation just attributed to it, fine art has the power to transform what is ugly in nature into something beautiful. Dreadful occurrences such as war and disease can be transfigured, so long as the subject matter is not disgusting. More generally, the artist is capable of giving form to an artistic expression simply by exercising her taste, that is, through educated judgement arising from study of many examples from art and nature. (So, even though the artwork may not qualify for taste, the artist has to exercise taste.) Is this what counted as a mechanism in Section 43 and as academic training at the end of Section 47? Yet education through examples reminds us of the way in which one great artist communicates with another. It is not entirely clear how the rule given by the artist and the training that provides the possibility of her doing so relate to one another. Kant could have said that the artist exercises taste in seeking out examples from history and from contemporary art, but only on the basis of her genius can she devise a new example for other artists. In the discussion of artistic beauty, his evaluation of rules and constraints becomes more positive. This new position is not inconsistent with the earlier one, as it remains the case that rules cannot determine the beauty of an artwork and can only foster the development of the budding genius.

Nevertheless, the identification of taste with education through exemplary forms and, possibly, as academic constraint signals a shift in its identity from the account given in the 'Analytic of the Beautiful' where taste was free of any rule. Later we will see Kant's position shifting further towards one where taste takes the role of disciplining the potentially wild freedom of genius and, even more radically, taste is either preferred over or subsumes genius. For now, he still insists that taste cannot produce anything and, thus, we can conclude that it could not be a substitute for genius [AA 313].

In Section 49 Kant investigates the powers of the mind necessary for genius. First among these is spirit [*Geist*], the principle that enlivens thinking through the deployment of material [*Stoff*] [AA 313]. This comment is important, suggesting that genius provides a material correlate for the formal correctness achievable through the exercise of taste. Spirit is 'the ability to present aesthetic ideas' [AA 313/4]. An aesthetic idea is an imaginative perspective that gives rise to much thought, but cannot be pinned down in concepts due to the wealth of material (or intuitions). A rational idea, contrastively, is one where no intuition is adequate to a concept or principle. For instance, elsewhere, in his moral philosophy, Kant suggests that there is no empirical act, however morally well intended, that lives up to the principle of virtue. [See Allison's *Kant's Theory of Freedom*, p. 170–1 on Kant's description of virtue as 'always in progress' in *Metaphysics of Morals,* Part II, XVI, AA Volume VI, p. 409.] I would suggest that the capacity for generating aesthetic ideas has a general significance beyond art, for all of us have a power of imagination that allows us to transform the reality of the natural world into something quite different. When we use our imagination in this non-reproductive way, it is appropriate to talk of aesthetic ideas, because we go beyond experience and seem to strive for something intellectual. Like rational ideas, aesthetic ideas cannot be completely captured in a concept. Thus we need not conclude that spirit is restricted to artists, but such creative spirits display a greater degree of this quality than most, as the artist does not merely entertain aesthetic ideas, she creates a sensory expression of rich associative material in an artwork. [See AA 313, where spirit is characterized as 'the animating principle in the mind', which suggests that it is a capacity shared by all human beings, while not to the same degree.] Aesthetic ideas entail a striving for completeness, as do rational ideas, although in this case it is imagination not reason that transports us beyond the sensory. Kant thinks that, of all the arts, poetry is most capable of transcending the sensory through aesthetic ideas. Artworks are able to set thought in motion through the richness of associations they evoke.

Aesthetic 'attributes' are features of an object that prompt a rich range of imaginative associations. The combination of particular aesthetic attributes amounts to an aesthetic idea. While we are also aware of logical attributes, that is, the empirical features of the object, aesthetic associations enrich our apprehension so that in looking at the object, we are prompted to think more. Kant's example of an aesthetic attribute is the association Frederick the Great makes in one of his poems between the ideal of cosmopolitanism and the sensory pleasure of a beautiful summer day. This particular attribute or association contributes to the poem's achieving the expression of an aesthetic idea. The mind of the poet is enlivened and this counts as spirit. In Frederick's case, thought is animated by a sensory image, but in other cases the relation may be reversed and we think more about something we see because it is associated with an idea. Kant gives the example of the academic poet Withof who, describing a beautiful day, associates the rays of the sun with moral goodness. In both cases a sensory intuition is set alongside a rational idea that cannot be expressed through the senses. Despite the impossibility of synthesizing these two elements, they interact with one another in a productive fashion just because they cannot be resolved into a unity. Looking makes me think more and thinking makes me see more acutely. This is the essential dynamic of aesthetic ideas.

An aesthetic idea is a combination of 'a multiplicity of partial presentations', that is, aesthetic attributes, where it seems as if a concept could be found that would capture the wealth of sensory associations, yet we are always defeated in finding one [P: AA 316]. The lack of a conclusion is, indeed, the reason why this product of the imagination is enlivening for thought. The poet associates concepts with ideas of something beyond the senses, stimulating her (and our) cognitive powers and rendering her use of language, not merely a mechanical facility, but an expression of spirit. (This is one of the few occasions when Kant discusses language, not just the role of concepts and he is prompted to do so by his discussion of poetry.)

The mental powers that are necessary for genius are imagination and understanding. These powers are also those that are necessary for cognition, but whereas there imagination follows the rule of understanding, now imagination is free and the understanding takes up sensory material not so as to achieve knowledge, but purely to animate our thinking. No cognition arises, but the cognitive powers are in operation and this is conducive to our general capacity for cognition. While Kant is careful to distinguish genius from cognition, we might think that his account of the former is extraordinarily close to that of taste. Yet, it's clear that taste and genius are distinct and thus we can assume that they are not based on exactly the same mental activity. My suggestion is that while the same formal apparatus is at work in genius and in taste, imagination and understanding operate differently in the two cases. This is the significance of the comment that the faculties combine 'in a certain relation' [AA 316]. In taste, sensory appearance and our capacity to think about that appearance harmonize in such a way that there seems to be a balance between sensing and thinking. Genius arises when sensory appearance urges thinking on to greater heights. While the dynamic achieved is harmonious, it is one of acceleration rather than contemplative equilibrium. I am not suggesting that our appreciation of something beautiful arises as a mental stasis, but the ebb and flow of the play of the faculties is, in comparison to genius, calm. So although the genius produces something that gives rise to taste in our reception of it, the relation of the cognitive powers necessary for the creative act of genius requires a specifically different, although formally similar, activity of the mind. In the terms introduced in Section 21, genius depends on a different mental proportion than does taste.

Genius first discovers aesthetic ideas capable of expressing a concept, strictly, a rational idea, but in such a way as to open up possibilities, rather than to determine or explain what can never be wholly grasped at the sensory level. Secondly, genius finds a way of expressing these ideas so that not merely the ideas but principally the mental attunement or state of mind accompanying them in the mind of the genius, can be communicated to others. Only the second of these requires spirit. The genius is able to go beyond sensory experience through her power of imagination, just as we all are. But only the genius is able to communicate in an artwork this expansion of thinking in an aesthetic idea that stimulates the broadened thought of the viewer. Spirit, thus, is particularly active in the genius, as is the imagination. The genius combines imagination and understanding by being aware of the imaginative possibilities of a phenomenon and finding a concept that is capable of communicating them. The 'concept' or mode of expression the artist devises must be original and not dependent on a rule, even though the artwork that emerges will itself serve as an exemplary rule for other artists who come after.

Genius is the originality that produces an example to be followed [*nachfolgen*] not imitated [*nachahmen*]. One artist is inspired by another, but does not merely repeat what has been already created. Thus the artwork provides an education – even a 'school' – for those who come after. The artist is not in a condition of splendid isolation, as there is a need for a positive, non-mechanical form of imitation. If the later artist were simply to copy all the particular details of someone else's work, this would count as 'aping', whereas repeating peculiarity just for its own sake counts as 'mannerism'. The problem with both negative forms of imitation is that they are incapable of giving an example to other artists, as they are too caught up in the passive reproduction of detail [Hughes, 2006a, pp. 317–20]. In this passage it seems clear that academic training cannot be merely mechanical if it is to be conducive to the development of a genius. Rule-following is only compatible with artistic production if it is exemplary, not merely academic.

Section 50 concludes the discussion of art, aesthetic ideas and genius with a further consideration of the role played by taste in fine art. Consistently, Kant has insisted that art does not arise through inspiration alone and requires constraint or schooling. He now asks if imagination, which at this point stands in for genius, is more important than judgement, that is, taste. Genius is necessary for inspired art, a new category in the discussion, while fine art requires taste. Kant suggests that art need not be a product of genius – presumably because it may not count as inspired – but must only give rise to the harmonious relation between the freedom of the imagination and the lawfulness of understanding required by taste and characteristic of fine art. Yet, in earlier sections, genius was established as the distinctive capacity for the production of fine art and taste was an ability to supply rules conducive to that production. Taste is now characterized as training genius, introducing civilization, polish, clarity and order, while making possible an enduring value for the artwork. This is quite consistent with what has gone before, but Kant concludes that if there is a choice between taste and genius, it is judgement not imagination that should win out. Yet, surely there is nothing to trim if genius has not produced the rich material without which the form would be merely academic and not art at all? Although the choice Kant poses is only speculative, even the contemplation of a resolution of the tension between the formal and material conditions of art seems to risk its dissolution and of falling into a formalism that is dead, not dynamic. At the very least, fine art risks falling back into the hands of the academy in contrast to an inspired – perhaps Romantic – art, feared for its lack of control.

In conclusion Kant says that fine art requires imagination, understanding, spirit and taste and that the first three are united in the fourth. Each of these mental activities is necessary for the production of fine art, yet it would appear that taste not genius or spirit, as was previously suggested, is paramount. And now taste subsumes spirit, rather than being an alternative to it as he argued earlier in the section. Yet, neither conclusion was necessitated by what went before or is representative of the rich account of artistic creation offered up until Section 50. Throughout the preceding sections, taste is a necessary educator for genius. How could this be if genius is simply a part of taste or, on the other hand, if they give rise to distinctive aesthetic products? Surely, Kant should have maintained that taste and genius stand in a productive tension with one another and must do, insofar as art cannot arise from rules and can only be the production of an original (even though disciplined) exemplarity.

Study questions
Can artworks give rise to judgements of taste? What, if any, is their shortcoming in comparison with natural beauty?
Does genius need rules? If so, what sort of rules might these be?
What makes a genius?
Does the mutual implication between natural beauty and fine art introduced in Section 45 help you in thinking about what might count as a good artwork?
Would good taste educate or repress genius?

6 THE RELATIONSHIP BETWEEN THE DIFFERENT ARTS

The following sections of the *Critique of Aesthetic Judgement* provide an account of the range of expressions of artistic creativity and the relation in which different arts stand to aesthetic judgement. The highest ranking is given to those arts which present an object capable of evoking a pleasure based on the formal activity of our minds.

Section 51 begins with the rather surprising announcement that all beauty – both artistic and natural – counts as an expression of aesthetic ideas. In the preceding sections it would be easy to conclude that aesthetic ideas are necessarily linked to the creativity of the artistic genius, although in my reading I have suggested that this is not the case. We saw that genius arises from two sources, first, an activity of the imagination that allows for an expansion of thought and secondly an expression of this in the production of an object. Thus there is a distinction between having aesthetic ideas and being able to express them in an artwork. Only the second is restricted to the artistic producer, while the first is possible for every receptive judging subject. Kant is now suggesting that even natural beauty counts as expression of an idea, although in this case the idea comes from our response to a natural phenomenon. We can understand this claim by referring to his previous suggestion that natural beauty is pleasing insofar as we view it *as if* it were an artwork. [See Section 45] It would appear that taste and genius are closely related abilities and that, just as Kant has already argued that the genius needs taste, we might also say that taste emulates genius in seeing aspects of the natural world as if they were artistic creations.

The identification of expression as central for beauty in general provides a key for Kant's account of the relation between the different arts. He sees expression as primarily the capacity to communicate in word, gesture and tone. These correspond to the art of speech, visual arts and what he calls the 'art of the play of sensations (as outer sense impressions)', but all are modelled on characteristics of verbal communication [P: AA 321]. I suspect that his preference for verbal over visual arts stems from a belief that expression is more direct when communication is verbal. We should not forget that communicability of feeling was established as characteristic of aesthetic judgement. While communication of beauty through determinate concepts is ruled out, there is no prohibition on communication through the indeterminate connotation of words. Poetry operates in just this way and is the highest of the arts from Kant's perspective. In contrast, oratory lies on the margins of the fine arts because it is not free, as it serves a purpose of persuasion.

The visual arts either present a figure in space, as in sculpture and architecture, or the illusion of figures in space, as in painting. In both, an aesthetic idea provides the original image or 'archetype', although a different artistic effect or, what Kant calls an 'ectype' or 'derivative image' is produced in each case. And if sculpture is purely concerned with the expression of an aesthetic idea, architecture always has to take into consideration the purpose for which the building has been constructed. Architecture, like oratory, is a candidate for inclusion within the fine arts and its status is likewise compromised by the unavoidable consideration of utility that arises.

Kant subdivides painting into painting proper and landscape gardening. Indeed he takes a very catholic position, including the decoration of rooms and fashionable dress within the category of painting, understood in a broad sense, just because these activities devise things that please the eye in their mere form. (Proust also elevates fashion to a fine art in his descriptions of the Fortuny dresses worn by Albertine in *In Search of Lost Time*.)[10] We saw earlier that Kant considers the beauty of English gardens particularly free: he now says that landscaping arranges nature's products – for instance, plants and trees – beautifully. He clearly thinks that gardens display the design that is a necessary characteristic for beauty, though, of course, only if the form achieved is purposive without there being a purpose. For this reason, French formal gardens do not qualify as free beauties.

The third category of fine art, arts of the beautiful play of sensations, includes music and the 'art of colour'. These arts produce a vibration in the senses. The 'tension', or specific degree of attunement, that arises counts as the sense's 'tone', by which Kant seems to mean that these arts operate by producing a heightened activity of our senses [AA 324]. Tone is either aural or visual. Hearing and seeing are necessary for our apprehension of the external world, but through them we are also capable of responding to phenomena we like even when we are not seeking to determine something about objects. Kant hesitates as to whether these 'special' sensations operate solely at the level of sense or, also, can be combined with reflection and, thus, qualify as potentially beautiful. The problem is a familiar one and first arose in Section 14 where Kant seems to endorse Euler's position that colour perception involves not only sense but also reflection. He now entertains the possibility that the sheer rapidity of tonal variation defeats our capacity for judging them, meaning that tone pleases us only agreeably, not aesthetically. At this stage Kant pronounces himself agnostic as to whether or not tonal arts are merely agreeable, however, for he adds that on the other side of the coin it can be argued that music builds on a mathematical ratio of vibrations and thus must involve reflection. Also, there are those whose perception is unimpaired and yet they cannot discern tonal variation. Kant's point seems to be that being tone deaf is not merely based on a deficiency of sense, but also on an inability to reflect.

A possible response to the objection that tone is simply too rapid to be captured by our judgement, would be to say that the reflective ability in an aesthetic judgement is not of the sort implied here. When we look at a painting or listen to a poem, we find it beautiful not because we can compute its complexity but rather because our minds are expanded in an indeterminate way. It is not so much that we judge the number of associations that arise, but rather that our power of judgement is encouraged not to make any conclusive judgement – other than 'this is beautiful' – but, rather, to exercise 'judgement as such' in an open-ended fashion. I do not see why aural or visual tones could not achieve this. The expanse of colour presented by Rothko's 'Seagram Murals' gives me something to look at and reflect on at the same time. The reason my looking counts as reflective is that it explores beyond the field of what is actually given and expands my thinking to a level beyond what is immediately sensed. While the 'beyond' may still be a sensory possibility and not a rational idea, it is arguable that aesthetic presentation of colour is not merely sensory, at least, not sensory in an everyday manner. My point is that even the instances that Kant counts as reflectively pleasing do not achieve the standard that is presented by this objection to the aesthetic status of the tonal arts and that, once the appropriate characterization of aesthetic reflection is established, there is no reason why they too cannot pass the revised test.

What qualifies a garden as aesthetic is that it pleases the eye alone. Earlier, when Kant spoke about pleasing the eye, he did not contrast vision to the other senses and we might have been tempted to think that aesthetic pleasure arises for any of the senses in conjunction with a reflective activity of the mind. As we have seen, the limitation on this is that Kant holds that only some sensory perceptions give rise to reflective activity. Now Kant suggests that touch cannot uncover the form distinctive of beauty [AA 323]. This is another occasion when Kant's formalism becomes restrictive rather than illuminating. While he is not alone in excluding touch from the range of aesthetic possibilities, it is arguable that he is wrong to do so. Certainly, Merleau-Ponty has argued that vision and touch are inextricably related to one another. [*Phenomenology of Perception,* Part 2, chapter 1] While it is not easy to see how Kant could have argued that touch gives us access to the forms of things and his conclusion that only vision can do so is unsurprising, he could have expanded his formalism arguing that aesthetic form always stands in relation to aesthetic matter, to which touch gives us access in a more immediate way than vision ever could. Indeed as we have seen in his discussion of art, Kant suggests that the power of genius is that of going beyond merely formal considerations, discovering a rich range of material for expression in an aesthetic idea.

Section 52 considers the combination of different arts within one and the same artwork. Oratory and drama may be combined, as may poetry and music in song; song and theatre in opera; and music and dance in ballet. Kant seems doubtful about the merits of such hybrids, while Wagner and Nietzsche later set up opera, in particular, as the ideal of the total artwork or *Gesamtkunstwerk.*

The main discussion in this section reinforces the formal status of fine art and the relative insignificance of matter. Yet, all Kant needs to say here is that the material content of an artwork must achieve a certain form if it is to be worthy of a liking that is purposive without purpose. He does not need to take the further step of suggesting, as he seems to here, that formal considerations are sufficient (not merely necessary) conditions of artistic creation. We have seen already on several occasions that he struggles to give a persuasive account of the relation in which form stands to matter, even though I have suggested his core account does not preclude this.

Kant now crucially suggests that only if we associate beauty with moral ideas, can we avoid being dissatisfied about its worth. He thinks this is easiest to achieve with natural rather than artistic beauty. He now is in danger of making too strong a connection between beauty and morality, something he has previously resisted both in his account of adherent beauty and in his account of the moral interest in beauty in Section 42. It could seem as if he is saying that artworks must be moral in order to sustain their formal status and thus be worthy of aesthetic appreciation. Yet all he needs say is that no beauty, whether natural or artistic, can arise merely from the causal impact of the senses. For something to count as aesthetic, it must open up a space for reflection in a way that emulates reason's ideas of a supersensible. The artwork takes us beyond the given, but it must not be already and wholly determined by moral purposes. The lack of sufficient precision and explanation at this stage of his argument has led to the impression that he now argues that beauty ultimately has a moral basis.

Having laid out a taxonomy of the fine arts, in Section 53 Kant proceeds to rank them. Poetry comes closest to pure expression of aesthetic ideas because it 'expands the mind' by discovering a form compatible with the greatest possible richness of thinking [AA 326]. Interestingly, Kant insists that although poetry makes use of illusion, it does not deceive, so we must conclude that not all artistic illusion is deceptive. This contrasts with his rather quick judgement of artistic semblance as equivalent to deception in Section 42. [But see also the more sophisticated account in Section 45.] As we are transported beyond nature, Kant holds that we attain the level of the supersensible, which here he seems to associate directly with morality, even though in our discussion of the 'Dialectic of Taste' we will see that such an equation is rather too simple.

Music stimulates the mind, although it does so only at the level of sensation, without giving us something to meditate on. For this reason Kant concludes that it is the lowest of the fine arts. Whereas in earlier discussions Kant hesitated about the role of reflection in the tonal arts and left open the possibility that music presents a temporal form worthy of aesthetic appreciation, he now concludes that music operates solely at the level of emotion. The visual arts are far superior in that they give rise to a reflective liking, sustained by the production of something that engages our contemplative attention. The visual arts' capacity for holding our attention during an extended period of time is crucial for their superiority over music, which in Kant's view gives only a transitory pleasure. Among the visual arts, painting is foremost because of its reliance on design [*Zeichnung*] and its ability to lead us *via* sensory perception to the realm of ideas.

This is surely an unconvincing account of music and leaves out of account the way in which a musical theme is capable of development over time, while also having a very reductive notion of an 'object' of aesthetic attention. Why shouldn't a musical work hold our attention as a phenomenon, even though it is not a material object? Kant says that music moves from sensations to indeterminate ideas, while the visual arts progress from determinate ideas to sensations. Yet he previously ruled out the possibility that aesthetic judgement could be based on determinate ideas. It seems much more representative of his position to say that beauty starts with the sensory, but moves beyond to an indeterminate idea analogous to, but distinct from, a rational idea. Kant's dismissal of music seems to have more to do with a mental – or aesthetic – block on his part, rather than arising from a coherent argument. Could it be that his experience of music leads him to believe that the pleasure arising from it is affective or corporeal in origin? Is it that lacking an aesthetic sense for music, he concludes that music is not aesthetic? It would be wrong to think we can explain his assessment of music through merely biographical details, but when he says that music extends its influence farther than people wish, it is difficult not to be reminded that Kant himself complained about nearby hymn singing that disturbed his philosophical concentration!

In the 'Comment' at the end of the first Division of the *Critique of Aesthetic Judgement,* Kant links music to wit (or humour), as each requires a play of thought through the expression of aesthetic ideas. In both we experience pleasure due to an extended series of associations which principally affect us through our bodies. The joke sets up an expectation that is then defeated and we laugh as a result. Although our minds are engaged, music and wit give us bodily pleasure and are not instances of free explorations of thinking. A purpose dominates both: the intention of bringing about a pleasurable response. The aim of achieving agreeableness is sufficient to disqualify these instances of the play of ideas for purely aesthetic status. There are at least two principal problems with Kant's evaluation of music and wit. First, it is arguable that neither are wholly reducible to bodily affects. Secondly, it is arguable that his conception of the body is too simplistic. An alternative account would open up the possibility that the body is a way of being aware of the world and not just causally affected by it. This is the phenomenological position introduced by Husserl (in his later works) and by Merleau-Ponty. Building on this new understanding of the body, it would be possible to argue that even if music and wit do have their impact at a corporeal level, they may still be capable of going beyond the merely sensory and thus could count as a form of reflective awareness.

We have come to the end of the 'Analytic of Aesthetic Judgement', comprising the 'Analytic' of the beautiful and of the sublime, as well as the 'Deduction' of taste, and should, we might think, have arrived at the conclusion of Kant's account of aesthetic reflective judgements about natural and artistic objects. However, this is not his view for he will now reintroduce the question as to the identity and even the possibility of a distinctive principle on which such judgements are based. This doubt has haunted the whole of the third *Critique* so far and it will be addressed, again, in the 'Dialectic'.

Study questions

Do the highest and lowest ranked arts deserve Kant's evaluation? What would your ranking be, if any?

What is the dispute about the tonal arts?

Is it surprising when Kant says that all beauty is an expression of aesthetic ideas?

What is 'painting' from Kant's point of view and how does it qualify as a fine art?

7   THE 'DIALECTIC OF AESTHETIC JUDGEMENT': BEAUTY AND THE SUPERSENSIBLE

The final sections of the *Critique of Aesthetic Judgement* move the discussion to the deepest sources of taste, which Kant calls the 'supersensible'. It may appear that Kant is now suggesting that taste is founded on something beyond this world or, at least, in our moral ability to transcend the sensory. If this were the case, the *Critique* would conclude by showing, finally, that taste is not autonomous, being founded on a higher principle of reason, as Kant suggested was possible in Section 22. However, by stressing the tripartite character of the supersensible and its identification with our cognitive powers, I will show this is not the case.

Section 55 announces a dialectic that arises in aesthetic judgement. A dialectic, generally speaking, is a conflict between opposing explanatory principles. One such conflict arose in the first *Critique* insofar as an attempt was made to use the power of reason to explain experience. Kant argued that rational principles necessarily generate a dialectic when they seek to determine experience as a totality. Reason, in its intellectual rather than moral use, seeks to grasp the infinite as a totality. There is no total explanation of experience, which is only open to cumulative determinations, resting on the principle of understanding. Nevertheless, there is a valid role for reason within experience if it is used regulatively, that is, as tending towards though not imposing an idea of totality. When experience is approached in this way, Kant says we introduce the idea of the systematicity of nature and avoid dialectic [*C.Pu.R.,* A 642–704, B 670–32].

Dialectic only arises at the level of principle, that is, when a judgement claims *a priori* universal status. It does not result from judgements operating without a principle, such as those of sense. Even a disagreement between people about their judgements of taste does not amount to dialectic. Kant says this is because no-one aims to make his own judgement a universal rule. This is surprising for surely he has characterized judgements of taste as claiming subjective universal validity? However, we have seen that, on occasion, Kant distinguishes between claiming that my aesthetic preference for a particular object is universally valid and claiming this only for my capacity to judge through a certain proportion of my mental powers. This distinction may be behind his suggestion in Section 8 that nothing is 'postulated' in a judgement of taste other than the universal voice on which it is founded [AA 216]. As we have seen, Allison suggests that a distinction between first- and second-order aesthetic judgements underlies Section 37 and that only the principle of judgement claims subjective universal validity and, thus, requires a deduction [Allison, 2001, p. 173–4.]. Nevertheless, elsewhere Kant seems to be concerned with the subjective universality of our particular aesthetic judgements. (See Section 20, for instance.) I have also remarked that it is not clear how restricting the critical task to the level of the principle alone would be sustainable, because an awareness of the activity of judging *per se* is only possible in and through a pleasure taken in an object considered beautiful. A possible solution to this problem, drawing on my reading of Section 37, is that the validity claimed in a deduction pertains to the principle, but as first-order judgements are grounded on the latter, they too aspire to subjective universality. Any particular aesthetic judgement could fail to qualify as an exercise of the power of judgement as law and object to itself and, thus, first-order aesthetic judgements' claims to subjective universality are fallible. In contrast, Kant believes he will now, finally, show that the principle of taste is a necessary condition of human experience and, thus, its subjective validity is not contestable. Yet taste is ultimately ideal, for we cannot ever be sure that we have applied the principle of taste correctly and thus can only require others to agree with us and cannot prove that they must do so. Read in this way, it is understandable why disagreements about taste arise, alongside our adopting as a goal the possibility of agreement.

So when Kant says that no-one seeks to make his judgement a universal rule, it would have been more precise to say that no-one *should* do so, just because of the fallibility of particular aesthetic preferences. In contrast, the transcendental philosopher can claim subjective universal validity for the principle on which the judgements of individuals are based, by providing a deduction of taste that traces it back to the subjective conditions of cognition, *sensus communis*. But the philosopher has to resolve a dialectic that puts in question the nature of the principle of taste and its capacity to legislate for our aesthetic preferences. If this problem is not answered it is questionable whether or not taste is lawful and, as a corollary, whether or not its principle qualifies as such. For if the power of judgement cannot legislate for our aesthetic apprehension of the world, then there is no distinctive capacity for aesthetic judgement in the first place.

Thus at the outset of the final section of Kant's investigation of aesthetic judgement, he raises yet again the spectre that was explicit in Section 22 and arguably has haunted the whole work: is it possible to establish that there is a distinctive capacity for aesthetic judgement? The curiosity of this admission is in announcing at the end of a work that its condition of possibility has not been established: for if taste is not possible, there is no justification for writing a critique of it. I have suggested that the mediating status of taste leads to its continually escaping philosophical determination and being approachable only through examples, indirectly.

So what is the dispute about the principle of taste? This is the question Kant addresses in Section 56. People often say that there's no accounting for taste, that is, everyone has his or her own preference. This is to say that taste is merely subjective and when we call something beautiful, we are not justified in requiring others to agree with us. Another commonplace about taste is the view that, because it cannot be explained through determinate concepts, it is impossible to enter into a rational dispute about it. Nevertheless, we may well quarrel about our differing preferences, while there is no way of arbitrating on the basis of principle. Kant suggests that we can identify an opposition within these positions once we realize that if we can quarrel about something then it cannot simply be the case that each individual's preference is wholly cut off from everyone else's. The conflict that arises in common opinion about taste can be traced back to a dialectical conflict or 'antinomy' concerning the principle of taste. On the one hand, a judgement of taste is not based on concepts, because we cannot enter into rational dispute about it with the view of achieving a definitive conclusion. On the other hand, a judgement of taste must be based on concepts, because otherwise it would make no sense whatsoever to quarrel about it and even demand that others agree with us.

The solution Kant offers to this antinomy in Section 57 is to clarify the way in which a concept is invoked in the two conflicting accounts of the status of the principle of taste. This precision uncovers a way of holding onto the sense behind both commonplaces considered in the previous section, while clarifying why taste unavoidably gives rise to such disagreement. This helps explain why Kant is still struggling to establish the possibility of taste, for if its status is viewed in two wholly opposed ways within everyday life, this could be because taste is a philosopher's dream, not something necessary for human life. Kant intends to show that there is a way of rescuing taste from this threat.

Judgements of taste cannot be based on a concept that determines the object as such and such a thing, as when a concept of understanding gives rise to knowledge. There is, however, an alternative in reason's concepts, more properly 'ideas', which express the 'supersensible' underlying intuition [AA 339]. Kant does not yet make clear what exactly he means by this term although he says it is both indeterminate and indeterminable. As a rule of thumb, it may be useful to remember that in his account of the sublime, the supersensible was the idea of a rational and, ultimately, moral capacity. At the most simple level, the supersensible is our rational capacity to transcend the sensory world through our power of thinking and in moral acts.

Kant now concedes that everyone *does* have his (or her) own taste, insofar as a preference for an object is an expression of a feeling of pleasure and hence is only private. At the same time, however, in judging aesthetically for ourselves we also judge more broadly, that is, for all other judging subjects. Thus we base our judgements on the second sort of concept, that is, the idea of something that goes beyond and even underlies both the sensory perception of objects and the judging subject, the supersensible.

The apparent contradiction at the level of its principle disappears if we see taste as founded on 'the concept of a general basis of nature's subjective purposiveness for our power of judgement' [P: AA 340]. This is the 'purposiveness of nature for our judgement' which Kant discussed extensively in both introductions, yet only alludes to occasionally in the main body of the text. (The re-emergence of this theme in the 'Dialectic' makes some sense of Kant's claiming at the end of the first Introduction that the main body of the text is devoted to 'the exposition and then the deduction of the concept of a purposiveness of nature'. [AA Volume 20, AA 251' in the 'First Introduction'.[1]]) This indeterminate idea – or second sort of concept – is now identified as the 'supersensible substrate of humanity', yet in the 'Analytic of the Sublime' the supersensible was identified with our rational power. Later we will see that there is, in fact, a tripartite taxonomy of the supersensible. In both introductions Kant suggested that our experience of the organization of empirical objects in accordance with laws would not be possible were we not able to presuppose that nature is purposive (or fitting) for our judgement. It now is clear that the idea of the purposiveness of objects for our judgement is also the deepest ground of the principle of judgements of taste. An aesthetic judgement points us beyond the sensory field to the combination of mental faculties that is a necessary condition of cognition in general and provides an instance where the object stands in harmony with the activity of the mind. This is a singular example of the possibility in general that nature is purposive for our judgement and that we may attain cognition of objects. While the connection between the purposiveness of nature and taste is intricate and difficult to establish, I have suggested in very general terms what this might mean. [See Hughes, 2006b, pp. 559–63.] For now it is not very clear what purposiveness has to do with the supersensible. The answer will come later in the discovery that the supersensible is nothing other than the exercise of our cognitive powers, one of which is judgement with its principle of the purposiveness of nature for judgement.

It is worth pausing to take in what we have just learned, for didn't the 'Deduction' establish that taste's ground is *sensus communis,* that is, the cooperative activity of our faculties? Yet we also learned both there and elsewhere that the attunement of the faculties arises when prompted by an object and that there is a dual harmony, first, within the mind and, secondly, between object and mind. While it is not possible to investigate adequately the relationship between the result of the 'Deduction' and the argument developed in the 'Dialectic' here, I will suggest a solution in a very general way. The *sensus communis* characteristic of taste is a harmonious cooperation of the faculties prompted by an object, which stands in a spontaneous harmony with our minds. It is as if the object were designed by our imagination. This heightened case is exemplary of the general purposiveness of nature for judgement, which Kant investigated in the Introduction. Thus there is no contradiction between the conclusion of the 'Deduction' and that of the 'Dialectic'.

Although Kant does not explain the way in which the principle of the purposiveness of nature for our judgement operates and even suggests that all we can do is 'point to it', he announces that he has solved the antinomy of taste by establishing that the latter is based not on a determinate concept, but on an indeterminate one [P: AA 341]. The dialectic of taste has been generated by assuming that the ground of taste is a determining concept or rule. This is what leads to the contradiction that we cannot prove the correctness of our aesthetic judgements and yet nor can we be indifferent to the disagreement of others. There is no necessary conflict between the two 'commonplaces' with which the 'Dialectic' commenced, if we understand taste as it has been characterized in the *Critique of Aesthetic Judgement*, that is, as based on an indeterminate concept of the purposiveness of nature for our judgement. This explanatory principle establishes that the validity of aesthetic judgements is universally valid, thus allowing for our 'quarrelling' about them. Yet the principle is also strictly subjective insofar as it is a presupposition, thus the judgements cannot be proven or 'disputed'.

If taste were understood as equivalent to the agreeable or to perfection, no such resolution of the dialectic would be possible [AA 341]. In defence of this claim, Kant could have said that whereas in the first case the aesthetic would stand in no relation to the supersensible, in the second the relation would be direct and beauty would immediately express moral value. Only if taste is reflective, occupying a middle ground between the sensory and the rational is it capable of being both singular and universal at the same time. When I judge aesthetically I must do so for myself in response to a singular phenomenon and yet do so on universal grounds, the mental powers that are shared by all judging subjects. And it is exactly because of this that such a judgement rests on no determinate concept and yet evokes an indeterminate one. We can now clearly see why indeterminacy features both at the surface and in the depths of taste: not only is it indeterminate which concept applies to a beautiful phenomenon, the very principle on which our judgement is based is also indeterminate.

Next come two sections, each of which count as a 'Comment' on what has gone before. In the first of these Kant rehearses the distinction between aesthetic and rational ideas, which he first introduced in his account of genius. It is important he does so, because the discussion so far in the 'Dialectic' could appear to resolve the aesthetic antinomy through identifying the ground of taste as a rational idea instead of a distinctively aesthetic principle. At the end of the first comment he makes another important clarification, speaking of 'the supersensible substrate (unattainable by any concept of the understanding) of all his powers' [P: AA 344]. Although I cannot give an adequate analysis of this extremely difficult passage here, I would argue that the supersensible is not another world, nor even a divine being but, rather, the activity of the mind understood in its fullest extent as incorporating a range of cognitive powers. This is the subjective standard behind the productions of genius.

The second 'Comment' develops the identification of the supersensible with the cognitive powers, situating the antinomy of taste within the context of Kant's wider philosophical project. He argues that each of the three critiques has an antinomy and that in each case reason's ability to go beyond the sensory world is reinforced. He then distinguishes three ideas of the supersensible: the supersensible in general as the substrate of nature, the principle of nature's subjective purposiveness for our cognitive power (which he has just been discussing) and, finally, the (possible) harmony between our moral principles and nature. This tripartite supersensible corresponds to the three principal cognitive faculties: understanding, judgement and reason. The supersensible substrate of all the powers, mentioned in the preceding section, is now spelled out as the range of cognitive powers that make possible our experience of the natural world and the possibility that arises from their operation, namely, that we might succeed in freely determining our actions within that world. It is not possible here to examine how each of the three ideas of the supersensible contributes to his account. What is clear is that taste depends on a supersensible distinctively associated with the power of judgement.

Section 58 begins by contrasting the interpretation of the principle of taste from an empiricist perspective, where beauty would coincide with the agreeable, from a rationalistic perspective, where beauty has an *a priori* basis. The rationalistic perspective can be further subdivided into realist and idealist versions. The preceding argument has established that judgements of taste are not determining, that is, cognitive and are, instead, subjectively purposive. But this can be understood, on the one hand, as an actual intention or purpose pursued by nature (or art) with the aim of harmonizing with our power of judgement; or, on the other, as something we presuppose in our judgements of nature, without taking the further step of claiming this is something in nature itself. The first option, which is realistically rationalistic, may seem plausible when there is so much beauty with so little apparent purpose, tempting us to think that this must all have been designed for our enjoyment. Yet Kant insists that this would be to indulge in finding explanations where none are necessary. There is no need to go beyond the normal 'mechanical' or causal understanding of nature: we must simply accept that many natural phenomena are beautiful, without looking to explain this further. Thus subjective purposiveness is something we presuppose in order to facilitate our judgement of nature, not something that is the result of a design or higher order. The idealistic rationalistic interpretation of purposiveness is compatible with a mechanical explanation of nature in terms of cause and effect. Kant gives the example of crystalline forms that can be explained through scientific analysis, yet this does not preclude that some of them are also beautiful. [See Hughes, 2007, pp. 284–90]

Kant concludes his defence of the idealistically rationalistic interpretation of the principle of judgement, insisting that we always look for the basis for taste within ourselves. He says that we do not look for beauty in what nature is, but only in 'how we take it in' [*wie wir sie aufnehmenI*] [G: AA 350]. His point is not that beauty arises from a pure introspection of the mental powers, but rather that a judgement of beauty has its ground in our general capacity to be receptive to nature and this is facilitated by our presupposition that nature is purposive for our judgement. Beauty is neither in the object nor in the subject and is, rather, traced back to our subjective ability to take up nature in such a way that it can be judged.

Kant now suggests that fine art is even more propitious for the idealistic interpretation than is nature. His argument is that if fine art rested on actual purposes, it would be merely mechanical and not fine. Thus, although art arises from purposes, the phenomenon that is produced must not display this. Fine art transfigures the conditions of its production. This is what Kant should have always said, whereas we have seen that he sometimes makes the (unnecessary) inference that art cannot escape from the intentions that motivate it, which would mean that it failed to achieve purely aesthetic status.

Section 59 begins by reinforcing the point that rational ideas are incapable of exhibition or demonstration at a sensory level. Making a concept sensible is called 'hypotyposis' and is either schematic, where knowledge arises, or symbolic, where an intuition stands for an idea without ever being determined by it. Symbols are analogous to explanations in that they follow the (subjective) formal conditions for cognition. Reflective judgement is exercised *as if* it were going to provide an explanation, yet it stops short of a conclusion and only a broadened way of thinking about a sensory perception results.

Symbols are not mere associations or 'characterisations', as they exhibit a concept, albeit indirectly. For Kant, symbols operate analogically, transferring a feature that can be demonstrated about a mechanically determinable fact of nature to something else, the full determination of which is impossible. He gives the example of symbolizing a despotic monarchy as a machine, whereas a constitutional monarchy could be seen as a living body. The exhibition is indirect because we are provided with a symbol for reflection, not an explanation. Interestingly, he suggests that many of the central concepts of metaphysics, for instance, 'foundation', 'dependence', 'flowing from' and 'substance', count as symbolic hypotyposes. Even our 'cognition' of God falls under this heading.

Kant now announces that beauty is the symbol of morality and it is only because we are compelled to go beyond the senses that we require the agreement of others. The claim is potentially confusing, as it might suggest that aesthetic communicability rests on morality, yet he has already argued in the 'Deduction' that the grounds of the claim for the universal validity of taste must be traced back to 'cognition in general'. While surely Kant means that the subjective universality of taste *also* requires a relation to the morally supersensible, he does not sufficiently distinguish his terms. If we recall that the link between beauty and morality is analogical, we must conclude that he cannot intend that beauty is merely an epiphenomenon of morality. He should have stressed the cooperation, not suggested a one-way relation, between these two fundamental ways of experiencing the world and the powers on which they are based.

When taste aims at the supersensible, as Kant has argued in the immediately preceding sections, it now seems that it was the morally good that was in question. However, having restricted the range of the supersensible in this way, Kant returns to the tripartite account introduced in the second Comment. All our higher cognitive powers – understanding, judgement and reason – finally 'harmonise' with the standard set by morality. We can make sense of this in the following way: all our mental capacities take us beyond the strictly sensory field and in so doing they open up an alternative level of reflection that counts as the supersensible. Moral action arises when we are no longer determined by external sensory causes and, instead, judge for ourselves on the basis of a purely rational principle, the 'Categorical Imperative'. Thus, the greatest degree of distance from sensory determination and the clearest expression of the supersensible arises in morality.

Despite the precision as to the range of the supersensible, the primacy afforded to morality within the tripartite structure may make it seem that beauty is now directly referenced to morality and that the 'Deduction' of taste, which traced beauty back to the subjective conditions of cognition in general, has been supplanted by a deduction of taste from morality [For an account of beauty's status as an 'extension' of the cognitively oriented direction, see Crawford, 1974, pp. 66–9, 145–59]. Focussing on the tripartite structure of the supersensible is the key to avoiding such a solution. My idea for understanding Kant's position, which I cannot explore in any depth here, is that our orientation to the morally good necessarily arises out of a combination of broadly mental orientations, all of which express the supersensible in a distinctive fashion. [For an initial account of this, see Hughes, 2007, pp. 299–302.] In particular, the beautiful symbolizes morality: this means that beauty stands in analogically for morality. Beauty can neither explain nor be traced back to morality in a direct fashion and thus no alternative deduction of taste is offered at this stage of the text. Nevertheless, taste's lineage is complex for not only can it be traced back to the general subjective conditions of cognition; it also stands in a necessary relation to the power of ideas. The supersensible is such, by definition, that it cannot be demonstrated for our senses. In the absence of a direct exhibition of what must remain at the level of rational ideas, beauty is able to give us an intimation of the morally good. Beauty's claim for subjective universality arises from the relation in which it stands to morality, but beauty and morality depend on one another, albeit in quite distinct ways. Beauty takes us beyond the merely sensory by allying what we perceive with an indeterminate idea. In doing so, beauty emulates the morally good and is worthy of universal approval. On the other hand, the morally good is and must remain an idea, incapable of demonstration within the sensory field. A particular beautiful phenomenon evokes a mental response that broadens and enlivens the activity of the mind, making us aware of our capacity for thinking beyond what is determined by external states of affairs. Through an imaginative expansion, we get a glimpse of our power of self-determination, that is, our moral rational being. Beauty is thus the facilitator of reason in the sense that, while we already have a capacity for reason, its exercise within the natural world is strengthened through the indirect insight into our mental powers afforded by a direct liking for a beautiful object. [This is an argument Schiller developed in his *On the Aesthetic Education of Man*.] The relationship between beauty and morality is thus mutually re-enforcing at a symbolic level, just as is the relation among the faculties on which they rely. Aesthetic judgement opens up a way of seeing what is ultimately unseen, while reason gives judgement a prospective beyond the sensory dimension. Both directions of this relation are propitious for the possibility that moral principles may come to be realized within the sensory domain, the goal Kant set for himself in writing the *Critique of Aesthetic Judgement*. However, it is important to emphasize that aesthetic judgement opens up the prospect that morality can be furthered and, in no sense, the certainty that it will be realized in a 'kingdom of ends' or a purely moral state. The morally good is, necessarily, a rational idea and can only be realized as an approximation. In other words, the morally good can only ever be exhibited symbolically. This is the distance between morality and reality bridged by the beautiful; a bridging that, as symbolical, can only operate as a hope. The singular beautiful object shows that the world is, in this instance at least, open to our cognition of it. At the same time, we can become aware of a further significance of this 'fit' between nature and our cognitive power. If nature is in harmony with one of our cognitive powers, the understanding, then, in principle at least, it is possible that nature could also be in harmony with our power of reason. If this is true, then we can at least hope that our moral purposes may be realized within the everyday sensory world in which nature holds sway.

Having made what seemed too direct a link between beauty and morality, Kant now reinforces their distinctiveness. We like beauty directly in our reflection on a sensory perception, while our liking for morality can be traced back to a concept or principle. Taste, unlike morality, is free from interest. Although both taste and morality require a harmonizing activity, in the first case the imagination harmonizes with understanding, in the second the free will harmonizes 'with itself in accordance with universal laws of reason' [G: AA 354]. The moral will is self-determining just because it is capable of obeying the Categorical Imperative, which is the highest maxim of morality. Finally, both taste and morality count as universally valid for everyone, but whereas the first is indeterminate, the second has a determining constitutive principle. Kant's point is that the Categorical Imperative is the test for what will count as moral and determines what we must do should we opt to be moral; in contrast, there is no principle that prescribes what will count as beautiful and only a standard for subjectively assessing the way in which we respond to an object.

The differential analogy between taste and morality allows beauty to be an educator for our action. Taste 'makes possible, as it were, the transition from sensible charm to habitual moral interest without too violent a leap' [AA 354]. Taste's right to claim universal validity arises in part from the structural similarity between it and morality, our hope for the possible realization of which is encouraged by beauty. But this does not preclude the analogical relation in which taste stands to cognition and if taste is to provide the bridge between cognition and morality, it cannot simply be traced to one side of the relation. Taste's importance for morality arises from the close connection it has to cognition: it could not be the mediator between nature and freedom if it did not maintain its distinctiveness from, as well as its similarity to, both.

In Section 60, which counts as an appendix to the 'Dialectic' and is the final section of the critique, Kant reverses the relation and makes morality the educator for taste. The fine arts, in particular, require an expansion of our human capacity for feeling sympathy with others and communicating with them. In the final words of the *Critique of Aesthetic Judgement* he says that only when we develop our moral feeling and transform the natural world so that it stands in harmony with morality, will 'genuine taste take on a determinate, unchangeable form' [AA 356]. If the sensory world were governed by moral law, taste would finally achieve a definitive standard. While this may seem like a rather dogmatic conclusion to the critique, its hypothetical mood is crucial. We can conclude that taste, prior to the realization of moral laws in the sensible world, is neither 'determinate' nor 'unchangeable'. We have often been told that the standard of taste is indeterminate, but now we may also conclude that judgements of taste make progress and thus are historical. Admittedly, Kant might seem to be guilty here of tempting his readers with a possibility of completion alien to the analysis of taste he has so far presented, but presumably he is only too aware of the ideal status of the aesthetic goal. While in the penultimate paragraph of the critique he makes the prescient prediction that future generations will become more and more distant from nature, he surely does not think that human beings will escape nature, for he is committed to the perspective that we are finite beings situated in a natural world that is not – wholly, at least – within our control. Insofar as we are human, we will continue to be both naturally determined and morally self-determining beings, so there simply is no possibility that sensibility will ever fully harmonize with morality and, thus, even less that taste will take on a definitive form. Kant does, of course, think that we can improve our ability to morally direct the world and, analogously, develop our taste as a free exercise of the mental powers, but he is not suggesting that either morality or taste will come to a conclusion. Achieving such an end, for Kant, would be the death of morality and of aesthetic judgement, both of which rest on an ideal towards which we, at best, strive in our everyday lives.

Study questions

What do you think is the purpose of the 'Dialectic' and how does it contribute to the *Critique* as a whole?

Why does the 'purposiveness of nature for our judgement' reappear in the 'Dialectic' of the third *Critique*?

How dangerous and/ or useful is it to trace aesthetic judgement
back to a supersensible?

Even some artists, for instance, Rodchenko, have suggested
there is an end of art. What could this claim mean and are
you convinced by it?

CHAPTER 4

RECEPTION AND INFLUENCE

In what follows, I first draw together the elements of the 'dual harmony' I have discovered within Kant's aesthetics. As is well known, Kant claims that aesthetic judgement is characterized by a harmony between the faculties. I have tried to excavate the way in which this first harmony is inextricably caught up with a second harmony between mind and nature. This complex relation within the mind and between mind and world reveals the conditions that make cognition possible, while also suggesting how we, as rational free beings, might exercise moral agency within the empirical world. In the second part of my conclusion I sketch out where the idea of a dual harmony might take us, tracing a possible lineage in later thinkers. While I do not pretend to mention every candidate, nor give a comprehensive account of those I do, I hope to show the importance of Kant's idea by drawing out its reception in writings by Schiller, Fichte, Schelling, Hegel and the German Romantics; Schopenhauer and Nietzsche; Husserl, Heidegger and Merleau-Ponty; Arendt and Adorno; and, finally, Lyotard. In conclusion, I suggest that the idea of a dual harmony plays a role in artworks, not just in philosophers' interpretations of them and that it helps explain why the *Critique of Judgement* is still relevant within and beyond academia.

1   THE IDEA OF A DUAL HARMONY

Kant placed aesthetics on the philosophical agenda, but he did not offer aesthetic answers for epistemological and moral problems. Rather, he suggested that when we respond to the beautiful and even to the sublime, we display a power of judgement that is also necessary, although not sufficient, for epistemic and moral contexts.

Aesthetic judgements reveal a relation between mind and world that makes epistemic and moral judgements possible.

In order to play this role, aesthetic pleasure must respond to an empirical object and arise within an inter-subjective framework. However, aesthetic judgement does not operate at the level of our empirical understanding of the world or at that of moral agency. Aesthetic response reveals a meeting of mind and world, prior to any determination, either theoretical or practical. Although Kant did not explicitly elucidate the ramifications of aesthetic judgement's status as a third term – between concept and intuition, knowledge and morality, mind and world – a rich resource is opened up for later thinkers, as I will presently suggest. One of the most important aspects of Kant's insights, also held by many whose ways of thinking were in other respects quite contrastive, is the suggestion that aesthetic judgement preserves a capacity to access aspects of the world, normally lost or, at least, hidden in everyday life.

Judgement is the capacity for joining together (synthesis) and for discrimination. When we make a judgement, we combine a sensory impression with a concept. This is the process of synthesis, which Kant investigated in the *Critique of Pure Reason.* Cognitive judgement holds together the sensory with the conceptual and yet is, for this very reason, the condition of holding one thing apart from another. When I synthesize some sensory input with a specific concept, I mark out this particular thing within a field of other impressions. And were we not able to identify objects in distinction from one another, no knowledge of them would be possible. Aesthetic judgement makes visible the process of cognition even though no specific knowledge arises. When I take aesthetic pleasure in a beautiful thing, I take in impressions through my senses and search out a concept that might pin down what I am looking at or listening to. There is no concept that finally explains the phenomenon, nevertheless I have engaged in the process that would be necessary for knowledge of it and, in so doing, have focused on the specificity of the beautiful thing, but, strictly, only with contemplative attention.

But we have seen that the power of judgement, when exercised in aesthetic judgements, also tends towards an ideal (hence not entirely realizable) resolution that would require the power of reason. Thus aesthetic judgement emulates not only understanding's power of synthesis, but also reason's power of transcending experience in ideas and thoughts. Aesthetic judgement discovers the ideal within the sensory and does not so much reduce experience to the rational, as find a balancing point or transition between the two. In this, too, judgement is a mediating power and qualifies as a third term.

The importance of aesthetic response for knowledge and morality is not that beauty is their foundation, but, rather, that the mental activity of combining and distinguishing, necessary for any judgement, is written large in our appreciation of nature and art, as too, is our capacity for going beyond the mere facts of the empirical world towards ideas expressing values. This makes aesthetics both crucial for and, yet, not centre-stage in the range of life's dominant concerns. The marginality of aesthetics situates it, not outside knowledge and morality, nor centrally at their core, but, rather, in a de-centred perspective that allows the process out of which they emerge to be perceived, albeit in an indirect and indeterminate fashion. As we have seen in 'Reading the Text', Kant's view is that the power of judgement is exercised in an autonomous form, detached from specific aims or objectives, only in aesthetic judgement. In this case, judgement achieves a delicate balance between an (apparent) opposite and its other. As we have seen, reflective aesthetic judgement combines sensory input and concepts without eradicating the distinctiveness of either. At the same time, it makes possible, but not actual the realization of a moral idea in the empirical world where objects stand in necessary connection with one another in space and time. Judgement bridges gaps, but does not eliminate them.

The power of judgement is at work in knowledge and morality; indeed, without it the rest of experience would lack meaning. The activity of judging, revealed in reflective judgement, starts from the presupposition that we can make sense of the world. While we sometimes, at least, doubt that we can succeed in this task, we would not be able to engage in judging did we not have some expectation, however fragile, that our minds are capable of grasping the contents of the world and, even, of intervening in it. Aesthetic judgements are singular instances where it appears that such a meeting between mind and world occurs. The parallel Kant makes with epistemic judgement is based on the claim that the form of the aesthetic object or event is in tune with the activity of our minds. There is a harmony between mind and world in this one singular case, for so long as I am capable of sustaining my aesthetic attention to it. The attunement, between a singular object and the judging activity through which I respond to it, is an intimation of the possibility that, in principle at least, we can know things in the world and, even, be able to act morally. This aesthetic epiphany can only ever express a hope that such a harmony of mind and world could be generalized, but even this suggests that the sceptic's denial that we have access to the world is an abstract one because in this one instance at least, we are not cut off from the world.

The completion of the critical trilogy is dedicated to establishing not only that it is meaningful to take pleasure in beautiful objects, but that the pleasure we take in them is significant for the possibility that experience in general can be meaningful. Beautiful natural objects are singular instances of the purposiveness of nature for judgement, in that, aesthetic judgements display a harmony between the powers of the mind, which in a distinctively different combination make possible a cognitive 'fit' between mind and world. Taste also opens up the even more fragile possibility that our moral intentions could have real effects.

The dual harmony – between our mental faculties and between mind and world – fragile and singular as it is, is the underlying message of Kant's aesthetics as reconstructed in this *Reader's Guide*. Admittedly, I have drawn out a particular direction in Kant's text and one that is not always evident. In so doing, I have emphasized aspects which other interpreters – and even, on occasion, Kant himself – have not brought to the fore, while I have left in the background other issues that would, had we more time, merit examination. But this is the fate of all readings, however long or short.

The same limitation holds for the account I will now give of the reception of Kant's aesthetics in subsequent writers. I do not intend to try to provide anything like a complete survey of the influence of the *Critique of Aesthetic Judgement* here. Instead I will attempt to point out some ways in which the idea of the dual harmony I have just outlined was rediscovered by other thinkers within their own distinctive style of thinking. While

I hope this discussion will help situate Kant's achievement in relation to later developments, like most conclusions, it is principally a starting point for further reflection and discussion.

2 THE FATE OF THE IDEA OF A DUAL HARMONY

A direct continuation of Kant's ideas is to be found in the work of Schiller, whose *On the Aesthetic Education of Man* (1795/ 1967) set out to establish aesthetic judgement as preparatory for moral education and, eventually, the establishment of a free republican political state where the duties and rights of all citizens would be safeguarded by just laws. Aesthetic judgement frees the mind in anticipation of a more concrete political freedom that is to come. Schiller thus shares Kant's Enlightenment project and, in particular, the belief that aesthetic judgement fosters a broadening of the mind conducive to political freedom. [See Kant's account of 'common human understanding' in Section 40, discussed in 'Reading the Text'.] Schiller maintains both sides of the dual harmony, for it is only through the play of the faculties, highlighted in aesthetic judgement, that access to the sensory world is possible. Schiller takes up the moral potential of aesthetic judgement more explicitly than does Kant, emphasizing the way in which beauty acts as a point of transition for the transformation of the sensory world into a politically just state.

Fichte also considered his work as a continuation and even as a correction of Kant's. As we have seen, Kant aimed to bridge the gap between mind and world and, in particular, between knowledge and morality, through the mediating role of aesthetic pleasure. However, Fichte was unsatisfied with the indeterminacy of the resolution this offered. For this reason, the harmony between mind and world aimed at in reflective judgement was to be replaced by a full determination of the 'I', on which all thought is grounded. This is the project of the *Foundation of the Entire Wissenschaftslehre* (1794–95/1982), establishing the starting point for all Fichte's further philosophical work. The singular source of mental activity provides a determinate ground for all human experience. While, for Kant, the subject is an irreducible source of experience, it can only be so in relation not only to an object, but an external one. The interconnectedness of the subjective and objective conditions of experience is highlighted in the dual harmony distinctive of aesthetic judgement. Fichte rejects the dualist solution and the philosophy of mind that accompanies it. He sees Kant as committed to a coordination of the three cognitive faculties, whereas he intends to unify them under the primacy of practical reason. [See his letter to Reinhold from 1795, cited in Neuhoser, 1990, p. 62.] And, while summing up his complex position in a few words is bound to lead to distortion, he leaves an, at best, problematic role for the object. While the founding of the object in the primacy of the 'I' is 'strived for' rather than actually achieved, the absence of the object from the foundations of experience is bound to be significant for the subsequent account of the relation between subject and object [Neuhoser, 1990, pp. 48–53]. Later Idealist thinkers certainly thought so and tried to re-establish a fundamental place for the object, while not falling back into treating the relation between subject and object as one between opposites. This, they believed, was the fate of Kant's dualism, although I have argued that his account of aesthetic judgement concerns the relation and not the opposition between mind and world.

Schelling, along with Hegel and the poet Hölderlin, energetically engaged with Kant's writings while still students at the theological seminary in Tübingen. They, like Fichte along with so many subsequent readers of Kant, saw his project as marred by an insuperable rift between subject and object. Hölderlin was quick to spot a central difficulty in Fichte's own position, namely, that if there is no object outside of the 'absolute I', then the 'I' cannot even be conscious of itself, for it would only be the activity of subjectivity and such activity could not be intuited *as* an object for consciousness. [See 1795 'Letter to Hegel' in Hölderlin, 1988, p. 125; Bowie, 2003, pp. 82–8] Unfortunately, it is not possible to explore further Hölderlin's insight, which was highly influential for the future of German Idealism. In *System of Transcendental Idealism* (1800/1978) Schelling explicitly argues for the thesis that art can achieve an expression of the indeterminate relation between the subject and reality. Kant, as we saw, is much more confident that natural beauty can play this role. However, this aspect of Schelling's position may not be as close to Kant's dual harmony as we might think, even if we ignore this important distinction. For Schelling, 'reality' is not the world of objects, but, rather, the supersensible and absolute source of any experience whatsoever. Rolf-Peter Horstmann argues that in his *System* the Absolute is construed as the relation in which the self stands to *itself* as supersensible [Horstmann, 2000, pp. 133–5]. This is not the same as the view I have attributed to Kant in my reading of the 'Dialectic of Taste', namely, that the supersensible is the ground of the possibility of relations with objects existing externally to the mind, as well as of our moral agency. At the end of Schelling's *System*, the Absolute finally becomes accessible in aesthetic experience. Despite the distinction I have just pointed out, an analogy can be drawn with the role Kant apportions aesthetics as completing his philosophical system, at the same time as revealing a possibility of unity in the heart of experience. However, this capacity for achieving access to a 'pre-objective identity of spirit with itself' derives from a new capacity for intellectual intuition, which for Kant was a contradiction in terms, not from a cooperation of the faculties necessary for any experience whatsoever, as it was for Kant [Horstmann, 2000, p. 134].

In later works such as *Ages of the World* [1813/1997], Schelling, encouraged by the insights of Hölderlin, moved beyond this largely Fichtean perspective and sought to find the Absolute not only in the self, but also in nature, understood, not as a mechanical or causally regulated order, but as alive and teleologically directed. Indeed, Andrew Bowie suggests that the early Schelling was already struggling between these two understandings of the Absolute and that the alternative to Fichte is Spinoza's determinist account of nature [Bowie, 1993, pp. 17–25]. Kant viewed aesthetic apprehension as a mode of access to the relation between mind and world that first makes knowledge of empirical objects possible and, thus, is prior to causal determinism. What mind relates to is no longer the surface level of empirical objects, so, in the *Critique of Judgement,* he too introduced an alternative, deeper notion of nature than the one familiar from the first *Critique*. Both Kant and Schelling insist on the reciprocal importance of subject and object, although the later Schelling does not see aesthetics as privileged in uncovering this. We might even be tempted to conclude that Kant's notion that it is *as if* nature were designed for our judgement is a precursor to Schelling's idea of nature as an absolute producing subject. However, Kant insisted that this way of thinking was, strictly speaking, exactly that, namely, heuristic, whereas Schelling considered it a genuine way of construing the absolute ontological being of nature.

Of great interest for this present discussion is the later Schelling's insistence (in particular, against Hegel) that the relation ('identity') between thinking and what we think about ('being') is not fully graspable within thought [Bowie, 1993, pp. 127–77]. He traces the relation between thought and being back to an absolute ground that has always already been. This is very different from Kant's solution where systematicity is aimed at as an ideal and unachievable end, not an originary source [Bowie, 1993, p. 140]. However, despite the contrasting temporalities of these two strategies, both philosophers share the insight that thought's capacity for determination or knowledge is limited and only rendered coherent in the light of a presupposition not capable of a full and explicit statement in rational (including philosophical) terms. For both Kant and Schelling, a presupposition is the necessary third term that lies between the apparent oppositions dominating post-Cartesian philosophical thinking.

Hegel, like Schelling, aimed to overcome what he saw as the abstract nature of Kantian dualism. Hegel held that the distinctiveness of his own position lay in overcoming the indeterminacy inherent in previous versions of idealism. While Kant only aimed at an 'ideal', Hegel was committed to a determinate 'idea' realized within history. [See his 1830/1975 'Second Draft' of *Lectures on the Philosophy of World History: Introduction,* pp. 47–68.] And if Fichte aimed to determine the subjective side of the relation between subject and object, he did so one-sidedly. Meanwhile Schelling's attempt to find a point of 'indifference' or identity between subject and object traced them back to a presupposition that cannot be determined, that is, known. Each of these 'solutions' is a failure from Hegel's perspective insofar as they fail to achieve full determinacy, or knowledge, of both subject and object. The advance Hegel thinks he makes over the previous subjective idealisms of both Kant and Fichte arises from situating the idea or what he, like Schelling, calls the 'Absolute', within the world and not at its boundaries.

[*Phenomenology of Spirit* (1807/1979), 'Introduction', p. 46.] The Absolute thus becomes knowable.

While the Absolute has become knowable or 'concrete', Hegel rejects any direct reliance on facts, insisting that the idea only becomes real through a process. 'Dialectic' starts from an immediate consciousness of an external object, which is then shown to depend on the self-consciousness of the subject and, finally, both subject and object are united in a fully mediated relation. [This is a sketch of the structure of the *Phenomenology of Spirit*.] Determinacy is not an empirical fact and can only arise as the dialectic's final term, which is dependent on the process of consciousness that makes it possible. A possible interpretation of Hegel's position is that this process must be continually repeated even once self-consciousness is fully achieved [Hegel 1830/1975, p. 149]. Despite the ongoing movement of the dialectic, however, the Hegelian system aims to achieve full determination of subject and object, whereas for Schelling the system will always presuppose an indeterminate remainder: the third term cannot become determinate, that is, can never be resolved in theoretical terms. While in the *System* he considered art to be a possible expression of the indeterminate union of subject and object, in his later philosophy 'God' plays the role of what both defies and yet makes possible determination. As Bowie has argued, while we may remain unconvinced for a number of reasons by Schelling's theological position, his philosophical insight into the impossibility of achieving complete determination within a system is still relevant today [Bowie, 1993, pp. 159–68]. The disagreement between Hegel, on the one hand, and, on the other, both Kant (as I have read him here) and Schelling concerns the possibility of finally overcoming indeterminacy and achieving total or systematic determinate knowledge. The highpoint of Hegel's Absolute Idealism comes in his *Science of Logic* (1812/1998). Kant, Hegel and Schelling aimed to discover a philosophical way of thinking the relation in which subject and object stand to one another. But, while for Hegel this relation must be determinate, for Kant and Schelling any attempt to fully determine subjectivity, objectivity or the relation in which they stand to one another unavoidably fails.

The ideal is the indeterminate and, necessarily, incompletely realized goal of Kant's reflective judgement, whereas the

Hegelian idea is concrete, being fully realized within experience and history. The final element of Kant's system is one that opens the mind to a reflection without end, the epitome of which is the process of aesthetic judgement. Hegel understood Kant's intent very well and rejected it. In contrast to Kant's open system where an aesthetic phenomenon suggests an ideal that lies beyond experience, Hegel insists we discover the idea within every phenomenon. It was not that he intended that the sensory should become conceptual, but rather that what he saw as the antinomian or divisive character of Kantian synthesis should be overcome in a genuine relation or dialectic between the sensory and the conceptual. I have tried to show in my reading of the third *Critique* how Kant's project was to uncover the relation within mind and between mind and world that makes synthesis possible. In this respect, Hegel did not see enough of Kant in himself.

But there is a difference between the way in which Hegel and Kant reconstruct the relation between thinking and sensing, even when Kantian dualism is no longer seen as simply antinomian. Hegel believes that thought aims at an end, which it can capture in its own terms, so long as thinking proceeds dialectically. The Kantian account of reflective judgement insists that the relation between sensory input and thought cannot be resolved on one side or another. Thinking, whether it operates through the concepts of understanding or the ideas of reason, must always return to the phenomena of the senses and *vice versa*. Hegel aims to incorporate the awareness arising from the senses within the wider orbit of thought through a process he calls 'sublation' [*Aufhebung*]. While his intention is not to reduce sense to reason and, rather, to include sense within a broader understanding of reason; his solution leaves no room for a genuine relation between two distinctive inputs to experience. Yet Hegel did not abandon the project of mediation so central to the *Critique of Judgement* and, arguably, also to Schelling and Hölderlin's thinking. He did, however, privilege the resolution of the dialectic over its process. In this respect, his version of the third term is not primarily focused on the relational status of the relation between mind and world.

There is an associated distinction between Kant and Hegel, due to the latter's hierarchical account of the mental faculties.

The primary faculty for Hegel is reason, now seen as combining the roles formerly played by both speculative *and* moral reason. Reason operates through dialectic, an ongoing process of distinction and comparison and in this respect is comparable to reflective judgement. Yet, unlike the conclusion to Kant's system, dialectical reason finally operates as thinking at the level of the concept or idea alone. A genuine relating of sensory input with concepts would require a combination of two faculties, sensibility and understanding, facilitated by the mediating power of judgement in collaboration with imagination. This is Kant's complex story of how experience can arise for a reasoning being who is at the same time embodied.

As Hegel agrees with Kant that aesthetic judgement is characterized by a balancing act between concept and intuition, it is not surprising that aesthetics is not the apogee of Hegel's system. For Hegel aesthetics is highly important, because it represents a mobilization of thought in response to sensory perception, but it cannot count as the highest level of reflection as it is still, in his terms, restricted to the sensory sphere. [This is his position in *Phenomenology of Spirit,* as well as in lectures given from 1818–28, which are the basis for *Introduction to Lectures on Aesthetics* and *Lectures on Aesthetics* (Hegel 1823/1998).] Philosophy and, to a lesser extent, religion are capable of going beyond aesthetics through their capacity to transcend the senses and achieve the idea. Aesthetics is a necessary step in the process of reason and even one of the most important stages, arguably still operating *in nuce* even within philosophy's thinking of the idea. This makes it difficult to set up a straightforward opposition between Hegel's and Kant's positions. The balancing act of the power of judgement has been transformed into a dialectical progression and, while both are marked by a process of complex differentiation and integration, the combination of sense and reflection that is always anticipated but never realized for Kant, is centred on the life of the mind for Hegel. Mind has become reason and world finally becomes mind, rather than its necessary other. The mind for Hegel is not an internal retreat, nor does it offer us the complacency of immediate self-knowledge; but it is effective, indeed dominant, within its world. The Kantian mind has to risk losing itself in the world if it is ever to find itself.

As we have seen in 'Reading the Text', whereas in the two previous critiques Kant had been concerned with the universal conditions for the possibility of cognition and morality, in the *Critique of Judgement* he finally turned to the possibility of discovering the universal within the particular. German Romantic thinkers, principally Friedrich Schlegel and Novalis, took Kant's insight into the importance of aesthetic response to another level, while offering an alternative to Kant's account of the relation between singularity and philosophical system. For these early Romantics, systematicity is not to be confused with totality, but, rather, transformed into a philosophy of singular, though associated, insights expressed in fragments. They, like the Schelling of the *System,* saw art as the possible resolution of the antinomies of the human condition. Unlike Kant, aesthetics is no longer a balancing point between two distinct poles, for the third term has incorporated knowledge and morality within its horizon. German Romanticism aestheticized experience, not in the superficial sense that art is presented as more important than anything else, but in the alternative sense that the true and the good are most clearly accessible in artworks. Aesthetic creativity is now the highest human potentiality, in contrast to Hegel's rational idealism and, indeed, to the main tradition of philosophy since Plato. Friedrich Schlegel rejected the foundationalism of Fichte's philosophy of the 'I' in favour of a whole arising as a 'chaotic universality'. But instead of simply rejecting his predecessor, Schlegel transformed the Fichtean project, saying in 'Critical Fragment' 37 (1797/1991) that 'irony' is at the same time self-creation, self-limitation and self-destruction. [Schlegel, 1797/1991, pp. 4–5; Speight, 2008, Section 3.] Schegel's philosophy thereby achieved both the realization and the nemesis of the Fichtean project.

A new faculty of 'irony' or 'wit' [*Witz*] is crucial for the Romantics. [See Bauemler, 1923/1967, Part I, A. Aesthetik, pp. 141–66] Wit plays a similar role to that of imagination for Kant, as it serves as a third term linking otherwise disparate insights. And if this is right, wit is a successor to the play of the faculties. The German Romantics also shared Kant's view that the mind strives towards the world, rather than dominates it. They expressed this in their appreciation of natural phenomena such as minerals and crystallization. [See Ziolkowski, 1990, chapter two, 'The Mine: Image of the Soul', pp. 18–63] But despite these parallels, both sides of the dual harmony are transformed by putting aesthetics centre-stage, rather than at the limits of the system.

Schopenhauer, mentor of the young Nietzsche, owed much not only to Kant but also to Schelling. He has a further importance in that he transmitted some principal ideas of German Idealism to later thinkers such as Freud [Bowie, 2003, pp. 267–8; 1993, pp. 96–7]. Aesthetic contemplation is, for Schopenhauer, an alternative to the striving of the will and the suffering it causes. [See *The World as Will and Representation* (1818–19/1969), especially Volume 1, Section 33] In our terms, aesthetic detachment offers an indeterminate third term beyond the determinacy of the world and the determining force of the will. But while for Kant, aesthetic response is a reflection on and ongoing engagement with objects in the world, albeit a disinterested one, for Schopenhauer appreciation of art and nature counts as a withdrawal.

As a result of a lineage via Schopenhauer, we can find traces of earlier German philosophy in Nietzsche. Is there anything in his writings of the dual harmony I have pointed to in Kant? Given Nietzsche's insistence on perspectivism in, for instance, *The Gay Science* (1882, second edition 1887/1974, Aphorisms 354 and 374), we might think it would be difficult to see how he could meaningfully talk about a purposiveness of nature for our judgement. Surely there could be no genuine point of relation between mind and world, which is nothing if we are not conscious of it. Yet, his view that our interpretations of the world are only that, namely, perspectives on something we will never know 'in itself', owes much to Kant's Copernican turn and its insistence that our experience is restricted to appearances or appearing things. Kant's principle of the purposiveness of nature does not concern something *in* nature viewed as wholly detached from human perception, but rather, as I have argued, it concerns the relation in which our minds stand to objects in the world. And while Kant denies we can have any knowledge of a thing detached from our experience of it or 'in-itself', he insists that we must be able to think about reality as existing beyond the mind. It is not that Kant changed his mind in the *Critique of Judgement* and held that there really is a pristine world out there, untouched by human thought, but rather he always thought that, within anything we think, there is a relation to something beyond our minds, which is accessed by our senses and *about which* we think. Reflection is an unending task just because of the impossibility of wholly grasping something that must nevertheless be sought out. Now while Nietzsche's perspectivism, as often interpreted, leaves no room for the unthought, there are some grounds for suggesting Nietzsche had an insight into the pathos of thinking, namely that we are not the commanders of our own thought. I cannot make good this claim here, but it is possible to make sense of some of his claims about our lack of freedom in this way, even though such passages are usually read as evidence for determinism. [See 1882–87/1974, *Gay Science,* for instance, Aphorism 335 on physicist creators, when he says that in order to know what is possible, we first have to know what is necessary. See Hughes, 2002, pp. 129–32. The balance he suggests is required between forgetting and remembering would also be relevant for showing that Nietzsche is not committed to a mind that imposes its order on reality. See Hughes, 1998.] If this is right, Nietzsche had a sense of the delicate balancing between thinking and what thought intends, which for Kant is at the heart of the notion of the purposiveness of nature for our judgement. And it is indisputably the case that in *The Birth of Tragedy* (1872/1988), but not only there, Nietzsche suggests that the birth of meaningfulness – or, rather, its rebirth – can be found in art. However, even if I am right in thinking there is more to Nietzsche than a new and irrational version of subjective idealism, his sense of the role played by art and of the relation between mind and world is more troubling and sublime, than hopeful and beautiful. Extensive further work would be necessary to establish that Nietzsche takes up the question of a relation between mind and world and, additionally, whether he sees such a relation as arising from a combination of distinctive mental faculties.

Husserl, the father of Phenomenology, took as his leading question: How does a mind have access to something given to it? [See, for instance, *The Idea of Phenomenology* (1907/ 1990), but also *Ideas Pertaining to a Pure Phenomenology and to a Phenomenological Philosophy* First Book (1913/1998) and

Second Book (1928/1989), as well as *Cartesian Mediations* (1929/1991).] While Husserl did not focus on the investigation of natural or artistic beauty as a route to understanding the mind–world relation, he remarked on various occasions that he considered his project to be one of 'philosophical aesthetics'. [See *Analyses Concerning Passive and Active Synthesis* (lectures given during the 1920s), 2001, Part 2.] However, 'aesthetics' here refers to the conditions of our experience in space and time, the terrain of the 'Transcendental Aesthetic' of Kant's *Critique of Pure Reason*, not to the pleasurable appreciation of objects that is the subject of the third *Critique*. Husserl saw the phenomeno-logical task as returning to the primary consciousness we have of things, the point at which a mind first takes up something given to it and prior to any conceptual determination of it.

For Husserl, intuition is the capacity that allows access to something other than mind. Although this suggests the primacy of one faculty, not the play of a plurality of faculties charac-teristic of the Kantian dual harmony, it is possible to draw an analogy between mental play and the phenomenological idea of *epoche,* that is, the method of mentally standing back from the contents of empirical experience in order to investigate our access to them. [See Hughes, 2006c] We can at least be confi-dent that Husserl's project of uncovering the mind's access to the world shares Kant's insight that empirical objects cannot in themselves explain our perception of them and that the phil-osopher's task is to uncover a deeper relation between mind and world than the one most evident in everyday life. However, later Phenomenologists, principally Heidegger and Merleau-Ponty, while aware of their deep indebtedness to Husserl, reacted rather as the later Idealists responded to Fichte. They considered Husserl's account of the relationship between mind and world unevenly balanced on the side of the subject.

In his later works, Husserl's pupil Heidegger took up 'aes-thetics' in the sense established in the *Critique of Judgement* as a phenomenological method. Art is the mode of access to truth, or, in Heidegger's terms, 'the being of truth'. [See 'The Origin of the Artwork' (1936/1971) pp. 39–57.] Artworks reveal the struggle between concealment and disclosure that is at the root of all existence. In this way of viewing the role of art Heidegger continues a Kantian theme, and as we have seen a

Nietzschean one also, namely, that aesthetic response crystallizes an existential truth otherwise difficult to grasp. The Husserlian project of grasping the phenomenon becomes realizable through the indirect route of appreciating an artwork. Heidegger's earlier work on Kant's first *Critique, Kant and the Problem of Metaphysics* (1929/1962), insists that access to phenomena in the world requires a third term beyond understanding and sensibility, the imagination. The imagination is the hidden root of the two opposed sides of Kantian dualism, which are now mobilized so as to facilitate access to the world. Thus Heidegger calls imagination the ontological faculty *par excellence.* [See, for instance, *op. cit.,* p. 93.] In Heidegger's opinion, Kant's prioritizing of understanding over imagination is central to the failure of his epistemically biased project and leads to critical philosophy's failure to show how consciousness can have access to objects. But we can conclude that Heidegger shares with Kant the aim of establishing the possibility of the relation between mind and world *and* the insight that artworks facilitate this project. They additionally share the insight that the solution to Husserl's problem lies in the mobilization of a plurality of mental operations, not in the dominance of one of them.

Merleau-Ponty's phenomenological writings are deeply indebted to the late Husserl, as well as to the late Heidegger. We have seen how his phenomenological predecessors sought to uncover a relation between mind and world prior to an objectifying attitude, characteristic both of science and everyday experience. Merleau-Ponty shares this goal and the phenomenological method of working through examples, rather than attempting to first establish theoretical principles. In Merleau-Ponty's late works, particularly in *The Visible and The Invisible*, he makes particular progress in the investigation of the internal structure of relations.

In Merleau-Ponty's early major work, *Phenomenology of Perception* (1945/2002), he used a number of neurological, perceptual and, to a lesser extent, artistic examples of how the mind perceives the world. In his late major work *The Visible and the Invisible* (1964/1968), he investigates the implications of a core example, namely, how one of my hands grasps my other hand, an image that stands for the reciprocal relations at the heart of all human experience. This exploration of the point of transition between one term of a relation and another is of great interest for a deeper understanding of relations. Written just before his death and published posthumously, like other works from this period, *Eye and Mind* (1964/1993) examines phenomenological questions of perception almost exclusively through the medium of artworks. Artworks open up an opportunity for reflection within which the problems earlier posed by Husserl in purely phenomenological terms can finally be unlocked or at least recognized in their true form. Especially in his later work, Merleau-Ponty shared with the late Heidegger and with Kant's third and final critique the view that aesthetic experience allows us to see the way in which we encounter things outside and, yet, related to the mind.

In a series of lectures originally presented in 1956–57 and only published in French under the title *La Nature* in 1968, he takes up the topic of nature. What is nature? Is it a 'thing in itself' wholly independent of our awareness of it or a mere appearance dreamed up by the human mind? Arguably, he suggests that nature is best understood as mutually implicated [*Ineinander*] in the human body or, in my terms, 'relational' [Merleau-Ponty, 1968/ 2000, pp. 209–15]. Surely this is very close to Kant's notion of the purposiveness of nature for our judgement, that is, the relation between world and mind? From the *Phenomenology of Perception* to his latest works Merleau-Ponty aimed to uncover the grounds of our perception of objects, lying beyond the opposition of subject and object. Again, this sounds very close to the harmony of mind and world made accessible through reflective judgement. Nevertheless, it seems unlikely that Merleau-Ponty would have conceded this parallel, as he considered Kant too 'intellectualist' and insufficiently attuned to the perceptual core of experience.

Is there also a corollary to Kant's notion of the harmony within mind that allows the second harmony between mind and world to get going? This would be more difficult to establish, but although Merleau-Ponty's philosophy of mind is somewhat underdeveloped, I think there is potential for drawing out his thinking. He clearly holds that phenomenological insight can only be gained by going beyond the polarities of everyday life, as well as the antinomies into which philosophy so often falls.

The way of relating to the world investigated in *The Visible and the Invisible* requires a mobility of mind, impossible for any one 'faculty' or mental orientation. Our minds must be capable of a variety of functions, it would seem, if we are to explore the relation of one hand to the other, a phenomenon where the impetus moves from one side of the relation to the other and thus can never be wholly determinate. We need, in Kantian terms, to apprehend with our senses, while at the same time imagining what might be hidden and reflecting on what is seen and unseen. For Merleau-Ponty, the seen and the unseen are always intertwined and this suggests that our awareness of such reciprocity requires an ability to move between one perspective and another, a sort of freedom of the faculties analogous to aesthetic judgement in the *Critique of Judgement*. This, however, goes beyond any explicit philosophy of mind to be found in *The Visible and the Invisible.*

One philosopher trained in the phenomenological tradition, but moving beyond its presuppositions, Hannah Arendt, developed a distinctive way of thinking of the political. Moreover, she found inspiration for her project in the *Critique of Judgement.* Although there is no overt political philosophy in Kant's aesthetics, in *The Life of the Mind* (1978) Arendt developed a model for political life based on his account of the free contemplative mind. The link she makes between aesthetics and politics is, however, not new as we already saw in our discussion of Schiller. Indeed, the author or authors of a short, enigmatic but highly interesting work from 1796, the so-called 'The Oldest System Programme of German Idealism', argued for a systematic link between political enlightenment and aesthetic renaissance. [This work was almost certainly written by Schelling, Hölderlin or Hegel. See Bowie, 2003 pp. 334–5 for a translation of this short piece.] Arendt allows us to understand the importance of aesthetics for progressive politics within the tradition of philosophy following on from Kant. Politics is, for Arendt, not an aspect of life, but life lived at its highest human potentiality and aesthetic response allows us to explore the possibilities for individual and communal life expressed in politics. In her belief that aesthetics opens up an insight into the deepest roots of human existence, she shares ground not only with Kant but also with Nietzsche, Heidegger and Merleau-Ponty.

She focuses, however, not on the first beginnings of perception, nor on the mental powers necessary for our apprehension of the world. In her view, the most pressing question of the relation in which mind stands to the world arises as political. This emphasis, however, is not so distant from Kant's view that aesthetic pleasure allows us to see how we might possibly intervene morally in the empirical world. While Arendt, like Hegel, prefers the more communitarian 'ethics' to the individualist connotations of 'morality', her project aims to show how we might reassert ourselves as responsible agents within everyday life. This, we have seen, in Kant's view, is a possibility – albeit a tentative one – opened up by judgements of beauty. The ethical promise associated with the dual harmony is also important for the authors we are about to discuss.

The Frankfurt School philosophers share Arendt's view that political life is, or should be, at the centre of philosophical reflections on human existence. The first generation of these thinkers, broadly inspired by Marx, but also by Freud and Nietzsche, waged their assault on a society they considered degenerative and consumerist through the development of an aesthetic or cultural philosophy. While, as Arendt has shown, Kant's aesthetics contain an indirect political message, the intent of Adorno, Horkheimer and Benjamin was to develop a direct, if complex, series of reflections on politics within the medium of aesthetics. Later generations of the Frankfurt School, including influential thinkers such as Habermas, show considerably less engagement with aesthetics and thus do not enter into our present concerns. Both Adorno and Benjamin were committed to art as a central human project and this was because both of them, in rather different ways, believed, like Nietzsche before them, that artworks operate as crystallizations of knowledge and values lost sight of in everyday life. Early Frankfurt School thinkers were committed to the idea that lost insights could be recuperated, partially at least, against the tide of Capitalism, which had replaced human values with a quantitative measure, based entirely on money. While these thinkers were no longer hopeful of total revolution in the Marxian sense, they saw artworks as distillations of potential resistance and hope for a better society. [This is a very simplified account of a central theme of Adorno and Horkheimer's

Dialectic of Enlightenment (1947/1997a)] Admittedly, they were not particularly interested in the specific notion of a purposiveness of nature for our judgement, but they were interested in the way in which we have lost touch with nature due to modern society's fixation on controlling the non-human world. At the same time, they were committed to the possible purposiveness of the cultural world for our freedom. In this they share, although at a very different time and in a distinctive way, Kant's overall project for the *Critique of Aesthetic Judgement,* namely, to establish the possibility of rational intervention in the empirical world.

I will now focus on how Adorno may be seen as developing one side of Kant's idea of a dual harmony, namely, that between mind and world. His *Aesthetic Theory* (1970/1997b) presents the artwork and, in particular, what is often called 'high art', as capable of opening up a utopian alternative to the actual world where alienation is the norm. Adorno does not see art as a means of escape from everyday suffering as Schopenhauer did. It is, rather, that certain artworks seem to be more than mere commodities, the worth of which arises only from the possibility that they can be exchanged for other useful things. This allows the artwork to open up an alternative to the prevailing ethos of the market, but not because Adorno thinks that such 'high art' escapes the ethos of the market: he was all too aware of the market in art. Rather, the alternative prospect offered by artworks operates entirely at the level of appearance: they appear to escape exchange value, just because they appear entirely useless [Jarvis, 1998, pp. 90–123]. Now, because all of this is apparent rather than real, the artwork does not qualify as an end in itself, as art for art's sake. Rather, a piece of music by Beethoven or Schoenberg, for instance, can be the beginning of an insight into a value for human life that lies beyond the perspective of useful products exchangeable for other products. The way in which the artwork seems to escape the values of the market becomes a cipher for recognizing human life as valuable in itself and not just as a means to an end, to use Kantian terms, or, in Marx's way of thinking, for seeing how we could move beyond our current alienated condition. The artwork allows us to glimpse – albeit in a distorted form because it, too, is part of the alienated world of the market – how life could be other than it is. The utopian alternative, which can only ever be thought in negative terms, that is, as a critique of the existing status quo, would be one in which we could emerge from our current alienated state. The background to Adorno's perspective is to be found in Marx's *1844 Manuscripts,* which diagnoses four stages of alienation. We are alienated, first, in relation to nature and the products we create from it; second, we are alienated from our own productivity or work; third, we are alienated from the humanity within ourselves; and, fourth, as a consequence, we are alienated from other human beings [Marx, 1884/2007, *Economic and Philosophic Manuscripts of 1844,* First Manuscript, 'Estranged Labour'].

With regard to Adorno's reception and transmission of the first and last of these four aspects of alienation first established by Marx, I believe it is possible to draw a limited, but illuminating, parallel with Kant's presupposition of the purposiveness of nature for our judgement. Kant's idea was that only through reflective judgement could we establish a relationship between the subject and the order of the empirical world. I suggested early in this section that the deeper truth of this idea is that, both epistemic and moral engagement with the world require a prior involvement with the world, most directly expressed in aesthetic judgement. Adorno sees artworks as opening up the tentative prospect of an unalienated relation to nature and to others; meanwhile Kant holds that aesthetic judgement prefigures our cognitive engagement with objects *and* our moral relations with other human beings. And, while Adorno found in aesthetic response a potential for moving to a less alienated relation between subject and world and between subject and subject principally in 'high art', Benjamin believed that more popular art-forms such as cinema have the potential to contribute to the construction of a society, where we would no longer merely quantify nature outside us, within ourselves and within other human beings. Art creates, at the level of appearance, an image of an alternative to the real world and in so doing makes possible the creation of an alternative reality. While the details of Adorno's approach are quite different from Kant's, he and other early Frankfurt School thinkers share the view that our capacity for aesthetic response is crucial for the possibility of human progress.

A philosopher who more recently and quite explicitly took up the mantle of Kant's project in *The Critique of Aesthetic Judgement* is Jean-François Lyotard. From his early work, *The Post-Modern Condition* (1979/1994), Lyotard insisted on the importance of combining a plurality of different perspectives and this can be seen as a revised version of the play of the faculties. For Lyotard, modern times, which he remarks are often referred to as 'postmodernity', are characterized by a drive to determine and control. Against this trend, Lyotard tries to identify moments of possible disruption where the calculations of the prevailing dominant order might be disrupted. An alternative and second 'postmodernity' – more properly called 'the postmodern' – opposed to all totalizing systems, is dedicated to identifying what Lyotard later calls the 'differend', this being a minuscule turning point where a pre-ordained pattern is unsettled. Lyotard, once a Marxist, came to think that revolution on a grand scale could not be expected with any certainty, while all that could be hoped for were minor revolutions and disruptions in everyday life.

In some of his latest writings and especially in *The Inhuman* (1988/1991), he turns directly to the role of artworks, particularly abstract modern art, in providing an alternative to the dominant productive or 'performative' mentality of modern life. At this point of his development, the parallels with Kant's 'dual harmony' become most interesting, although they are complex, for Lyotard's deepest insight concerns the disharmony associated with the sublime, not the harmony of the beautiful. Aesthetic experience reveals our place in the world and our access to it, not, principally, by showing the way in which the world is congenial to our judgement of it, but by disrupting that relation and going beyond our power of thinking. When we respond to an artwork, such as a painting by the Abstract Expressionist, Barnett Newman, we take on a wholly different relationship to the world than is the norm, most particularly to its temporality. We no longer approach what we perceive quantitatively or with a view to achieving a certain goal: we look at a line – for Newman, a 'zip' – of painted colour that has no meaning beyond itself. Lyotard does not suggest that such a disruption of our normal perception has a direct pay-off in political or cultural terms. There is no agenda for this disruption, this differend. An alternative is implied simply in the possibility of perceiving in a different way, one that allows for an intimation of something that cannot be perceived or even thought. This is what Lyotard understands by the sublime, which offers hope only as a specific moment of disruption of the normal order of the modern world. The Kantian hope in a singular moment of harmony has been replaced by an even more fragile hope arising from a particular moment of disharmony.

3 IS THE IDEA OF A DUAL HARMONY PRESENT IN ARTWORKS, NOT JUST IN OUR INTERPRETATION OF THEM?

I have suggested how various philosophical thinkers carry forward Kant's idea of a dual harmony, or, in his terms, the purposiveness of nature for our judgement. Is there any reason to think that this idea is important, not just for philosophical aesthetics, but, also, for artists? While it may seem odd to switch our attention from theory to the practice of art at this stage, I believe it is important to remind ourselves of the other side of the story I've been telling. I have shown how the thinkers I have been discussing discover an expression of the theoretical idea of the relation between mind and world in our response to beautiful nature and in artworks. My intention is not to give a list of artists who have taken up a philosophical idea, but, rather, to suggest briefly how an insight that is taken up in a philosophical form also has a distinctively aesthetic expression in artworks.

While we may discover much about ourselves in the course of appreciating beauty in the natural world, artistic creativity has always been, explicitly or otherwise, a way of interpreting our place in the world. While it would be naïve and, worse, reductive to suggest that an agenda of self-explication motivates every artwork, it seems plausible to suggest that greater self-understanding is one of the results – intended or otherwise – of responding to art. Sometimes, the self-understanding that ensues can be quite specific, especially if works are strongly motivated by and directed to particular historical circumstances. But many artworks and most modern artworks are not aimed at documenting specific events. This, however, is not to say that artworks no longer tell us anything about our place in the world, it is just that they do not do so, or at least not solely, by documenting specific events.

It would be equally unwise to generalize about how artworks operate, because they do so in many different ways. We can say, however, that artworks make us see differently and in so doing we become aware of the very process of perceiving, something we usually take for granted. The general process of relating to the world becomes apparent in the particular artistic instance with which we are presently preoccupied. It is my view that Kant correctly identified the importance of aesthetic experience in opening up a world accessible to, but not ultimately controlled by, us. Yet, he also concluded that artworks are not capable of revealing the relations in which we stand to nature, which he viewed, principally, as the field of objects external to the mind. But while an artwork does not usually immediately present an encounter between the human mind and a world beyond, it can do so indirectly through layers of meaning that may be even more suggestive than a direct encounter with a natural phenomenon. The painting 'Lake at Annecy' [*Lac d'Annecy*] by Cézanne can help me become more aware of ways of seeing the lake for myself when I visit the French Alps. The painting opens up a way of seeing the buildings on the other side of the lake, the tree on the grassy bank in the foreground and even the mountains beyond as drawn towards the lake. Cézanne makes this way of seeing possible through the deployment of a play of reflections in the water and on *terra firma,* emphasizing the sense of enclosure through omitting any reference to the sky. The result is claustrophobic and is intensified by the use of sludgy colour. When I visit the lake and look at the scene with my own eyes, I rediscover the qualities in nature and its cultural environment of which the painting has made me aware. This mountain lake, usually viewed as a relaxing leisure destination, now appears trapped in a narrow space between mountains on either side, while, at the same time, dominating its environment. It is as though nature has become Cézanne's painting. [See Kant's comment on nature looking as if it were art in Section 45.] The fact that a painting is produced by an artist, who unavoidably has intentions even in the course of aesthetic production, does not mean that the viewer cannot draw on the artwork to expand her perception of nature. Moreover, in a world where pure instances of nature are more and more difficult to encounter and even to conceive, we must recognize that our world is not a purely natural one, but one that is highly culturally determined. Artworks have the capacity to aid our reflection on a world that is hybrid, even one in which natural beauty still operates as an ideal. If this is right, then the purposiveness of culturally mediated nature for our judgement is a problem for us and one on which artworks help us reflect.

4   WHY STILL READ *THE CRITIQUE OF JUDGEMENT*?

The continuing relevance of *The Critique of Judgement* arises from its insight into the contemplative reflection that allows for aesthetic appreciation both of nature and of artworks. Yet, as we have seen, such reflection does not require detachment from other aspects of life, but, rather, reveals our complex involvement with the world. Aesthetic appreciation reveals our capacity for relating to something without controlling or even knowing it. And yet we are not indifferent to it: we are engaged, but we are not appetitive, nor operating as moral agents, although we must be so on other occasions. The ability, without a further agenda, to pay attention to and even feel liking for something, reveals that we have a prospect beyond the material world, with which we are, nevertheless, inescapably engaged. Kant says near the outset of the *Critique* that only humans feel aesthetic pleasure. Whether or not it is right to restrict aesthetic feeling to human beings, surely Kant is right in suggesting that whatever human beings might be, an ability to like and dislike without agenda is crucial for our sense of identity – or at least, for what we hope we could be.

CHAPTER 5

NOTES FOR FURTHER READING

1 THE ORIGINAL EDITIONS AND THE EDITIONS WE USE NOW

'Kant is the most frequently edited German philosopher.' These are the words of Norbert Hinske and Wilhelm Weischedel at the outset of their concordance to the six major complete editions of his works in German. [*Kant-Seitenkonkordanz* published in 1970 by the *Wissenschaftliche Buchgesellschaft Darmstadt,* 'Foreword'.] However, while the original editions of works published in Kant's life time, along with other editions published much later, remain of interest to Kant scholars, there can be no doubt that the touchstone for Kant studies today is the *Akademie-Ausgabe,* the academic edition, the page numbering of which is now used in all scholarly discussions of Kant. The *Critique of Judgement* (*Kritik der Urteilskraft*) is included in Volume V. References to this standard edition are marked by the abbreviation 'AA' (which I have used) or *'Ak'.*

In references to the *Critique of Pure Reason* I have used 'A' and 'B' to refer to the first and second editions of the 'Original Edition' from 1781 and 1787, respectively, as is standard. They are to be found in Volumes III and IV of the *Akademie Ausgabe* with the 'Original Edition' page numberings at the side of the page.

For those who wish to acquire a German edition of Kant's works, Kant's *Werke in sechs Bänden*, edited by Wilhelm Weischedel and published by the Wissenschaftliche Buchgesellschaft, Darmstadt is the best option, being reliable and relatively inexpensive. (Unlike the *Akademie* edition, it is printed in modern script.) *Die Kritik der Urteilskraft* is included in Volume V of the 1998 reprint of the 1983 edition. Alternatively, there is a single volume edition published by Reclam, Ditzingen.

2 TRANSLATIONS AVAILABLE IN ENGLISH

Until 1987 a translation first published in 1911 by James Creed Meredith was the only complete translation into English of both the first (aesthetic) and second (teleological) parts of the *Critique of Judgement*. Meredith's translation has recently been revised and edited by Nicholas Walker and published by Oxford University Press (2007). Walker also offers a new translation of the 'First Introduction'. Especially in this new edition, Meredith's translation continues to be of interest to those who are not specialists in the field and are looking for a stylistically accessible version.

The year 1987 saw the appearance of Werner Pluhar's translation, *Critique of Judgment*, complete with substantial introductory material and critical apparatus [Indianapolis: Hackett]. A major strength of Pluhar's translation is the sense it gives of the systematic positioning of the third *Critique*, alongside his acuity in rendering passages that in the original German are often long and complex and can sometimes also be unclear. Pluhar quite often interjects additional words in square brackets, in the interest of clarification. Some readers, especially those who work closely with the German text, have been irritated by additions that go beyond the letter of the text. Nevertheless, this is an excellent translation.

In 2000, a new critical edition with the title *Critique of the Power of Judgement* was published, jointly translated by Paul Guyer and Eric Matthews and edited by Guyer and Alan Wood within Cambridge University Press's ongoing edition of Kant's complete works. There can be no doubt of the attractiveness of an edition of the third *Critique* produced under a consistent and scholarly editorial plan for Kant's opus as a whole. Moreover, this edition does not have editorial additions in the text. The Cambridge edition also has a clear and interesting introduction by Paul Guyer.

Both Pluhar's, and Guyer and Matthews' translations are based on the second corrected edition prepared by Kant himself and included in the *Akademie* edition in Volume V.

3 SELECTIVE BIBLIOGRAPHY REFERRED TO IN *READER'S GUIDE*

Adorno, T. and Horkheimer, M. [1947] (1997a), *Dialectic of Enlightenment*, trans. J. Cumming, London: Verso Books; [*Dialektik der Aufklärung:*

philosophische fragmente in *Gesammelte Schriften,* herausgegeben von R. Tiedemann unter Mitwerkung von G. Adorno, S. Buck-Morss und K. Schultz, Frankfurt am Main: Suhrkamp Taschenbuch, 1997, Band 3].

Adorno, T. [1970] (1997b), *Aesthetic Theory,* trans. R. Hullot-Kentor, London: The Athlone Press; [*Ästhetische Theorie* in *Gesammelte Schriften,* Frankfurt am Main: Surhkamp, 1997, Band 7].

Arendt, H. [1971] (1978), *The Life of the Mind,* Orlando, Florida: Harcourt Brace and Company.

Allison, H. (1990), *Kant's Theory of Freedom,* Cambridge: Cambridge University Press.

—(2001), *Kant's Theory of Taste,* Cambridge: Cambridge University Press.

Ameriks, K. (1992), 'Rudolf A. Makkreel, *Imagination and Interpretation in Kant',* *Man and World* 25, 227–34.

Bauemler, A. [1923] (1967), *Das Irrationalitätsproblem in der Ästhetik und Logik des 18. Jahrhunderts bis zur Kritik der Urteilskraft,* Tübingen, Niemeyer and Wissenschafliche Buchgesellschaft, Darmstadt.

Bowie, A. (1993), *Schelling and Modern European Philosophy: An Introduction,* London and New York: Routledge.

—(2003) (2nd edition), *Aesthetics and Subjectivity: From Kant to Nietzsche,* Manchester: Manchester University Press.

Brandt, R. (1998), 'Zur Logik des ästhetischen Urteils', *Kant's Ästhetik, Kant's Aesthetics, L'esthétique de Kant,* Herman Parret, ed. Berlin and New York: Walter de Gruyter, pp. 229–45.

Crawford, D.W. (1974), *Kant's Aesthetic Theory,* Madison, Wisconsin: The University of Wisconsin Press.

Derrida, J. [1978] (1987), 'The Parergon', in *The Truth in Painting,* trans. G. Bennington and I. McLeod, Chicago: The University of Chicago Press, pp. 15–147; [*La Vérité En Peinture* (Paris: Flammarion)].

Fichte, J.G. [1794–95] (1982), *Foundation of the Entire Science of Knowledge* (1794–95) in *The Science of Knowledge* ed. and trans. P. Heath and J. Lachs, Cambridge: Cambridge University Press; [*Grundlage der gesamten Wissenschaftslehre (1794–95), Fichtes Werke,* hrsg. von Immanuel Hermann Fichte, Berlin: W. de Gruyter, 1971, Band 1].

Fricke, C. (1990), *Kants Theorie des reinen Geschmacksurteils,* Berlin and New York: Walter de Gruyter.

Gotshalk, D.W. (1967), 'Form and Expression in Kant's Aesthetics', *The British Journal of Aesthetics* 7(3), 250–60.

Grayck, A. (1986), 'Sublimity, Ugliness, and Formlessness in Kant's Aesthetic Theory', *Journal of Aesthetics and Art Criticism* 45, 49–56.

Guyer, P. (1977), 'Formalism and the Theory of Expression in Kant's Aesthetics', *Kant-Studien* 68, 46–70.

—(1979), *Kant and the Claims of Taste,* Cambridge, MA and London, England: Harvard University Press.

Hegel, G.W.F. [1830] (1975), *Lectures on the Philosophy of World History: Introduction,* trans. H.B. Nisbet, Cambridge: Cambridge

University Press; [*Vorlesungen über die Philosophie der Weltgeschichte*, herausgegeben von Johannes Hoffmeister, Georg Lasson Berlin: Akademie-Verlag, 1970].

—[1807] (1979), *Phenomenology of Spirit*, trans. A.V. Miller, Oxford: Clarendon Press; [*Phänomenologie des Geistes*, Frankfurt am Main: Suhrkamp, 1981].

—(1993), *Introductory Lectures on Aesthetics*, trans. B. Bosanquet, London: Penguin.

—[1818–28] (1998a), *Aesthetics: Lectures on Fine Art*, trans. T.M. Knox, Oxford: Clarendon Press; [*Vorlesungen über die Ästhetik* Auf der Grundlage der Werke von 1832–1845, Redaktion E. Moldenhauer und K.M. Michel, Suhrkamp Verlag, Frankfurt am Main, 1970].

—[1812] (1998b), *Science of Logic*, trans. A.V. Miller, New York: Prometheus Books; [*Wissenschaft der Logik*, hrsg. von Friedrich Hogemann und Walter Jaeschke, Hamburg: Meiner, Band 1, 1978; Band 2, 1981].

Heidegger, M. [1929] (1962), *Kant and the Problem of Metaphysics*, trans. J.S. Churchill, Bloomington, Indiana: Indiana University Press; [*Kant und das Problem der Metaphysik*, hrsg. von Friedrich-Wilhelm von Herrmann, Frankfurt am Main: Klostermann, 1991].

—[1936] (1971), 'The Origin of the Work of Art', in *Poetry, Language, Thought*, trans. A. Hofstadter, New York: Harper & Row 1971. An abridged version is available in (1978), D.F. Krell, (ed.), *Martin Heidegger Basic Writings*, London: Routledge and Kegan Paul; ['Der Ursprung des Kunstwerkes' (1935/6) in *Holzwege*, Frankfurt am Main: Vittorio Klostermann, 1950].

Hölderlin, F. [1795] (1988), 'Letter to Hegel' in *Essays and Letters on Theory*, trans. and ed. T. Pfau, Albany: State University of New York Press; [*Werke und Briefe*, herausgegeben von F. Beissner und J. Schmidt, Frankfurt am Main: Insel Verlag, 1969, Bd. II].

Horstmann, R.-P. (2000), 'The early philosophy of Fichte and Schelling', in *The Cambridge Companion to German Idealism*, ed. K. Ameriks, Cambridge: Cambridge University Press, pp. 117–40.

Hudson, H. (1991), 'The Significance of an Analytic of the Ugly in Kant's Deduction of Pure Judgments of Taste' *Kant's Aesthetics*, ed. R. Meerbote, Atascadero, CA: Ridgeview Publishing Company, pp. 87–103.

Hughes, F. (1998), 'Forgetful All Too Forgetful: Nietzsche and the Question of Measure', *Journal of British Society for Phenomenology*, 29(3), October 1998, 252–67.

—(2002), 'Nietzsche's Janus Perceptions and the Construction of Values', *The Journal of the British Society for Phenomenology*, Summer 33(2), May 2002, 116–37.

—(2006a), 'Taste as Productive Mimesis', *Journal for the British Society of Phenomenology*, 37(3), October, 308–26.

—(2006b), 'On Aesthetic Judgement and our Relation to Nature: Kant's Concept of Purposiveness', *Inquiry*, 49(6) December 2006, 547–72.

Hughes, F. (2006c), 'Kant's Phenomenological Reduction?', *Études phénoménologiques*, tome XXII, n° 43–44, 163–92.

——(2007), *Kant's Aesthetic Epistemology: Form and World,* Edinburgh: Edinburgh University Press.

Husserl, E. [1928] (1989), *Ideas Pertaining to a Pure Phenomenology and to a Phenomenological Philosophy:* Second Book, trans. R. Rojcewicz and A. Schuwer, Dordrecht: Kluwer; [*Ideen zu einer reinen Phänomenologie und phänomenologischen Philosophie* (Band 2), herausgegeben M. Biemel, Den Haag: M. Nijhoff, 1952, *Husserliana* Bd. IV].

——[1907] (1990), *The Idea of Phenomenology*, trans. W.P. Alston and G. Nakhnikian, Dordrecht: Kluwer; [*Die Idee der Phänomenologie*: fünf Vorlesungen, herausgegeben und eingeleitet von Walter Biemel, 2. Aufl., Den Haag: M. Nijhoff, 1973, *Husserliana* Bd. II].

——[1929] (1991), *Cartesian Meditations,* trans. D. Cairns, Dordrecht: Kluwer; [*Cartesianische Meditationen und Pariser Vorträge*, herausgegeben und eingeleitet von S. Strasser, 2. Aufl., Den Haag, M. Nijhoff, 1973, *Husserliana* Bd. I].

——[1913] (1998), *Ideas Pertaining to a Pure Phenomenology and to a Phenomenological Philosophy*: First Book, trans. F. Kersten, Dordrecht: Kluwer; [*Ideen zu einer reinen Phänomenologie und phänomenologischen Philosophie*, (Band 1) herausgebeben W. Biemel, Den Haag: M. Nijhoff, 1950, *Husserliana* Bd. III].

——[1920–] (2001), *Analyses Concerning Passive and Active Synthesis,* trans. A.J. Steinbock, Dordrecht: Kluwer; [*Analysen zur passiven Synthesis*: aus Vorlesungs – und Forschungsmanuskripten 1918–26, hrsg. von M. Fleischer, Den Haag: M. Nijhoff, 1966, *Husserliana* Bd. XI].

James, W. [1890] (1981), *The Principles of Psychology*, Cambridge MA: Harvard University Press.

Jarvis, S. (1998), *Adorno: A Critical Introduction*, Cambridge: Polity Press.

Kant, I. [1793] (1960), *Religion within the Limits of Reason Alone*, trans. T.M. Greene and H.H. Hudson, New York: Harper and Row; [*Die Religion innerhalb der Grenzen der blossen Vernunft*, herausgegeben von Rudolf Malter, Stuttgart: Reclam [1974], *Akademie-Ausgabe* Bd. VI].

——[1797] (1964), *The Doctrine of Virtue: Part II of The Metaphysic of Morals*, trans. M.J. Gregor, New York: Harper and Row; [*Metaphysik der Sitten,* neu herausgegeben von Bernd Ludwig, Hamburg: F. Meiner, 1986–; *AA* Bd. VI].

——[1795] (1991), 'Perpetual Peace', in *Kant: Political Writings*, ed. H.S. Reiss, trans. H.B. Nisbet, Cambridge: Cambridge University Press; [*Zum ewigen Frieden. Ein philosophischer entwurf, hrsg. von Theodor Valentiner, Stuttgart: Reclam,1971, *AA* Bd. VIII].

——[1781–87] (2007), *Critique of Pure Reason*, trans. N. Kemp Smith, Basingstoke: Palgrave Macmillan; [*Kritik der reinen Vernunft*, Hamburg: Felix Meiner, 1956; *AA* Bände III and IV].

Llewelyn, J. (2000), *The HypoCritical Imagination. Between Kant and Levinas*, London: Routledge.

Lyotard, J.-F. [1979] (1984), *The Postmodern Condition: A Report on Knowledge*, trans. G. Bennington and B. Massumi, Manchester: Manchester University Press; [*La condition postmoderne: rapport sur le savoir*, Paris: Editions de Minuit, 1979].

—[1988] (1991), *The Inhuman*, trans. G. Bennington and R. Bowlby, Cambridge: Polity Press; [*L'inhumain: Causeries sur le temps*, Paris: Gallilée].

Makkreel, R. (1990), *Imagination and Interpretation in Kant*, Chicago: University of Chicago Press.

—(1992), 'Response to Guenter Zoeller', *Philosophy Today*, 36, Fall 1992, 276–80.

Marx, K. [1844] (2007), *Economic and Philosophic Manuscripts of 1844*, trans. M. Milligan, New York: Dover Publications; ['Ökonomisch-philosophische Manuskripte' in *Karl Marx Friedrich Engels Gesamtausgabe*, herausgegeben von der Internationalen Marx-Engels Stiftung Amsterdam, Erste Abteilung, Band 2, Berlin: Dietz, 1982 (Erste Wiedergabe pp. 187–318 & Zweite Wiedergabe pp. 323–464)].

Meerbote, R. (1982), 'Reflection on Beauty', in T. Cohen and P. Guyer (eds), *Essays in Kant's Aesthetics*, Chicago: The University of Chicago Press, pp. 55–86.

Merleau-Ponty, M. [1964] (1968), *The Visible and the Invisible*, ed. C. Lefort, trans. A Lingis, Evanston, IL: Northwestern University Press; [*Le visible et l'invisible*: suivi de notes de travail; texte établi par Claude Lefort, accompagné d'un avertissement et d'une postface, Paris: Gallimard, 1964].

—[1964] (1993), 'Eye and Mind', in ed. G.A. Johnson, *The Merleau-Ponty Aesthetics Reader*, Evanston, IL: Northwestern University Press, pp. 121–49; [*L'œil et l'esprit*, Paris: Gallimard 1964].

—[1968] (2003), *Nature: Course Notes from the Collège de France*, trans. R. Vallier, Evanston, IL: Northwestern University Press; [*La Nature: Notes. Cours du Collège de France*, Paris: Éditions de Seuil, 1995].

—[1945] (2002), *Phenomenology of Perception*, trans. C. Smith, London: Routledge; [*Phénoménologie de la perception*, Paris: Gallimard, 1976, reprinted 1983].

Neuhoser, F. (1990), *Fichte's Theory of Subjectivity*, Cambridge: Cambridge University Press.

Nietzsche, F. [1882–87] (1974), *The Gay Science*, trans. W. Kaufmann, New York: Vintage; [*Werke: kritische Gesamtausgabe*, herausgegeben von Giorgio Colli und Mazzino Montinari, Berlin: de Gruyter, 1967–, Band III].

—[1872] (1988), *The Birth of Tragedy and The Case of Wagner*, trans. W. Kaufmann, New York: Vintage; [*Werke* Band I].

Proust, M. [1924] (2000), *In Search of Lost Time*, trans. C.K. Scott Moncrieff and T. Kilmartin. Revised by D.J. Enright, London:

Vintage; [*A la recherche du temps perdu*; édition publiée sous la direction de Jean-Yves Tadié, Paris: Gallimard, 1988, Volume III].

Schelling, F.W.J. [1801–04] (1978), *The Philosophy of Art*, ed. and trans. D.W. Stott, Minneapolis, MN: University of Minnesota Press; [*Philosophie der Kunst*, Darmstadt: Wissenschaftliche Buchgesellschaft, 1980].

—[1800] (1978), *System of Transcendental Idealism*, trans. P. Heath, Charlottesville: University of Press of Virginia; [*System des Transscendentale Idealismus (1800), Historische-kritische Ausgabe. Reihe I: Werke*. Band 9, 1–2, herausgegeben von H. Korten und P. Ziche, Stuttgart: Frommann-Holzboog, 1975–2005].

—[1813] (1997), 'Ages of the World' in *The Abyss of Freedom/ Ages of the World*, trans. J. Norman with an essay by Slavoj Žižek, Ann Arbor: The University of Michigan Press; ['Weltalter-Fragmente', *Schellingiana* Band XIII, 1–2, Stuttgart: Frommann-Holzboog, 2002].

Schiller, F. [1795] (1967), *On the Aesthetic Education of Man*, ed. E.M. Wilkinson and L.A. Willoughby, Oxford: Clarendon Press; [*Über die ästhetische Erziehung des Menschen* in *Werke in Drei Banden*, unter Mitwerkung von G. Fricke, herausgegeben von H. G. Göpfert, 5. Auflage, Darmstadt: Wissenschaftliche Buchgesellschaft, 1984, Band II].

Schlegel, F. [1797] (1991), *Philosophical Fragments*, trans. P. Firchow, Minneapolis: University of Minnesota Press; ['Kritische Fragmente' („Lyceum") [1797] in *Kritische Schriften und Fragmente Studienausgabe*, herausgegeben von E. Behler und H. Eichner; Paderborn: Ferdinand Schöningh, 1988, Band 1.]

Schopenhauer, A. [1818–19] (1969), *The World as Will and Representation* (in two volumes), trans. E.F.J. Payne, New York: Dover Publications; [*Die Welt als Wille und Vorstellung*, Stuttgart: Reclam, 1987].

Shier, D. (1998), 'Why Kant Finds Nothing Ugly', *The British Journal of Aesthetics*, 38(4), 412–18.

Speight, A. (2008), 'Friedrich Schlegel', *The Stanford Encyclopedia of Philosophy* (Fall 2008 Edition), Edward N. Zalta (ed.), http://plato.stanford.edu/archives/fall2008/entries/Schlegel.

Ziolkowski, T. (1990), *German Romanticism and Its Institutions*, Princeton: Princeton University Press.

4   SUGGESTIONS FOR FURTHER READING ARISING FROM 'READING THE TEXT'

4.1   The place of aesthetic judgement within the critical system

Allison, 2001, pp. 13–64.

Baz, A. (2005), 'Kant's Principle of Purposiveness and the Missing Point of (Aesthetic) Judgements', *Kantian Review*, 10, 1–32.

Gibbons, S. (1994), *Kant's Theory of Imagination*, Oxford: Clarendon Press, pp. 79–123.

Guyer, 1979, pp. 33–67.

Hughes, F. (1998), 'The Technic of Nature: What is Involved in Judging?', in H. Parret (ed.), *Kants Ästhetik/Kant's Aesthetics/L'esthétique de Kant*, Berlin/New York: de Gruyter, pp. 176–91.

—2006b.

—2007, pp. 248–76.

Kitcher, P. (1986), 'Projecting the Order of Nature', in R.E. Butts (ed.), *Kant's Philosophy of Physical Science*, Dordrecht: D. Reidel, pp. 201–35.

Pippin, R. (1996), 'The Significance of Taste: Kant, Aesthetic and Reflective Judgement', *Journal of the History of Philosophy*, 34(4), October: 549–69.

4.2 The four 'moments' of a judgement of beauty

Allison, 2001, pp. 67–159.

Ameriks, K. (1983), 'Kant and the Objectivity of Taste', *The British Journal of Aesthetics*, 23(1), Winter: 3–17.

—1992.

Brandt, 1998.

Burnham, D. (2000), *An Introduction to Kant's Critique of Judgement*, Edinburgh: Edinburgh University Press, pp. 40–74.

Crawford, 1974, pp. 29–57 on Moments 1 and 2; pp. 96–124 on the formalism of taste.

Derrida, 1978/ 1987, *passim*, pp. 15–147.

Gotshalk, 1967.

Grayck, 1986.

Guyer, 1979, pp. 68–255.

—1977.

Hudson, 1991.

Kemal, S. (1997), *Kant's Aesthetic Theory: An Introduction*, London: Macmillan, pp. 23–68.

Meerbote, 1992.

Merleau-Ponty, 1964/1993.

Savile, A. (1987), *Aesthetic Reconstructions: The Seminal Writings of Lessing, Kant and Schiller*, Oxford: Blackwell.

Shier, 1998.

4.3 Judgements of the sublime and the defeat of the senses

Allison, 2001, pp. 302–44.

Burnham, 2000, pp. 88–105.

Crowther, P. (1989), *The Kantian Sublime*, Oxford: Clarendon Press, especially pp. 78–135.

Gibbons, 1994, pp. 124–51.

Kant, 1990.

Lyotard, J.-F. [1991] (1994), *Lessons on the Analytic of the Sublime*, trans. E. Rottenberg, Stanford: Stanford University Press; [*Leçons*

sur l'analytique du sublime Paris: Galilée, 1991], especially Sections 4–5.
Makkreel, 1990, pp. 67–87.

4.4 The Deduction of judgements of beauty

Allison, 2001, pp. 160–92.
Ameriks, K. (1982), 'How to Save Kant's Deduction of Taste', *Journal of Value Inquiry*, 16, 295–302.
Burnham, 2000, pp. 74–86.
Crawford, 1974, pp. 58–74, 75–91, 92–6, 125–33, 145–59.
Guyer, 1979, pp. 256–330.
Hughes, 2007, pp. 151–60, 169–206.
Kemal, 1992, pp. 73–115.
Makkreel, 1990, pp. 48–51.
—1992.

4.5 Aesthetic ideas and the artistic genius

Allison, 2001, pp. 271–301.
Burnham, 2000, pp. 106–18.
Guyer, 1977.
Hughes, 2006a.
Kemal, S. (1986), *Kant and Fine Art*, Oxford: Clarendon Press, pp. 35–67.
Podro, M. (1972), *The Manifold in Perception*, Oxford: Clarendon Press, pp. 7–35.

4.6 The relationship between the different arts

Crawford, 1974, pp. 171–6.

4.7 Beauty and the supersensible

Allison, 2001, pp. 236–67.
Burnham, 2000, pp. 118–23.
Crawford, 1974, pp.133–41.
Guyer, 1979, pp. 331–50, 351–94.
Hughes, 2007, pp. 299–302.

NOTES

2 OVERVIEW OF THEMES

1 The phrase is from James, 1890/1981, p. 462.

3 READING THE TEXT

1 References to the *Critique of Judgement* are to the *Akademie-Ausgabe*, the 'Academic Edition', Volume 5. References to this standard edition are marked by the abbreviation 'AA'.

2 Translations in this *Reader's Guide* are, unless otherwise signalled, my own. When I use translations by Pluhar, Guyer and Matthews or Meredith, I signal this by a 'P', 'G' or 'M' prior to the Kant page reference e.g., 'P: AA 204'. In references to the 'Introduction', such as the current one, I have also provided the section number in Roman numerals.

3 References to the *Critique of Pure Reason (C.Pu.R.)* refer to the 1781 or first [A] and 1787 or second [B] editions.

4 Guyer and Matthews translate *Vorstellung* as 'representation', which is literally correct. I follow Pluhar in using 'presentation' in order to avoid suggesting, without further argument, that Kant's theory of perception is representational. See Pluhar's Note 17 to AA 175. See also his Note 4 to AA 203, pointing out the broad range of connotations of this German term, which can refer to any species of mental awareness from sensory intuitions to rational ideas. Importantly, Kant insists that the aesthetic *Vorstellungen* central to the third *Critique* are directly apprehended by – or presented to – our senses. Consequently, I, like Pluhar, use 'exhibition' for *Darstellung,* which is rendered by Guyer and Matthews as 'presentation' and has the sense of the demonstration of a concept or idea in an intuition. See AA 343.

5 Admittedly, it would be more difficult to establish that music requires an elaboration in space. However, I think it would be possible to develop an account of the spatial characteristics of sound. Moreover, at the end of Section 14 Kant suggests that design, more strictly 'form', is not only spatial but also temporal. So, we could argue that the aesthetic form of music is principally temporal, while it necessarily stands in some relation to the spatial world.

6 Taste's mediating status owes much to the way in which it depends on imagination. John Llewelyn writes of 'a basic tonality of imagination as the hinge between reason and sensibility'. [Llewelyn, 2000, p. 28]

7 Kemp Smith's translation.

8   Guyer and Matthews give a correct literal translation as 'the faculty for judging itself'. Pluhar's rendering better captures the spirit of Kant's original phrase.

9   Guyer and Matthews's translation is 'the power of judgement in general'.

10 See, for instance, Proust, 2000, Volume V, 'The Captive', pp. 40–1 where he discusses a Fortuny dress as an 'original' unreproducible by lesser designers.

11 This reference to the 'First Introduction' is marked with a prime sign – AA 251' – to avoid any confusion with references to the published or second 'Introduction'.

INDEX

Absolute 154–6
    Hegelian 156–7
abstract modern art 170
academic training
    genius and 120, 121–2,
        125–6
accessory beauty *see*
    adherent beauty
adherent beauty 61, 62–4, 113
    examples of 61–2
Adorno, Theodor W. 167–9
aesthetic art 117
aesthetic ideas 122–4, 140
    artistic creativity and 127
    genius and 125
aesthetic judgements 5, 94–5, 96
    analogy between cognitive
        judgement and 38
    between knowledge and
        morality 10–12
    characteristics of 12–16,
        21–2
    cognitive *vs.* 29–30
    distinctiveness of 27–8, 31
    philosophical emergence
        of 5–6, 149–50
    pleasure connected
        with 66–74

politics and 166
    within critical
        philosophy 18–25
aesthetic measure 84–6
aesthetic necessity 67
Aesthetic Theory
    (Adorno) 168
Ages of the World
    (Schelling) 155
agreeable 31–2, 33, 34, 35, 57,
    92, 140
    arts 117
    charm and 52–3, 117
    music and wit 133
    sociability of 38–40
Akademie-ausgabe
    (Academic edition) 174
alienation 168–9
    stages of 169
Allison, Henry 19, 36, 54, 56,
    57, 58, 69, 72, 73, 102,
    105, 122, 135
*Analyses Concerning
    Passive and Active
    Synthesis* (Husserl) 163
'Analytic of Aesthetic
    Judgement' 4, 15–16,
    27, 134